The Seduction of Sarah Marks

A THOSE MAGNIFICENT MALVERNS NOVEL

The Seduction of Sarah Marks

A THOSE MAGNIFICENT MALVERNS NOVEL

KATHLEEN BITTNER ROTH

Entangled Publishing, LLC
2614 South Timberline Road
Suite 109
Fort Collins, CO 80525
Visit our website at www.entangledpublishing.com.

Edited by Erin Molta
Cover design by Heidi Stryker

ISBN   978-1502915719

Manufactured in the United States of America

First Edition June 2014

To my assistant, Gloria Erickson. You've kept the fires burning on my behalf for a long while.

Chapter One

Sarah was in bed with a stranger.

In a room bordering on the objectionable.

She lay on her side, her trembling fingers tucked beneath her cheek. If the galloping of her heart grew any louder, she was certain to awaken whoever *he* was before she could make her escape.

Who was this man?

Where was she?

Her befuddled mind tried to sort things out. Nothing came. Nothing at all.

Why can I not remember?

She had to get out of here, get out the door at least. Door? Where was it? There had to be one, but since she couldn't locate it by simply moving her eyes, it must be behind her.

If only she could manage to slip out of bed without waking him. She moved a bare inch.

He flopped onto his back with a small groan.

Oh, Heaven help me! She lay rigid for what seemed an eternity. Whoever he was, he appeared to be fully dressed, in clothing befitting a gentleman—at least based on what she could see from the shoulders up, for his shirt was white and he wore a gray pin-striped waistcoat. She was fairly certain she was clothed as well since the blue sleeve on her bent arm looked like a day gown, not a nightrail, but at the moment, she dared not move anything but her eyes.

He shifted again, facing her, and she held her breath until his returned to soft, rhythmic whiffles. She studied his face, so close as to be nearly blurred. Rich brown hair curled over his forehead and around his ears while a fringe of dark lashes lay against chiseled cheeks. An aristocratic, aquiline nose rested above a set of full lips, slightly parted. Still no recognition.

She eased backward again, shifting her weight ever so carefully. Pressing one foot against the cold floor, she slid from the bed and backed away.

A board squeaked, sounding like cannon shot in the quiet room.

His eyes opened.

"Oh!" A quick glance at the door, and she scrambled backward, one hand flailing behind her.

He rose on an elbow. "What are you up to?" Despite the sleep in his voice, authority rumbled through it.

Afraid to take her eyes off him, she felt around for the door's latch. "Who are you?"

He cocked a brow, and his expression grew quizzical.

"Are you quite serious?"

She nodded.

"Last I knew, I was Augustus Malvern, Lord Eastleigh." Remarkably clear brown eyes studied her. "Door's locked. Key's in my pocket."

"Where am I?" she croaked. "How did I get here?"

He scowled. "At the Golden Hen, near Hampshire. You don't recall?" When she shook her head, he threw back the covers and stood. His height and the breadth of his shoulders nearly swallowed the small room.

The room swayed—or was it her doing the wavering? She braced her shoulders against the door.

His booted feet pounded the floor, closing the distance between them. *He wore his boots to bed?* He paused before her and canted his head, puzzlement reigning in his regard of her. Reaching to her temple, he gently fingered a bump.

She gasped at both the pain and his touch, and craned her head away from him. Whatever had occurred, she feared him.

"Dear God," he muttered, and turning on his heel, strode to the window. Flinging the faded curtains aside, he backed off as a cloud of dust motes swirled about. He brushed at his shoulders, stepped again to the window, and clasped his hands behind him.

Despite the grime on the bubble-filled glass, the morning sun, still pink and fresh from its rising, shone through bright and clear. Off to the right, a rooster crowed. Lord Eastleigh turned an ear in that direction. "Let me get this straight. You do not recall where you are, or how you got here?"

"No...no, I do not." Despite her faltering voice, she stiffened her spine and gathered courage.

"Have no fear, madam. I won't harm you." His voice had gentled, and for whatever reason, she wanted to trust his word. "And except for that nasty lump, which I did not inflict, none has come to you."

When she said nothing in response, he asked, "By any chance, do you know your name?"

She took in a breath and managed a strong voice. "Yes. Sarah Marks."

He whipped around, a deep frown furrowing his brow.

She touched the nasty bump on her head and hissed. "How…how did I get here?"

"We rode in a hired carriage, which was overtaken by thieves. We walked here—or rather, I carried you a good deal of the way." His voice softened measurably. "Do you recall any of those events?"

Her mouth formed a silent, "No."

Fighting the panic trying to take root again, she perused the room. A dingy space, this. One window, an iron bed with a small, raw-wood table alongside, a few hooks on the wall— one holding a man's dark jacket and what looked to be a white cravat draped over its shoulder. A robin's egg blue cape hung over the back of the single chair in the room. A matching hat rested on its seat, while black kid gloves were stacked beside the bonnet. Tucked neatly beneath was a pair of black walking boots. Everything appeared well-made. The dress she wore matched the blue-sprigged muslin lining the cloak.

His scowl faded. "You suffered a blow when you stepped between me and the thieves—"

"Good heavens, why would I have done such a foolish thing?" She fingered her wound again.

"Folly, I would suspect." He lifted a brow. "Or perhaps you are so adamant regarding right and wrong, you could not stand to see someone's life threatened?"

She stared boldly at him while she fought to keep her chin from trembling. "I do not have the slightest idea how I would react, sir. In fact, I do not know if I am adamant about much of anything at all." Oh, her heart wouldn't hold out much longer—neither would her knees. "Please, sir. What can you tell me about me?"

Closing the distance between them, he reached out and swept back a tendril of hair that had caught at one corner of her mouth, grazing her cheek with his thumb as he went.

Lord, his touch was gentle, soothing in fact. And his scent. So clean. But an odd tremble moved through her. Any desire to lean into his hand dissipated. Instead, she stiffened and stepped away, her heartbeat kicking up. Something told her that it was not just this man, but all men she feared. Could that be why she'd left her home? "Please, do not touch me."

"Beg your pardon. I'm not much good at this sort of thing. Not that I've ever been in such an odd predicament before." The crease between his eyes deepened. "As I said, I mean you no harm. You are obviously suffering amnesia from the knock on your head."

"Me? Amnesia?" Dear blessed Mary!

He nodded. "You seemed in possession of all your faculties when you nodded off for the night, but now—" He shrugged a shoulder and made his way back to the window. "You're likely feeling as though pieces of your mind have been scattered to the four winds, but I caution you not to panic or things could very well worsen."

"How could you possibly know how I might feel?" Her

words sounded like ice cracking.

He glanced over his shoulder, perused the length of her with those fathomless brown eyes, and turned back to the window. "I suffered from amnesia following an injury in the Crimean War, so I recognize the same in you. My own experience taught me to tread lightly while recovering, so as not to suffer setbacks. Or worse, lose the past entirely. There are chunks of my memory still missing."

Her mind a blank, Sarah nonetheless managed to maintain her dignity. "Tell me whatever you know. How we came to be traveling together. Where I am from."

She studied him for a moment and then said, "How did a man such as you, a lord, come to be traveling on a public coach?"

He turned and leaned a shoulder against the window's sash, making it impossible for her to see him clearly with the halo of sunlight surrounding him. "I rode in a hired coach because I was on my way to a ship for…ah…an extended holiday on the Continent."

"How did I come to be in the same conveyance? Was I on my way to the sea as well?"

"You were traveling by way of one of those over-crowded public coaches. You, and what I assumed was your companion, were bemoaning the dire conditions, and since we were headed in the same direction, I offered both of you my carriage. While you were an innocent, I'm afraid the other woman was not. She used being amidst your proper company to soundly dupe me."

"Was she the thief who injured me?"

He shook his head. "Her thieving friends lay in wait down the road a measure. Suffice it to say, you and I lost everything, including the hired carriage since the coachman teamed up with the filthy lot. He exchanged transportation for a cut of the bounty, the blackguard."

Her teeth slid over her bottom lip. "Did we turn back to the coaching stop from whence we came, or did we travel forward? Was where we came from my home?"

"Insightful questions." Eastleigh sketched a slight bow in deference, his curly locks tumbling over his forehead. "I overheard you tell the other woman that the stop where we encountered one another was your third, but you did not disclose to her your starting point." He scoured the small room with disapproving eyes. "And as for this rather questionable inn, we were nearer here than turning back."

"Then what?" She brushed her hands down her hips in an attempt to cease their quaking.

He eyed her movement. "Then we stumbled in here after dark. With a crowded inn, we were fortunate to capture the only room available." He looked around the sparsely furnished space with a look of distaste. "You are known below as Lady Eastleigh, by the by."

She glanced at the bed and her lips pursed. "You should have slept on the floor."

"Bloody hell on the hard floor!" He winced. "Beg pardon, a slip of the tongue."

Her hand crept to her throat. "But we are perfect strangers."

He paused as if in thought while regarding her through narrowed eyes. "You were not opposed to sharing a bed in order to get the rest we needed. We were both fully clothed, and it's not as if such an undertaking is an uncommon practice." He raked his hair back from his brow and heaved a sigh. "God knows if I'll be able to hire something out of here today that will give either of us a modicum of comfort.

We have a long road ahead, so I thank you for not insisting I take to the floor."

"To where do you intend this carriage take us?" Renewed panic hammered her heart in her chest.

He rubbed the back of his neck. "To my home in Kent."

She gasped and fought to regain her composure. Perhaps parts of her memory had been misplaced, but her instincts told her that traveling alone with a man to his residence was highly inappropriate. "I could not go there with you, sir. It isn't done."

His regard of her intensified until her skin felt seared. "Then tell me, madam," he said in little more than a murmur, "where else am I to take you?"

Chapter Two

From inside the carriage, Eastleigh scanned plowed fields bursting with the promise of spring. A dull beat at the base of his skull told him another megrim was about to roll through his head like a thundering herd of horses. He took in a long, slow breath and counted down from ten on the exhale, as he'd been taught.

What the devil had he been thinking leaving Easton Park? He had no business traveling even five miles from home, let alone trying to tour the Continent for three months with the idea of bringing home a bride. And painful as it was to admit, he was not ready to take on a wife, after all. Blast it all, Doctor Hemphill had been right. He rubbed at the back of his neck. Now he had to return home as quickly as possible and deliver the doctor yet another patient. "I am fully aware this might well be the worst day of your life—"

"That, sir, I would hardly know," she interrupted softly.

"Your pardon." He ran a sweaty palm down the side of

his leg. Damn the headache. Another breath, another count of ten. No, he should never have left home. But he had to hold himself together at all costs. The responsibility sitting before him wouldn't know the first thing about getting them to Kent if he sickened. "Madam, I know what it is to awaken not knowing anything with regard to one's self. If you wish for no conversation, we shall have none, and I shall leave you to yourself for the duration, or we can muddle through this together. Lord knows, I'm giving it my best."

Fringed lids closed over those great blue eyes, and her head fell back against the squabs. A tear trickled from one eye and trailed into her hair. He checked an urge to reach over and wipe it away—along with her pain. Instead, he fished inside his coat pocket, retrieved a handkerchief, and gently tucked it in her hand.

She pressed the square of cloth to her temple and looked again out the window. "Do you know the road from here?"

"Not as yet, but I'm told we'll turn onto a main highway near noon. I know that particular route well."

"Will we reach your home today?"

"Hardly," he responded. "We've a two-day ride, but there are far better inns ahead."

"I refuse to be Lady Eastleigh tonight."

He couldn't help the chuckle. "You'll become my youngest sister, Rose."

"We shan't share the same room."

He lifted a brow. "And if there is only one available?"

She said nothing but overtly perused the interior of the carriage.

He patted the hard seat. "Indeed. This will serve, if necessary."

"Rose lives with you?"

"No."

Her chin lifted. "Is there a Lady Eastleigh at home?"

"God, no!" He nearly laughed. "Mum will act as chaperone."
She went back to staring out the window.

Lord, but even under duress, she was a lovely sight. "I should warn you of my family before we arrive."

"Warn me?"

Good, he'd managed to distract her from her predicament. He grinned. "Everyone should have fair warning of the Malverns."

She tilted her pretty head. "Tell me of your parents."

Oh, wouldn't he like to pull her onto his lap and murmur his response in her ear? "Father's illness confines him and my mother to their estate, which lies an hour north of mine. Mum, who lives with me, is actually my grandmother. Mum is…that is—" Devil take it, he sounded like a schoolboy.

"She raised you?"

He laughed outright. "Isn't that a rich thought, but no. Mum is a bit…shall we say…" He scratched his head. "We aren't quite sure whether it's her age or the gin she tipples, but suffice it to say, her memory isn't much better than yours."

When her cheeks flushed, he could have kicked himself. "Sorry, ghastly turn of words." Bloody hell, where was her sense of humor? She'd likely not had much to begin with, since an amnesiac's personality rarely changed. "She's called Mum, by the by, because she fancies herself the Queen Mother and thinks my mother to be the Queen. Whenever Mother visits, we refer to her as Your Majesty. Pacifies Mum, it does."

He swallowed another chuckle. "When I sent a messenger

to alert Doctor Hemphill, I also sent word to Mum. Hard to tell how you'll be greeted."

Slowly, she turned her head his way. "What an odd way of putting things."

A corner of his mouth curled. "Isn't it though, madam?"

She turned back to looking out the window.

They grew quiet for a long while, with only the rattle of chains and the grind of the wheels on the hard-packed road to keep them company.

Despite the dire circumstances under which they traveled, Eastleigh found himself once again occupied with the exquisite profile of the woman who called herself Sarah Marks.

Uncommonly refined for a country girl, she was. And prettier than anyone had a right to be, given the circumstances. Loose tendrils of flaxen hair framed a heart-shaped face one would expect to appear drawn. But she looked refreshed— and fragile as spun glass, yet pugnaciously strong.

Amazing.

"You stare at me, sir," she said, without turning his way.

"My apologies." Fighting an impulse to squirm, he rested his elbow against the window's ledge and thumbed the edge of his broken tooth—an old habit he'd long ago given up trying to break. How could he not help but look at her? Bloody hell, despite her prim and perfunctory manner, she captivated him.

A thought struck him that there hadn't been a mirror back at the inn. "Your eyes match your cape. Are you aware of their color, madam?"

She shrugged, her cornflower blue eyes reflecting the sunlight passing through the carriage. "I should care little about my looks, my lord, when I have more dire things to ponder."

Blast his stupidity. "Of course, but since your eyes are striking enough to comment on, I thought you might like to know."

"Oh."

His gaze drifted to her pink mouth that formed a plump circle and had yet to return to its natural shape. Pure lust shot up from nowhere. Had they come together this morning under other circumstances, he would have found her kissable-looking lips irresistible. And in all likelihood, he'd have found a way to entice her into settling on his lap, where he would have entertained the both of them on this tedious journey.

Another turn of her head, and she spied where he stared. She let out a small gasp.

The wave of pleasure that had run through him at the sight of her sensuous lips evaporated like morning mist off a sunlit pond.

Bugger! He took to watching the spring flowers along the roadside and unobtrusively managed his breathing exercises. "Once again, my apologies. Although I have experience with amnesia, I'm finding it exceedingly difficult to deal with it in another."

Thoughts of what he'd endured over his many months of recovery swept through him like an angry gale. He didn't want those particular memories, thought he'd brushed them aside, but he found they only lay in hiding for as quickly as they could descend upon him. Damnation! He couldn't get home soon enough. And blast it all, he'd even left his powders behind.

He searched for words to alleviate the uncomfortable silence. "Do not dwell on your situation or try to think beyond this moment or you'll only buy yourself trouble."

Pain washed across her countenance. He was right—she had been trying to make sense of things.

Her chin quivered until she set her mouth against it, but she said nothing. "You've been trying to imagine your future and you cannot."

She gave a slight nod. "So it would seem."

"Which is normal." Good God, what had he got himself into?

"Normal?"

"You cannot project into the future because you have no memory of your past."

She let out a burdened sigh and tucked a stray lock behind her ear with gloved fingers that had a tremble to them. "I do not understand."

He had to keep her talking, keep her mind off her dilemma lest she panic. He leaned forward. "It's impossible to imagine a future without using your past as reference, so you must live in the present until your memory returns. Actually, in the whole of my recovery, learning to exist in the moment turned out to be the most valuable thing I gleaned from my experience."

He resisted a terrible urge to rest a comforting hand over hers. "Think on it—what do we really ever have but this moment?"

Her shoulders visibly relaxed. He offered her a small grin, pleased she made sense of what he tried to convey. "The physician who saw to my recovery has retired on a parcel of my land. I sent a courier ahead, so Doctor Hemphill awaits your arrival." *And so does Mum, with whatever opinions she'll have in the matter.*

Sarah rubbed the back of her neck. "Perhaps I should be thanking the good Lord someone with knowledge of this condition rescued me, but I am too angry with Him at the moment."

Guilt wound its way through Eastleigh. Had he never left home, this wouldn't have happened—to him or to her. "Does that mean we might enjoy a truce?"

Her refined features took on even more softness. "Between you and me, at least."

Something hitched low in his belly. He managed a smile, "Good," and realized he'd also managed to dispense with the headache. He was pain free at the moment—except for the constant throbbing in his right leg, which he'd learned to live with—bloody swords. They should be outlawed in battle.

• • •

She studied him for a long moment. "You may call me Miss Marks." She clasped her gloved hands tightly together. "I presume I'm unmarried since I wear no ring." Oh, dear, she was back to thinking of her predicament. "Or was one taken from me in the robbery?"

He shook his head. "They took a pair of ear bobs from you is all."

"Of any worth, could you tell?"

"Not much, I would suspect." He offered her a bit of a smile and then propped his elbow on the window sill.

My, but he was handsome—and growing more so with every passing hour. His upper teeth were white and even, except for a small triangular chip where a front tooth butted against the other. A small scar ran alongside his upper cheek.

She regarded his supple fingers while his thumb fiddled at that broken tooth, something she'd seen him do often during the ride.

When he caught her staring, he dropped his hand. "For what it's worth, madam —"

"Miss Marks."

He shifted in his seat and frowned. "I shall call you madam until I have grown used to the other."

Her heart went to galloping again. Lord, she had to take her mind off her predicament if her sanity was to remain intact. She took in a slow breath and exhaled just as slowly. "Tell me of your siblings."

He nodded, seeming more at ease with this question. "I'm the first of four sons and four daughters."

"Your rank? Certainly not a duke if your father remains alive."

His eyes sparkled whenever he smiled. "Ah, a knowledge of ranking. You see? Your memory will trickle in as it chooses. I am merely a viscount. My father is an earl."

"Tell me of your four sisters."

He was playing with that broken tooth again. "Perhaps there are only three. We aren't certain at times." When her brow rose, he laughed. "Willamette came along smack in the middle of a raucous bunch of boys. Being profoundly stubborn, she insisted on dressing and acting like her brothers and does so to this day."

"Oh, my."

"Mother claimed the name Willamette, shortened to Will by her brothers, did the deed, so my other sisters were named after flowers — Rose, Iris, and Violet."

Sarah fought to recall if she had any siblings.

Nothing.

Frustrated, she heaved a sigh.

Eastleigh leaned forward. She caught his scent. Familiar, but of what, she couldn't put to tangible thought. His hand covered hers. The heat emanating from his fingers went right through her. She tried to pull away, but he held her steady.

And as if in defiance, he leaned even closer. "You are here, as am I, as is John Coachman," he said in a low, commanding voice. "As are the flowers beside the road, the blue sky overhead."

His scent and the intimacy of his hands upon hers sent another shockwave through her.

"Here and now is truly your only world, madam, as much as it is my only world, with or without our memories intact. Will you send yourself to Bedlam trying to recollect your past and worry over your future? Perhaps you might try trusting that I know of what I speak and force your thoughts to remain in the present."

"You're right, of course." Oh, she had to exercise a little faith that somehow this would all be set to rights, or she would surely fall apart. Her hand beneath his relaxed. "Thank heavens it was you that I ended up with in this miserable condition."

He let go of her and leaned back, regarding her through heavy lids. "Pray, tell me more."

Those velvet-edged words may as well have been his fingers trailing over her tingling breasts and settling beneath her skirts. God help her if keeping her mind in the moment meant focusing on him.

Chapter Three

When the flavor of beef and fresh vegetables stewed in herbs burst in Sarah's mouth, a small moan escaped her lips, despite the impropriety. "Lord, thank the cook."

"And the innkeeper," Eastleigh responded.

They'd barely secured the last two rooms when the skies poured forth a deluge. She and Eastleigh sat at a table in the dining room, close to the fire. The warmth, the crackling of wood, comforted her amidst the raucous thunder. She'd already inspected her chamber, much to Eastleigh's humor. How consoling to know hers was fit for a well-bred traveler. She *was* well-bred, wasn't she? How otherwise would her sensibilities have been so knocked about?

Eastleigh studied her with an odd demeanor. Her heart missed a beat. She dismissed the way her toes curled at his regard, or how the air fairly quivered between them.

She shifted in her chair. "Will you dispense letters on my behalf when we arrive, Lord Eastleigh?"

"Indeed."

"Will you leave no stone unturned?"

That queer expression fell across his face again. "God knows, I am excruciatingly aware of your quandary, and I shall do all I can to help you find your place in the world."

An unidentifiable sensation wended through her. Strange the way he said that, as if his meaning went beyond his spoken words.

She searched for another topic of conversation. "Do you seek a wife?"

• • •

"No." God, that had been foremost in his mind when he'd set out on this journey. He'd fully expected to be gone three months, return from the Continent with a wife in hand, and surprise his meddling family, who'd constantly nagged him about his bachelorhood. After living alone on his estate with only a daft grandmother for company, lonely had become an understatement. But he'd needed time to heal from his war injuries, not to mention he could no longer tolerate the cacophony of London, or the shallow debutantes. Not after the brutalities of war. When he'd left home, he'd told no one but Hemphill of his plans to marry. Oh, wouldn't the good doctor greet him with a relentless, "I told you so," every time he looked his way? Just as Hemphill had foretold, Eastleigh was in no way ready to traipse all over the Continent.

His thoughts returned to Sarah. Firelight danced across her petal-soft skin and cast golden glints in hair that framed her face like a halo. Lovely, she was. And he wanted her. Those beautiful eyes, bold and without guile, and that delicious, little mouth of hers parted, as if ripe for a kiss. She wet her lower lip with a slide of her tongue. He was going to have to bide his time, allow her to heal until hopefully, he could claim her as his in every sense of the word. Sweet Christ, now his loins ached. "Enough of this talking of me."

She set her fork to her plate. "Well, it wouldn't be much of a discussion if we engaged in patter about me, now would it?"

"Beg pardon." If her situation weren't so deplorable, he could have laughed at her acerbic remark. "I suppose we could speak of the weather."

"Indeed." Her chin hiked. "Dreadful, isn't it?"

"Indeed." A corner of his mouth twitched. "Now wasn't that a long and worthy conversation?"

Her lips pursed.

"Why, madam, I do believe you fight a smile." When she said nothing, he lifted a brow. "It wouldn't hurt to let that grin take hold and see what comes of it. Providing you don't think me impertinent for suggesting you do something so outrageous under such serious circumstances."

She paused, regarding him again in that comely, frank way with her lips barely parted. And then it was as if the world shifted. She smiled—not only with her mouth, but from her eyes and by the bare bend of her head.

Beautiful.

His groin tightened. Damnable cock. Had a mind of its own, it did. He signaled for the waitress. "Would you care for something sweet to end your meal, madam? A tart, perhaps?"

"Only if sent to my room. Apple, if they have it." She set her fork and knife on her plate in a precise manner that indicated she'd completed her meal. The lady knew high manners.

He gave a nod to the innkeeper's daughter. "Make that two, each to our respective rooms."

They settled into a comfortable silence before the fire, although he fought glancing at her every chance he got. Was it the good food and ale, the decent lodgings, that did things to his mind or was she growing more enticing by the hour?

With her head held in a dignified manner, she surreptitiously perused the dining room. "I hadn't thought of this until now, and it's certainly none of my concern, but how do you intend to pay for all this?"

"A gentleman's word goes far. The courier I sent ahead will see to my debts on his return."

"What if he pockets the lot?"

"I'll have his bloody arse…I'll have his neck."

She acted as if he hadn't spoken, but there went her pursed lips again.

He chuckled. "Ah, don't fight that grin. However, I do apologize for my *faux pas*." He paused. What the hell, he may as well say it. "It seems you've been privy to crude language at one time or another."

"Indeed. I used to take my father's horses to be shod, and whenever the smithy got hold of a stubborn one, he'd use the most vile of words—" Her jaw dropped. "Oh, my. That bit of memory flew in from nowhere." She rubbed at her temples "But the rest…it went out like the wind." Tears flooded her eyes. "Can't seem to recall anything else."

Eastleigh reached across the table and squeezed her hand. "Give it up. And for pity's sake, don't let it sink you."

She nodded, slid her hand out from under his, and

blinked away tears.

He pulled a handkerchief from his pocket and handed it across the table. "You cannot judge your progress by these kinds of moments."

She discreetly wiped a corner of her eye with the white fabric.

Not knowing what else to do, he raked his fingers through his hair. "When I returned from the Crimean Peninsula, I had no idea who I was, didn't recall a single family member, nor my surroundings. Yet, I went directly to the piano and played. I found solace in spending hours there. My memory returned in pieces. One day I recalled how I had detested learning to play, swore I would burn the blasted instrument for firewood, given the chance. Who would have guessed the thing I disliked most would become my saving grace?"

Sarah laughed—a small tinkle of laughter that could have been a piano's top keys trilling.

He smiled. She was probably unaware that she took in several quick breaths while her luminous blue gaze fixed on his. Certainly she was unaware of what the rise and fall of her breasts did to him.

"You're a complicated man, I would suspect."

There went his body again—overreacting to his mind's risqué fantasy. "Let's get you upstairs. I've arranged a little something for your pleasure." *But not that kind of pleasure, damn it.* He stood, gave her his arm, and they exited the dining room.

As they neared the stairs, the front door crashed open, and a young couple, she with a babe in arms, rushed in. Bitter cold swept the space before the innkeeper slammed the door shut against the biting wind. The man looked to the innkeeper while shaking off the wet. "Devil of a storm. Not fit for mankind to get caught in."

The woman, impossibly young and with her hair plastered to her head, shivered and held her babe, blankets dripping, close to her chest.

"Oh, dear," Sarah murmured.

Without a word, Eastleigh escorted her up the stairs and to her room. Retrieving a key from his pocket, he handed it to her. "Lock yourself in when I'm gone in case there are strangers wandering about."

He swung open the door.

At the sight of a small bathing tub in front of a roaring fire, she beamed, the smile brightening her features like a lit candle. "How thoughtful. Have you done the same for yourself?"

"Indeed. Since yesterday's folly and today's long ride left a bit of grit behind my ears, we'll likely lounge in our respective tubs at the same time." Oh, hell, her spine stiffened again. Was a discussion indicating nakedness even too intimate for her?

A pounding of feet on the stairs caught his attention. The innkeeper bounded toward them, his generous belly bouncing beneath his stained apron. "A word, Lord Eastleigh."

"What is it?"

The innkeeper wrung his hands. "The young couple, sir. They have a babe, and I have no rooms available."

Foreboding sluiced through Eastleigh's veins. "What could this possibly have to do with me?"

"Well, sir...I...ah. With you being a gentleman and all, could you find fit to give up your room so as not to put a family out in the cold? Your sister is in the largest room with the biggest bed. Ample enough to share, sir."

Sarah gasped. "Do something, Eastleigh." And then, as if she'd recovered from the idea of sharing a room and fully realized the situation, she calmed. "Mother would have our necks if she learnt we'd left those poor people to wander about in a storm."

Oh, hell. Eastleigh slapped his key into the innkeeper's hand.

Sarah's brow furrowed. "Might they be without adequate funds? The babe's blankets appeared rather threadbare, and if I'm not mistaken, the couple seemed a bit hollow in the cheek."

Eastleigh leaned back on his heels. Well, if that didn't take some keen assessment whilst traipsing past the couple for mere seconds. "Accommodate the family in the dining room, as well, sir. And leave the charges to me. Good eve."

The innkeeper's head bobbed in a series of nods as he backed away. "Very kind of you, your lordship." He turned and hurried down the steps.

Eastleigh set his hand to Sarah's back and ushered her into the room.

Her gaze settled on the large bed in the center of the room. Blotches colored her cheeks. "Oh, dear. I…I don't believe I can—"

"Take your bath when the water is delivered," he snapped, and stepping to the four-poster, he ran his fingers across the soft comforter turned down to expose crisp linens. "Then climb into your nice, clean bed."

Another thought of the tub next door—in the room that should have been his—soured his disposition. That tell-tale throb started at the base of his skull.

"I'll be downstairs drowning any expectations of my own warm bath and soft bed in what I hope is decent whisky." *As well as drowning a few damnable thoughts of you.* "When the innkeeper thinks I'm sotted, I'll make my way to the privy and then stumble into the carriage with an excuse that I was too sauced to find my way back. Good night."

He turned to leave and nearly ran into a chambermaid carrying the warm tarts. Stepping aside, he caught the sweet scent of cooked apples and cinnamon as she passed by. Setting his jaw, he headed for the stairs and tossed his curt words over his shoulder. "Give both to my sister. She'll appreciate having my share."

• • •

While one chambermaid helped relieve Sarah of her clothing, two others filled the tub sitting next to the cozy fire with water hot enough to send steam spiraling in the air. It wasn't a small amount of guilt that plagued her every time lightning lit the sky or thunder rattled the windows. Well, the carriage shouldn't leak, so why concern herself with Eastleigh's well-being? Still, he was out there in the cold, and she was in here—warm and toasty.

"'Tis a new bed, milady," the maid proudly announced and ran a hand across the floral counterpane that matched the curtains.

More guilt traipsed through Sarah's bones. She bit her lip. They'd shared a bed once, hadn't they?

"Right proud of it, Mrs. Whistlethorpe is. Bedding is brand new as well. The Missus sent in a nightrail. Ain't fancy like yer probably used to, and much larger than befits your slim frame, but 'tis clean. We surely hope you have a nice bath and pleasant sleep."

Sarah silently groaned. Well, it simply wouldn't do to have Eastleigh in here. It wouldn't.

"Pardon me, milady, but yer brother sure turned out to be a fine-looking gent."

The others tittered.

Startled, Sarah glanced over her shoulder at the gray-haired maid working the laces on her corset. "You know Lord Eastleigh?"

"Only in passing, milady. Don't know if you recall, but years ago, your family stopped in once or twice on yer way to the sea, but can't rightly say as I can form a picture of you amongst them."

Sarah's insides trembled at the idea of being found out. "I…I'm the youngest. 'Tis said I've changed a great deal."

"Aye. Don't no one recognize me from me youth, neither." The maid laughed. "Had all me teeth back then fer one thing."

Sarah's spine went ramrod straight. This was an entirely inappropriate conversation to be having with anyone, let alone a servant. Something akin to gloom washed through her. What in heaven's name had her life been like if servants were not to be spoken to? Still, she didn't know quite what to say. "If you'll excuse me, I'll see to my bath alone."

The air crackled with sudden silence. Only the rain battering the window could be heard.

Oh, dear. "Beg your pardon, but I am used to my privacy. I did not intend to appear rude."

"As you wish, but would you like me to tend to yer hair first?"

And with that, Sarah realized how utterly fatigued she

was. "That would be wonderful. If there's an inch layer of dirt residing on my scalp, I wouldn't be surprised."

With an easy grin that exposed the many gaps in her teeth, the maid pulled a footstool over to the highest end of the tin tub. "If'n ye'll lean back here, my lady, I'll see to yer hair and then have the water freshened so you don't have to bathe in soap scum."

Sarah sat as instructed and reached for the pins in her hair. The maid shook her head. "Leave that to me, my lady. Ye've shadows under yer eyes, so if'n ye'll close them, I'll see to the rest."

Just the gentle act of setting her long hair free was soothing in itself, but when warm water washed through it, and strong fingers massaged chamomile soap throughout, Sarah could have moaned aloud. She sighed instead and let her mind wander.

"I'm curious about something. When my brother and I arrived, and while he instructed the hostler, I noticed a rather unusual looking dog with a litter of pups just around the side of the stable."

"Oh, they be Mr. Whistlethorpe's latest whelps. Ugly as sin, but they make powerful good sheep dogs. The farmers in these parts are quick to snatch them up soon as they's weaned."

"There's one that appears to be less than half the size of the others, and with only three fully formed legs. What will happen to it if it's not fit to be sold?"

"Ah, yes, poor thing. Like as not, it'll be put down."

A shudder ran through Sarah. "Killed?"

"Yes, my lady."

"But that would be awful."

The maid nodded. "Ain't nothing wasted around here, I'm afraid. Everything's put to good use exceptin' a pig's squeal, so having a worthless dog serves no purpose."

Whatever life was handing Sarah at the moment, at least she could darn well take charge of a piece of it. "Have they been weaned, yet?"

"Just the other day. They'll be left with the mother another ten days, and then Mr. Whistlethorpe will sort them out according to their worth. Soon as he notices the deformed runt, it'll be dealt with."

The idea of something to call her very own lifted Sarah's spirits. And the notion of saving the wretched little animal gave her a sense of purpose that was near to exhilarating. "Please notify Mrs. Whistlethorpe that I'll be taking the puppy with me when we leave."

Color rose in the maid's cheeks. "You mean to take that little runt?"

Sarah nodded. "If you can have a basket prepared in the morning that can accommodate it, I'd be glad to."

The maid pressed her fingers to her lips. "Oh, won't Mrs. Whistlethorpe fairly dance with joy. The poor pup is the sweetest little thing. We couldn't bring ourselves to do it in. I'll see meself that Lord Eastleigh gets the basket. Victuals for it, too."

"No! What I mean is, since this will be my doing entirely, my brother has no say in the matter." It wouldn't do to slip and let on that she wouldn't be staying long with the Malverns. "You'll take care of the matter for me?"

The maid's wide grin nearly split her face in two. "Oh, indeed, milady. We done lied to Mr. Whistlethorpe. Told him there were six pups, not seven, so he'll never know the difference. Been trying to figure out what to do with the poor thing for nigh on eight weeks, so both the missus and I will be resting a bit easier now."

"Good. Then if you will, deliver the basket to the carriage right before our departure, and place it on the seat that faces forward."

While the maid towel-dried Sarah's hair and ordered in more hot water for the bath, the storm worsened. Guilt piled upon guilt at the idea of Eastleigh being out in it. Oh, how she would have loved to have inquired about him. And the Malvern family. But what a brainless thing to do.

A light tapping sounded on the door, and a young maid marched in with warming pans. Behind her came two more maids with steaming buckets of fresh water. Lightning lit the edges around the window curtains, and thunder shook the room. Sarah jumped. Oh, dear, to think *he* was out in this. Well, he couldn't be. Not enough time had passed for more than a few sips of whisky. She had nothing to feel guilty about. Absolutely nothing. *Tell that to my conscience.*

The warming pans went between the sheets along with another layer of guilt.

"Yer gown seems to be clean enough, but if ye would care to hand over yer chemise and unmentionables, I'll see to having them washed and fresh for in the morning."

"Oh. Yes. Of course." While it only made sense to have her underclothing cleaned, somehow Sarah had the feeling she'd never bathed naked. "If you'll wait outside the door, I'll hand them over to you."

A curious expression ran through the maid's eyes. "I'll leave ye, then, milady."

When the door closed behind the woman, Sarah divested

herself of her remaining clothing, rolled them in a ball, and handed them through the smallest opening she could manage. Slamming the heavy panel shut, she twisted the key in the lock and scurried to the tub where she lowered herself into the scented water. Naked or not, she doubted a bath had ever felt so welcome. The water flowed around her and over her skin like heated silk.

Heavenly.

She picked up the soap and sniffed. Chamomile and lavender. How lovely. Lord Eastleigh was right—keeping her thoughts in the present kept panic at bay.

Eastleigh.

Try as she might, it didn't matter that he was not part of her present moment, thoughts of him overtook all else. The viscount was a presence, to be sure. All heads had turned when they'd entered the inn, with none focused on her, thank heavens. And it wasn't merely his large stature or the low timbre of his voice. Something else about him captivated, and she wasn't at all certain what it was.

Her hair clean and her body scrubbed, she donned the oversized nightrail, blew out the candle, and settled beneath the warm, downy comforter.

Don't try to figure out anything. Live in the present. What matters but the moment, anyway? Wise words, those. Lightning flickered again. She counted the seconds—One. Two. Three. Thunder boomed three miles away. A fast moving storm. *It'll be clear tomorrow when he climbs out of the carriage. Just you wait and see.*

An image flooded her mind of Eastleigh twisting and turning while he tried to fit his long legs into some kind of comfortable position, his damp, curly locks flying about.

Good heavens, she'd shared a bed with him, knew how unruly his hair looked in the morning. Her cheeks heated. She pressed the back of her hand against one. She'd been in bed with a stranger. Imagine that!

But this wasn't just any stranger.

The servants were right—he was a handsome gent. So handsome, she had trouble keeping her eyes off his every move. And his voice, the way it went husky at the oddest times. Thoughts of him set off a pulse thrumming deep in her belly. Worse, her nipples puckered.

Somehow, she didn't think this had ever happened to her before.

A blaze of lightning lit the edges of the curtains, and thunder shook her to the core. What if the carriage leaked?

Oh, she would never sleep knowing he was out there in this mess and it was all her doing. What did it matter if they shared a room? They'd done it before without harm coming to her. Besides, everyone below thought them brother and sister.

More lightning lit the room. Thunder boomed and everything around her shook. "That does it!"

She scrambled from the bed and yanked on the bell pull. Setting a candle aflame, she unlocked the door and waited for the maid.

"Milady?"

Sarah handed the key to the servant. "I fear I neglected to give this to my brother." Her stomach twisted at her lie. "Please lock me in and see he gets it straight away. You'll find him in the pub."

After the maid secured the room, Sarah made her way back to bed, pulled the covers to her neck and kept to the edge of the mattress, her heart hammering. She hoped he hadn't gone out in all this mess. Then again, she half-hoped he had.

It seemed an eternity before the door opened and Eastleigh stepped inside. Slipping the key into his pocket, he leaned a shoulder against the wall, folded his arms across his chest, and gave her a lop-sided grin, his eyes filled with mischief. "I don't suppose you'd consider turning your head while I bathed?"

Chapter Four

Oh, for heaven's sake! Sarah kept her back to Eastleigh, her head buried beneath a pillow, and clung to the edge of the mattress opposite the tub. If she wasn't careful, she'd tumble over the side. The arrogance of the man, announcing in front of the chambermaid that he was claiming his right to a hot soak since his sister had enjoyed one. But humming while sitting naked in a tub she'd only recently vacated? The nerve.

With every break in the booming thunder, his happy little tune vibrated through the metal bedframe and into her ears, breaking down what little remained of her sensibilities. He was taunting her outright. Getting even for his near banishment to the carriage.

With a muffled "*Humph*," she yanked the covers over the pillow. Low laughter rumbled through the mattress. The beast. He hadn't slept in the carriage after all, so he should be thankful, not provoking. Did the man have no conscience? Here she was, in a terrible fix, and tomorrow—oh, she mustn't think about her predicament and what might become of her. Except, if she didn't, there was only one other thing to consider—the present moment. And *him*. Naked. Not ten feet away. Oh, dear.

The bed shook. She jumped. What *was* he up to now? She managed to gather the bedclothes tighter around her.

"Madam," he commanded. "Come out from under there before you suffocate."

She inched the covers down and lifted the pillow. Damp curls clung to his forehead, he was clean shaven, and…and… good heavens! She slammed the pillow back in place.

He shook the mattress again. "Don't be such a turtle. I gave you my word I wouldn't harm you."

Slowly, she lifted the pillow and peeked at him again. Firelight shot shadows across the walls. Long shadows. Of him. She sucked in her breath. "Sir, you are wearing nothing but a nightshirt!"

A chuckle came from him and hovered in the air above her. He climbed into bed. She scrambled out the other side. "You are indecently clothed."

He craned his neck and gave her an up and down glance. "And you aren't? Perhaps I should rethink my assessment of *you*—that rag you wear is rather offensive the way it flops around your feet and pools on the floor. And in case you haven't noticed, the sleeves hang well past your fingertips and the neck of it rises to your chin." He crossed his arms behind his head. "Ugly as sin…the gown, not you. Now if you please, get into bed. We've a long journey ahead of us on the morrow, and I am fatigued."

She shoved her sleeves to her elbows. They fell right back down.

He watched her intently, and then a slow burn of a smile worked its way along his mouth.

A shiver ran through her.

"I'll blow out the candle once you are in bed, madam. Otherwise, you'll likely tangle yourself in that ungodly thing, trip and fall, and then where will I be? Out of the bed to look after you…me in a nightshirt and you in a nightrail. How positively *indecent*. How would that appear to someone running in here to see what the racket was about? Only to find me helping my clumsy sister to her feet, and both of us in an *improper* state of dress, daring to don the very rags they loaned us. *Tsk, tsk, tsk.*"

"How dare you mock me." She stomped toward a chair where an extra quilt lay folded, but her feet snagged the hem. She caught herself before she fell.

He snorted.

Kicking free from the tangle and ignoring his sarcasm, she lifted her skirt past her ankles and carried the blanket to the bed. She rolled the bulky quilt lengthwise, and setting it firmly between them, crawled into bed.

He lifted on an elbow, all humor gone from his countenance. His dark gaze shifted back and forth from the bundle to her. "Is this your way of seeing that I don't come near you?"

Lightning flashed and thunder boomed again, jarring her senses. Shaken by the storm and the way he regarded her, Sarah gave him her back and yanked the covers up to her ears. "Will this devil of a storm never cease?" She bit her lip and hauled in a shaky breath. How in the world had her life come to this?

"I hope you realize, madam, that what you have just done is called *bundling* and is meant to separate an unmarried couple who are promised to one another, but caught in a circumstance where they must sleep in the same bed for lack of space. Might I remind you that we are supposed to be seen as brother and sister, that we are not in a heated state where we cannot keep our hands off one another, and we have no parents monitoring us?"

"You are crass and unforgivably rude."

"How so?"

"Humming merrily along in a bathing tub in the middle of a storm." Her words trailed off into little more than a mutter. "Whilst I am beside myself with worry." She couldn't think of another response, she was so embarrassed.

He blew out the candle, leaving only the flicker of dying embers to cast shadows across the ceiling. "Forgive me, but since I was certain you'd be most uncomfortable upon my return, humming a tune was my pitiful attempt at a bit of levity."

A pause and he heaved a sigh. "Truth be told, if I hadn't done something to diffuse this dynamite of a situation, I'd likely be deep into a headache, one that's plagued me since my war injuries. Once it takes hold, you wouldn't see me out of this bed for days. I am bearing with your troubles, so if you please, do try to bear with mine."

Was that anger in his voice? Certainly irritation. Now she was the one who should make amends. "Pardon. I was merely seeing to both our comfort is all." Feeble apology, that.

He blew out a muttering breath in a great exhale and rolled onto his side, taking a good deal of the covers with him. "The last thing I would want to do is fondle a woman who does not wish to be touched. Now, good night!"

Even though guilt speared her conscience anew at

his remark of fighting a headache, Sarah turned over and yanked her share of the blankets back.

He sat up with a growl, his eyes flashing ominous in the flickering light. "There may as well be three people in here with that god-forsaken quilt stuffed between us!"

Grabbing up the bundle, he flung it across the room. "How bloody wide do you think this bed is, anyway?" He flopped onto his back.

"Well," she huffed, trying to sound more courageous than she felt. "There's no need to bully and curse."

"Madam, in case you haven't noticed, I am not a small man. And in case you have yet to notice, I have not harmed you. At this point, I would rather shag the innkeeper's horse-faced wife than place a finger half way to your side of the bed. Go to sleep!"

He snorted and went back to lying on his side, with Sarah left to stare at his broad back. She ogled his shoulders while lightning etched pale white around the edges of the curtains, and thunder gave off a muffled rumble in the distance. At least the storm was no longer overhead. Soon, it would be far enough away to allow a modicum of rest.

His breathing grew steady. Lord, he lay so close, his body heat radiating into her, smelling so fresh and turning her insides into knots. Odd, but at the same time, his closeness also gave her a peculiar sense of comfort. If she lifted her hand only a little, she could easily touch his hair. From the moment she'd laid eyes on him, she'd been drawn to those messy curls. The way they appeared so silky soft. Were they? She'd done fairly well at avoiding such consideration this evening, but now, with the storm settling and the quietude in the room, he stole any other thoughts.

Little good it did to tell herself over and over to think of him as a brother. A couple inches closer and she'd be nestled against him like spoons in a drawer. Her cheeks flushed at the improper thought, and her stomach curled at the notion of having shared a bed with him. But *he* acted as though such an event was a daily occurrence. Well, perhaps it was. Was he used to such behavior? After all, he was an unmarried viscount, handsome as sin, and most likely wealthy. Women probably fell all over themselves at his invitation to crawl in beside him. Maybe all it took was a simple lift of his eyebrow. That particular habit spoke volumes. And one he managed rather well. Yes, in all likelihood, women were eager to climb into his bed, while here she was desperately trying to figure a way out.

She took in a long, slow breath, only to catch his scent again. They had shared the same soap, so why did he smell different? It was as though a heady musk settled about him. Oh, dear. There went her senses again, running wild until she wanted to squirm.

It wouldn't do to rustle about and wake him. She held still until her legs ached. The air felt suddenly stifling, the room boxing her in. All because she was having an unholy reaction to his nearness. She didn't like this, not at all. And what was more, she was thoroughly disgusted with herself for being so entirely attuned to his every breath — and to the fact that he lay so close.

She couldn't help it. She fidgeted.

His breath hitched.

Well, she couldn't sleep, and lying still had turned into a painful impossibility. She reached out and set the tips of her fingers on his shoulder, but retracted them as though she'd touched fire. "Are you awake, Lord Eastleigh?"

"I am now," he responded.

"I'm sorry to awaken you, but I forgot to recommend something."

"Dear God, what now? That blasted quilt stays where it is."

"I wanted to ask you to remove yourself from the bed first thing in the morning, get yourself downstairs straight away, and allow me to see to my needs in private."

"Indeed, madam. I had planned on it. I was raised with a few manners, in case it's not apparent."

That went swimmingly. She inched back until her hips fairly hung off the bed. "Oh. I see. Well, good night, then."

• • •

What a blasted lie, pretending to be asleep. And what had he been about, telling her the last thing he wished to do was touch her? That flimsy nightrail she wore had seen so many washings it was practically threadbare. It did nothing to hide her breasts. With nipples that peaked like they were just begging to be nipped between his teeth. And despite their firmness, those splendid breasts had bounced when she'd raced across the room with that bloody quilt. And the way her round little arse jiggled and her hips swayed when she ran to fetch it. Not to mention the glimpse he got of those slim ankles when she'd lifted her gown. He could've watched that delightful little show all through the night.

His cock hardened, and an ache set in. He tried ignoring it and sought sleep, but the woman next to him breathed quietly, and with every inhale, he pictured her breasts rising up to meet his mouth.

Those perfect little peaks.

Damn it!

He rolled onto his side, away from her, but he swore he could feel her heat. Perhaps he should've chosen the carriage, after all. Nothing like cold rain to dash lascivious thoughts right out of one's head. He'd have gone there, knowing what a prude she was, except for the chance at a hot bath. God, the way his leg had set to aching in this foul weather, he had been desperate for a soak. He'd not had one the night before, the first time he'd missed out since he'd been removed from the battlefield. Still, here she was. He'd be a bigger liar if he told himself the thought of lying beside her didn't light a fire in him.

He snorted. If she knew what he was thinking, she'd be the one flying out of the room and into the carriage—bloody quilt and all. He snorted again.

"Are you quite all right?" Her voice sounded even more silken in the darkness.

"Quite, madam. I was in the beginnings of a dream and nearly dead asleep until you said something. Again." Lord, come morning, he'd find himself in Hades if he didn't stop fibbing. What he wouldn't give to pull her into his arms and order her to fall asleep curled against him. He set his teeth together at the renewed stiffness of his erection—so rigid as to be painful. And there was nothing he could do about it. Bloody, bloody hell!

Tossing and turning would do no good or she'd be kept awake as well, so he decided to figure out how many lambs might have been born by the time he returned home. Almost the same as counting sheep, but at least the numbers held purpose.

And fall asleep he must have, for when he opened his eyes, the essence of morning light shown through the edges of the curtains. But Lord Almighty, he faced a sleeping woman tucked up closed to him whose one hand rested beneath her cheek while the other curled around his waist. And his arm was slung around the top of her pillow, nearly cradling her against his shoulder. When had that happened?

He watched her sleep, so innocent, so lovely. He'd better rise before she opened her eyes and saw where she'd landed during the night. Not to mention the embarrassment of his physical state. Blame it on the morning, that. *Oh, yes, don't blame it on wanting her.* Never blame it on wanting the hell out of her.

He touched his lips to her forehead, caught the lovely scent of her hair and slowly, carefully, slid from the bed.

When he'd finished dressing, he made his way back to where she lay, still unmoving. What he wouldn't give to reach out and run the back of his hand across her cheek and gently wake her, but he dared not. She'd only fly from the bed and trip all over herself in that ridiculous nightrail.

"Wake up," he murmured, and gave the mattress a little shake. Her eyes fluttered open. She brushed a wisp of hair off her cheek, a blank look in her eyes until she remembered where she was. "Oh!"

There went the covers, up around her neck.

"And good morning to you, madam." He backed away from the bed. "Now then, I'm on my way downstairs. I'll see to having breakfast waiting for you, so if you're of a mind to make haste, we should arrive at my home in time for afternoon tea."

She sat up, pulling the bedding with her. "Truly? In time for tea?"

He nodded and couldn't help but grin. Damn she was beautiful, even sleepy-eyed. "Indeed." How he'd like to lean over and kiss that luscious mouth. Instead, he tossed the key onto the bed. "I'll be off then, hungry as a bear in spring, so do hurry." Like an idiot, he stood staring at her.

She shoved a lock of hair behind an ear, her eyes darting about the room as if in a panic.

He frowned. "What is it?"

"Well, you see, sir, I don't quite have all my clothing by which to properly…"

He opened the door and a basket sat in front of it. He took it up and lifted a corner of the fabric. "These are yours, I take it?"

Her cheeks flushed. "Oh, do put them down, you… you…"

He chuckled, set the basket inside the room, and made his exit.

· · ·

When the door snicked shut, Sarah scrambled from the bed, turned the key in the lock, and went about getting dressed. How she had managed to sleep so well with him next to her was puzzling, but she felt fully rested and renewed. Well, she had been exhausted. And he'd confessed to extreme fatigue, so he must have slept soundly, as well.

Dressed, she made her way down to the dining room and to the same table from the night before. Eastleigh sat facing the fire, his back to the room. As if sensing her presence, he glanced over his shoulder. His gaze, dark and delicious, rolled over her, from the tips of her toes to her head and back again. A tingle ran up her spine and landed at her nape, raising the fine hairs there. *Heavens.*

"Good morning, brother." She spoke loud enough for anyone nearby to hear, and slid into the chair across from him.

A corner of his mouth curled. "Good morning, Rose. Slept well, I suspect, seeing as how you didn't even hear me leave the room."

"Indeed," she replied, snapping the serviette over her lap. "So very different from how we grew up when you and the rest of our brothers bounded down the corridor like noisy rapscallions."

He grinned at his plate, muttered something she couldn't make out, and stuffed the last of his eggs into his mouth.

The innkeeper's wife approached and set a plate before Sarah filled with sausage, eggs, baked tomatoes, and beans. A crock of butter, a jar of marmalade, and a stack of toasted bread sat on the table between them.

Eastleigh placed his fork and knife on his plate, took a swig of coffee, and settled back in his chair. "Remember not to dawdle so we can make Mum's high tea. But then, you would know that, wouldn't you, Rose? You and Mum have always been so adamant about sharing your tea-time."

She flashed him a hard glare. "I refuse to gobble my food, Eastleigh."

He only grinned in response. And then, he watched every bite she slid into her mouth. After a while, his eyes took on an odd look she could've sworn was hunger. But that couldn't be—he'd already eaten.

Chapter Five

By the time Sarah and Eastleigh exited the inn and reached the open carriage door, the pup Sarah had taken on was out of the basket and sprawled on the leather seat, a wet spot spreading over one end.

"What is *that*?" Eastleigh growled.

"A puppy. What does it look like?" She glanced over her shoulder at Mrs. Whistlethorpe, who stood in the doorway, looking harried. No sign of Mr. Whistlethorpe, thank heavens. "And would you please lower your voice, you'll wake the world."

He squinted. "Does that thing only have three legs?"

"So it would appear. Which is why I laid claim to it, lest it be cruelly murdered."

"Well, you may not drag it along. I won't have the flea-bit thing."

Sarah's heart sank to a new low. She swept the puppy into her arms. "I can and I will. It's not flea-bit, and who are you to order me about?"

Eastleigh leaned forward and squinted into the carriage. "Bloody hell if it hasn't piddled on the good leather."

"Good leather? This is a rented carriage, for heaven's sake." She turned to the stable boy. "Could you please find a wet rag and clean off the bench?"

The boy looked to Eastleigh, who nodded. "You cannot keep the dog. I forbid it."

Those very words—*I forbid*—gripped her. They were as familiar as the skin attached to her bones. Somehow she knew she'd been prohibited many things throughout her life—to the point of having to endure unending bleakness. "Since I shan't remain with you very long, you will *not* be telling me what to do. I'll have this dog and that's that."

She ignored him and urged the pup back into the basket. Calm as she tried to appear on the outside, her insides shook like a leaf in the wind.

Eastleigh hooked an arm over a corner of the carriage door and shoved a hand into his pocket. "Since I rented the carriage, I suspect I might have a say in things."

"Fine. I shall remain here until my memory returns. I won't be bullied, and I won't have this dog's fate left to your arrogance and conceit."

He guffawed. "Remain here, at the inn? And do what? Live on air soup and rabbit track stew?"

"There's a chamber maid who just left the innkeeper's employ. I'll see to being hired in her stead."

"You are well bred, madam. You cannot possibly consider such a task. Now, please return the little beast from whence it came and join me in the carriage, or we will not make it to my home this day."

She managed to get the puppy back into the wicker basket, and slipping the handle over her arm, used her other hand to hold the dog down. She stared squarely into Eastleigh's eyes. "Then my upbringing will have educated me on what is expected of a maid, won't it?"

With her heart in her throat, she turned on her heel and headed back to the inn, where Mrs. Whistlethorpe stood wringing her hands. "Oh, milady, if Mr. Whistlethorpe catches you with that runt, he'll have my head."

Eastleigh's boots pounded the earth. He halted directly behind Sarah. "You can keep the blasted hound. Get in the carriage. Or will you have the rest of our brothers coming after you?"

She smiled at Mrs. Whistlethorpe. "I'll be on my way then. Thank you for everything." Without another word, she turned and marched back to the carriage.

Eastleigh took her elbow with one hand and reached for the basket with the other. "Give me the wretched beast whilst you get yourself inside."

Sarah settled into the far side of the carriage. A sense of victory flooded her being when Eastleigh slid the basket over to her with a gentle push and climbed in opposite her.

By the time the carriage pulled out of the drive and lurched onto the road, the dog was already working its way out of the basket, whining and carrying on. Sarah sighed and lifted it belly-up into her arms. She cradled it like one would a babe and went about lightly scratching its tummy. This dog was important to her. Very important. Here was the only thing she could anchor herself in—the only thing to call her own at present.

To her surprise, the pup settled right down as if it had

been delivered a drug. Within moments, its head lolled about and the tip of its little pink tongue hung out one side of its mouth. A bit of joyfulness settled in Sarah's heart.

Eastleigh snorted. "That's the ugliest thing I've ever seen."

She wanted to laugh. With a purposeful glance at Eastleigh's head, she said, "So it is. With its brown, curly hair, I see some resemblance."

He was silent for a moment. "So did you choose it because it looked like me?" His voice had changed, grown husky in that manner that both thrilled and frightened her.

When she didn't answer, he said, "What do you intend naming the thing? I can see it's a she."

Sarah thought for a moment, her fingers tracing little circles on the plump stomach. "I think I shall call her Daisy."

Eastleigh jerked. "You cannot name her that."

Sarah paused with her scratching and settled an angry gaze on Eastleigh. "There you go again, ordering me around. Something tells me I've been told what to do all my life, with no recourse but to comply, and here I am with you, a perfect stranger, trying to intimidate me and deliver imperatives."

"Perfect strangers?" A corner of his mouth twitched. "Might I remind you, we've twice shared a bed."

She narrowed her eyes. "That was low of you, Eastleigh. Very low."

He looked out the window and thumbed at his tooth. "Indeed. I do apologize." Nonetheless, his lips twitched.

"Then why don't you look me in the eye and say it like you mean it?"

He failed to turn her way. "Perhaps, I don't, then. Have it your way. Daisy it is."

The carriage knocked along for hours, halting every so often for the puppy to relieve itself. When they reached another inn and stopped for lunch, Sarah slipped the basket over her arm and carried it to a far corner of the dining room. Tossing bits of meat inside kept the pup quiet. Once back in the conveyance, however, there was no settling Daisy down until she was well ensconced in Sarah's lap.

Sarah dozed, and when she awoke, she found herself rolling along in an emerald green countryside. "Sheep," she announced.

With a startled jerk of his head, Eastleigh opened his eyes and peered out the carriage window. He covered a yawn with the back of his hand. "Home at last. The longest three days of my life."

What insolence. "Are they your sheep, sir?"

With a nod, he straightened in the seat. "At least I enjoyed a decent room our last night on the road. Not to mention a much needed bath and shave."

Heat pricked her cheeks at the idea of him naked in a bath, and in her bed. "So, this is all your land?"

"Indeed." His mouth lifted at one corner, which Sarah doubted had little to do with her question and more to do with guessing why her cheeks flamed.

"How much?"

"As far as the eye can see."

She caught sight of two ugly bronzed statues. They stood several feet apart and appeared to be misshapen back ends of horses facing the road. "What is *that*?"

"My cousin's idea of a joke. He claims his creation is art and will shoot anyone attempting to remove them."

"Why would you allow such an atrocity on your land?"

"Unfortunately, that little piece belongs to him."

"I thought you said the land as far as the eye could see belonged to you."

"Except for that fifteen-yard-wide strip he claims."

"Obviously, a sore spot." The carriage turned onto a long drive. Sarah caught sight of a grand entry flanked by two magnificent bronze statues of horses. She laughed. "Oh dear, that grotesque artwork back there has an odd resemblance to these two splendid ones."

"As I said, my cousin has a wicked sense of humor."

"Oh, do tell me the story."

"What story?" Something akin to a warning that she may have crossed a proprietary line flashed in his sharp gaze.

His eyes were remarkable. They should be considered quite plain, as there was nothing notable about brown eyes, but they fairly sparkled when something tickled him and seemed to withdraw like a tortoise into a shell when perturbed. Guilt or embarrassment shone through like a lit torch. And there were times when he seemed lost in thought, which was when those eyes seemed to pierce her very soul and send odd sensations sailing through her.

She wasn't about to back down from his current regard of her. "And if your cousin created his art, then who created yours?"

"I did."

"Do tell." What an unusual man. Despite the traumatic events, she realized she'd actually enjoyed moments of pleasurable company while they traveled. She'd learned a good deal about him in a few days, yet neither knew a speck about her.

He stretched his long legs to one side and propped his booted feet on the cushion. "This was all un-entailed Malvern land until the day my father let loose a team of mules and challenged us boys to head off in every direction. We had until sundown to circle back to the point of departure and lay claim to whatever land we'd traversed. First off, we drank ourselves into the ground, and then laid bets as to who could ride out farthest on the stubborn beasts—without saddles, mind you. My cousin, who'd been included, imbibed more than his share and rode in jagged circles, finally reaching the stables before dark with not much more than fifty acres to claim, including the odd shaped bit cutting right through my claim."

Sarah covered her mouth to keep from laughing. "Don't tell me you've been at odds ever since?"

When he merely shrugged, she clasped her hands in her lap. "How long ago was this?"

"Let's see, I was six and twenty. Four years ago."

"You are still angry with him."

His eyes sparked. "Oh, he's angry as well. Just look at those god-forsaken statues."

"I should like to meet your cousin."

"You shan't." He made to rise but quickly sat back, staring at her with those piercing eyes. "I mean, I hope you have your memory back by then and you can live your life as you see fit without ever having to run across the good-for-nothing."

"Are those mulberry trees lining the drive?" *Quite proper to change the subject, wasn't it?*

"Indeed."

Oh, here was heaven. Green rolling hills dotted with sheep, many with newborns appearing no bigger than puffs of cotton from where she sat. Streams cut through the land, looking like blue ribbons clipped from a spring bonnet. Pink cabbage roses the size of saucers hugged fences, their roots mingling with a low border of colorful flowers. She intended to pick them on her walks. She suddenly realized that she loved to walk.

Stands of trees grew thicker, and when she spotted mares and foals, she slid to the other side of the carriage and poked her head out the window. "Oh, my. This is why I love springtime."

Remembering her manners, she pulled her head back inside the carriage and primly folded her hands in her lap. "You've a beautiful estate."

He used his tongue to fiddle with that broken tooth, a half-smile on his lips. Her heart skipped a beat and her mouth went dry.

The carriage made a turn in the circular drive, and a pale limestone mansion, stately looking, but welcoming, loomed before her. Servants lined either side of the steps. A scruffy mongrel raced to the carriage, its tongue lapping in and out in a way that signaled happiness.

A tall and lean, gray-haired man looking to be in his late fifties stood beside a short, white-haired lady dressed in bright red and wearing an enormous hat to match. Did hats actually come so large? And was that a stuffed bluebird on top? Sitting in a real nest? Who in heaven's name was she expecting dressed that way?

"Is that the good doctor and your grandmother?"

Eastleigh chuckled. "Welcome to my home."

A footman opened the carriage door and helped Sarah out. Eastleigh followed while he petted the dog. "Good girl, Daisy."

"Daisy? Why, you deceitful brute. No wonder you argued the name. Well, what does it matter if there are two with the same moniker? It's not as if my stay is permanent. "

Eastleigh regarded her with an intensity that was palpable, but said nothing.

Mum marched toward Sarah, and for all to hear called out, "It's about time you returned with my ward."

"That'll work," he muttered.

Sarah stiffened her spine further and paused. Eastleigh stepped to her side, placed his hand at the small of her back, and discreetly nudged her forward.

"Do this for Mum," he murmured and bowed his head to his grandmother.

"You are *not* required to instruct me on what I well know how to do," she whispered back and genuflected to his grandmother. "Your Grace."

When she lifted her head, the doctor and Eastleigh were exchanging knowing glances. *What was that about?* Despite his pleasant smile, the doctor's countenance held a serious demeanor when he regarded her.

"Gel, aren't you the one, though," Mum said. "Just look at you. Meat on the bones, that's what this one needs."

Good heavens, Sarah couldn't take her eyes off the red hat and the stuffed bird. Were those tiny eggs in the nest real? And oh my, were those walnut-size stones in Mum's brooch actual rubies?

Mum turned and opened her arms to Eastleigh with a glow on her face that bespoke adoration.

All formality dropped, and he bent to give her a hug. "Missed you, Mum."

"Aye. You haven't aged a day."

He laughed. "I've only been gone a week."

She stepped back and looked him over from head to toe. "Is that all? You said you'd be gone three or four years."

"Months, Mum. Three or four months. But my plans changed, and I returned home with...ah...your ward a bit sooner than expected."

She started at the top of Sarah's head and scanned her to her toes. "Well, then, do come along. Time for tea."

Eastleigh turned to the man beside her. "This is Doctor Hemphill, madam. I expect he's here for full tea since he never misses it."

His words were a nice cover in front of the servants, but Sarah was acutely aware of Hemphill giving her a thorough looking over. Had she ever been to a doctor before? She wished she knew. He seemed kindly enough, but there was something rigid about him that indicated a hard taskmaster and left her feeling ill at ease. How she wished she could disappear into the chamber set aside for her. "You live nearby, Lord Eastleigh tells me."

"Should you need any physicking, I am down the lane." He nodded to a shaded stone path leading beyond the stables. "I think you'll find Easton Park a pleasant place."

She turned to Eastleigh. "Easton Park? Might I guess the direction in which you rode the mule?"

Eastleigh's cheeks flushed. He raked his fingers through his hair. "Tea time, right-o, Mum?"

Mum took his arm and marched toward the entrance. "'Tis that. Hemphill, see to Miss Marks. I sent notice of your arrival to your siblings and Her Majesty. I told them of my *female* ward you were bringing to me."

Eastleigh groaned. "You didn't."

"Of course I did. I just said so, didn't I? Would I lie?"

He lifted a brow at his grandmother. "That's debatable, Mum."

"I said lie, not fib."

"Well, whatever it is you do or do not," Eastleigh said, "they'll be descending upon Easton Park like locusts soon enough."

Sarah bit her tongue to keep from smiling. It wouldn't be proper, after all.

Doctor Hemphill touched the small of her back, and at the same time, motioned for the servants to follow in behind Eastleigh and Mum, leaving the two of them alone.

Sarah turned to regard the doctor and found a deep frown sculpting his brow. Deftly, she eased away from his touch. She knew one thing with certainty now: as innocuous as he appeared, he was a man—and not only did men make her quite uncomfortable, danger lurked in a mere touch. "You have something you wish to say to me, sir?"

"I'd like to remind you that you are not my only patient."

A cold chill ran down her stiffening spine. "Your meaning?"

"I *mean* Eastleigh has not yet fully recovered from his time at war, as I think he's made you well aware."

Anger overpowered her embarrassment at being pulled aside when she'd barely arrived. "If you think I have designs on him, think again, Doctor. I only wish to recover my memory and make my way home." She lifted her chin. "You don't care much for me being here, do you?"

"Dear God, that's not it at all." He pinched the bridge of

his nose. "I think it only fair to inform you that while yours was a knock on the head that broke no flesh, Eastleigh's condition came out of a war, where not only did he sustain severe wounds to his body, but to his soul as well. Carving out the heart of an enemy, if required, can do terrible things to a person."

Hemphill's dark eyes bore into Sarah's, and a sickening feeling curled in the pit of her stomach. "What are you inferring?"

"He's been wounded in more ways than you will ever know. Ways even his family is unaware."

"But you have knowledge of everything, don't you? Weren't you on the battlefield with him?"

He nodded, sorrow filling his eyes. "It was two years before he could look in the mirror and identify the image as his own. Perhaps there are things he doesn't wish to recall. Take care, Miss Marks."

He turned and motioned to the front entry, this time clasping his hands behind his back and well away from her. "Shall we?"

The entrance into the manse was lined on either side with carved benches in dark wood, candelabras, and one lone set of shining armor in the nook where the stairs made a turn. Sarah dared not ask about the relic since to inquire would be impolite.

Instead of showing her to her room, Mum and Eastleigh led her onto a sunny terrace where a table was set for full tea—sandwiches, delicate platters filled with meats and cheeses, fruits, and carved vegetables. A tiered confectionery held several layers of desserts.

Surely, they didn't expect her to take tea without offering

her a bit of privacy? She desperately needed a privy. "I beg your pardon, Mum, but may I see to freshening up a bit first?"

"Why? You look just fine. Doesn't she, Hemphill? Not a hair out of place."

Eastleigh's lips curled at one corner. He whispered something in his grandmother's ear.

"Oh, that." She waved her hand about. "Well, then, why didn't she say so?"

A female servant stepped forward. "This way, Miss Marks."

"I'll show her to her chamber." Eastleigh offered his arm.

Sarah pretended she hadn't noticed and walked past him, too embarrassed to make eye contact.

"Nice enough gel," Mum said in a voice loud enough for anyone within shouting distance to hear. "A couple of weeks around the Malverns ought to loosen that rod up her arse."

"Sink me," Eastleigh muttered.

Stunned, Sarah paused. A rod up her nether regions? At that moment, she was certain, quite, quite certain, she had never been around the likes of this grand old lady. From somewhere deep within, a bubble of laughter threatened to surface. With a flip of her head, she tossed her words over her shoulder. "Thy rod and thy staff, they comfort me."

Chapter Six

Mum was about to pour tea. She always poured tea. It was how she held court. Eastleigh raised a brow when a footman rolled in a tea cart laden with an intricately carved silver pot, the spout towering above its round belly like a crow's nest on a ship.

When Mum told the naughty tale of how a Turkish sheikh had gifted her with the distinctive vessel after she'd given him the night of his life, Sarah blushed until her ears pinked. Eastleigh nearly burst into laughter.

Sarah. Despite wearing the same dress, she appeared fresh as the morning sun, spine straight as a tailor's chalk line, with not an inch touching the back of the chair. So proper. So lovely. Most likely, she ached for a bath and fresh clothing, but one would never know.

The servant lined the cups in front of Mum and then set two small pots beside her. Mum poured, and then gripped the handles of the small pots and regarded Sarah. "Milk or gin, dear?"

Sarah blinked, wide-eyed, at Eastleigh.

He chuckled. "And you thought the question would be one lump or two?"

It wasn't anything he could name, but something spirited washed over Sarah's countenance. Her chin lifted. "Gin, please."

Hemphill jerked. "Easy, Mum."

She waved him off with flippant fingers, poured a good dollop of gin into her own cup, and splashed a bit into Sarah's. She lifted the matching sugar bowl. "You'll need three lumps, dear. Two for the cup, one for the cheek."

Sarah deposited two lumps into her gin-laden tea and held the other aloft with the silver pincers. "For the cheek?"

"It's the Russian way," Mum replied. "Works as well with gin as vodka. What have you, gentlemen?"

Sarah took the sugar cube in her fingers, turned it about like a single die, then tucked it inside her cheek.

"Small sips, madam," Eastleigh said, certain this was a first for her.

She gave off a little shiver as the liquid coursed down her throat. "Gads." A pause, and then another sip.

Mum beamed. Hemphill studied Sarah. And as for Eastleigh himself? Well, he might well be in love. Could one fall in love in a mere three days? Or was it merely lust? Of course, it was lust. He desired her—no doubt—and not in a room three doors from his, but in his bed, both of them naked, their mouths all over one another. He'd take the starch right out of her spine in a matter of minutes. Heat rolled through his groin. He set his serviette across his lap and silently thanked Mum for the overblown tablecloths she insisted upon.

Who would have thought his life would take such a turn? He could have scoured the Continent from Saint Petersburg to Rome and never found anyone who heightened his senses the way this woman did. Despite her prim ways, he was certain there was undiscovered passion running through her. And just look how Mum took to her.

But there was the bloody amnesia. What would come of that? Or her, once she regained her memory? She could be gone in a flash. It didn't matter that he stirred something in her—and he well knew he did, no sense playing games about that. He'd had three days to do nothing but sit in the damn carriage and stare at that sultry mouth of hers or watch her rein in emotions running rampant across her countenance every time he'd caught her studying him.

"Ahem," Hemphill coughed into his closed fist. "As I was saying, Eastleigh—"

He cocked a brow. "Yes?" Deuces take it, how long had his thoughts drifted?

"I was instructing Miss Marks on the significance of keeping a journal during her recovery. Since you kept one, are there any insights you'd care to convey?"

Eastleigh bunched the serviette over his fading erection and cleared his throat. "I cannot stress enough the importance of following that particular directive, madam..."

"Sarah. You may call me Sarah while in private."

Sarah Marks. He still couldn't get used to the name. "Patterns began to appear in my journal, and reading through them triggered recollections. My dreams were also helpful. They revealed things about myself and helped me recover pieces of my mind and string them together in a proper order. But don't force anything—your memories will surface of their own accord."

"At least until the cherries ripen," Mum put in.

He turned to his grandmother. "The cherries?"

Mum ignored him and gave Sarah's hand a squeeze. "I make the best cherry cordial, dear. And then there's apple season. I do a very nice cider. If your memory returns before then, perhaps you can fib that it hasn't. I'd hate to have you leave before winter sets in."

Hemphill rolled his eyes. "It's only May, Mum."

"That, too." Mum's face lit. "A right good spring we're having, isn't it? Did I tell you about my affairs in the desert, dear?"

Eastleigh shook his head, warning Sarah not to ask.

A wisp of a smile danced across her precious lips. "Please, do go on."

"Then let the cards fall where they may," he muttered.

Mum wiggled in her chair with her eyes mere slits from her grand smile. "Well, Lady Hester Stanhope and I...you do know of Lady Hester Stanhope?"

Sarah shook her head. "At least, I don't recall."

"Oh, my, you do have amnesia, don't you? More tea?"

"With cream this time, please."

"Lady Stanhope was my dear friend. She's dead now. Toes tipped up in a monastery out in the high desert. Two lumps, dear. You don't need the other in your cheek." Mum plopped the sugar into Sarah's cup.

"The gel was awarded a grand pension—which she flagrantly enjoyed. We were both deplorably bored with our stiff lives, she no longer involved in politics, and I with a passel of brats and a husband as bland as morning porridge, so we took off for parts unknown."

Sarah's eyes widened. "Oh, my, you left your family?"

Mum shrugged. "What was I to do with nannies about, sit and watch the grass grow?" Her eyes squeezed shut again with that infectious smile that brought roses to her cheeks.

Eastleigh chuckled. "Might I remind you, Mum, your first husband had passed away—before you had any children—prior to you sailing off with Lady Hester."

Mum regarded him with a brief quizzical look. "The nerve of him dying so young." She turned to Sarah. "Well, anyway, off we went by sea, eventually heading for Constantinople, but we never made it after our ship crashed on the rocks in Rhodes."

"Oh," Sarah jumped. "How dreadful."

"Not at all. We lost every stitch of clothing and had to borrow the Turks'. That's when we discovered how we loved the way they dressed—the men, that is. Lady Hester never wore anything but robes, turbans, and slippers thereafter. We tramped about in the desert for several years, slept in the tents of Bedouin sheikhs, traipsed through Turkish palaces, visited a Pasha or three, and learned to smoke water pipes. As for what happened within the tents, well, that remains private, if you will."

The color ran high in Sarah's cheeks.

Mum turned to Eastleigh. "I do believe I've shocked the gel."

"And I do believe you intended to," he responded in a monotone.

Despite the blush to her cheeks, Sarah boldly regarded him. "Lady Hester Stanhope and Mum running around the desert in men's clothing? *Humph*. They would not have survived a day."

A corner of his mouth twitched. "I've seen the letters from Lady Hester. Perhaps you'd like to study them since your... ah...interest is duly piqued?"

She said nothing while those plump lips of hers parted. Whatever was passing through her mind—or body—he'd bet it had to do with him. Damn if his own body didn't respond the only way it knew how—flaming and stupidly.

Hemphill leaned forward. "I do believe Miss Marks is fatigued, Mum. She's endured a long trip and shouldn't be overtaxed. She needs the privacy of her chambers for the rest of the evening, including dinner served in her room. Agreed, Miss Marks?"

Sarah looked down at her clothing and frowned.

"Not to worry," Mum said. "Augie's youngest sister grew so rapidly over the winter, she left some of her wardrobe behind. We'll send a lady's maid handy with a needle to your room should anything require adjusting."

"Augie?" Sarah's lips pursed as if to fight a smile.

Eastleigh rolled his eyes.

"Why, yes, Prince Augustus here," Mum said. "But I've called him Augie since he was in leading strings."

Augie. Damn if he didn't detest that name. "Which is precisely why I think of myself as Eastleigh, and nothing else."

Sarah mouthed the words "Prince Augustus" with quivering lips. "Of course, he'd be a prince since you are the Queen Mother."

"Indeed," Mum responded. "And tomorrow we shall begin your lessons in properly greeting the queen. Since I sent word of Augie's homecoming, the entourage is sure to arrive soon."

Eastleigh grunted. "Like locusts."

Mum rose and turned to Sarah. "Come, dear, let me see you to your rooms. But first you might like to view…"

Eastleigh stepped around the table. "No, Mum. Miss Marks can peruse your collections later. At the moment, she requires rest."

Disappointment ruffled Mum's countenance, and she appeared confused for a moment. But then her eyes cleared. "Yes, yes, you only arrived today, didn't you? Well, gel, tomorrow we shall begin anew. So very much to do." She wandered off.

Hemphill stepped between Eastleigh and Sarah. "A word, Eastleigh. Miss Marks, the servant here will see you to your chamber." He turned on his heel. Once out the door, he veered left.

Eastleigh cocked a brow. "The library, is it? Must be serious." He turned to Sarah, who'd grown pale.

He resisted the urge to take her in his arms. "You're safe here." God, he wanted to kiss her. "Rest well."

She gave a little nod. "Everything is so strange when one has no recollections."

Those sorrowful blue eyes nearly undid him. "Imagine what it was like for me to return home and feel the same way about my family who knew and loved me—all strangers."

"You'll see to sending off inquiries on my behalf?"

He nodded. "First thing in the morning."

She backed away. "Thank you. You've been more than kind."

He regarded the gentle sway of her hips as she departed, and then he strode into the library and closed the door.

"Don't touch her, Eastleigh." Hemphill's face was a stern mask, his bushy brows drawn together. "Do not so much as take her by the elbow to escort her anywhere. Not until she has her memory back, at least." He picked up a book and leafed through it.

Fury shot through Eastleigh, along with a good dose of guilt. "Look here. I have no intention of doing anything unseemly."

"Come, now." Hemphill tossed the book back on the table with a thud. "I see the way you look at her—any blind fool can see right through you."

"I can't help it if I am attracted to—"

"Have you forgotten what we are dealing with here?" Hemphill's voice rose to a shout. "One wrong move could erase her memory forever, damn it. We need to do all we can to see she recovers and remembers her life."

Eastleigh shoved his hand through his hair. "Perhaps never remembering is not such a bloody bad idea."

"You can't mean that." Hemphill's tone softened. "For God's sake, think what it's been like for you. Look at the setback you had when you ran into your cousin come home from the war."

A muscle in Eastleigh's jaw twitched. "We'll never settle our differences."

"You will, in due time. For now, you have a woman above stairs who has no idea who she is, where she came from, or anything beyond the past few days. Until her full memory returns—until she can think freely and without constraint—leave her the hell alone!"

Chapter Seven

Sarah slipped out of bed and made her way to the balcony doors where she flung open the curtains. A soft glow spilled into the room. No matter which way the window hangings were drawn, either open or closed, the full moon raised havoc with her ability to sleep. But then, she'd kept to her chambers since her arrival and had taken so many naps after her exhausting trip, no wonder she'd grown restless.

Her stomach growled. She ran a hand over her belly. Why did her appetite have to return full-force in the middle of the night? She ignored the inner grumblings and decided to spend some time writing in the journal Doctor Hemphill had insisted she keep.

Lighting a small lamp on her desk, she sat, dipped her pen into the inkwell and poised her hand over the open diary. Nothing. She propped her elbow on the table, set her chin in her hand, and stared at the moon. Her stomach bit at her backbone. She glanced down at the journal where she'd mindlessly scribbled the word "cake." Would it be wicked to sneak down to the kitchen? Wherever that might be? Surely no one would mind. Another noisy rumble, and her stomach clenched.

Perhaps some milk. There'd likely be no sleep at all if she didn't at least fill a bit of empty space. Donning a silk dressing gown, she took up the oil lamp, and shutting little Daisy in the room behind her, went in silent pursuit of sustenance. Reaching the main floor, she stood in the corridor a moment, pondering. Where to find the servant's stairwell that led to the kitchens below? The dining room. Of course. She headed toward the rear of the house.

A subtle change in the air, and she paused. Then she *felt* more than heard a door snick open behind her. *Oh, dear.*

"Are you lost?"

No mistaking that deep, husky voice sliding across her skin and leaving a tingling in its wake. And her in a nightrail! With the lamp in one hand, and clutching the buttons at the top of her robe—as if that would lend a bit of dignity—she turned.

At the sight of him, her breath hitched. She'd not seen him since their arrival. If anything, he'd grown more gloriously handsome.

He slipped his hands into his pockets and casually leaned a shoulder against the door's frame. He wore a shirt with the sleeves rolled back, a pair of dark trousers, and black slippers. That curly hair of his hung softly over his forehead as though he'd swiped his hands through it so many times, he'd given up and let it fall where it may.

Her skin prickled. "Lord Eastleigh. I am so sorry to disturb you."

Pushing away from the threshold, he strolled over to where she stood. "You don't bother me in the least. I often have trouble sleeping when the moon is full. Tonight being no exception."

"It's kept me awake as well."

He studied her through lowered lids.

Her stomach decided to harangue her again. Had he heard? Heat crawled up her neck and spread through her cheeks.

"Hungry?"

Oh, yes, he'd heard. "How utterly embarrassing."

"Don't be." His eyes, dark and curious, settled on her mouth. The prickling that had been skating on the surface burrowed deep beneath her skin and raced along every nerve in her body.

She stood there, staring into those mesmerizing eyes as if she'd lost all reason. Gathering her wits, she took a step back.

He came forward, closing more distance between them than what she'd managed to carve out in her retreat. "Hemphill has been a bit concerned about the way you've been playing with your food. You ate a good meal that one night at the inn, but other than that, you've apparently eaten little these past three days."

She could smell him now, the scent of soap and musk and a hint of liquor. Her hand tightened around the top button of her dressing gown.

His gaze dropped from her mouth to where she clutched her robe, skipped back up to her lips, and then to her eyes. The pulse low in her belly struck a new beat. What was happening to her? She cleared her throat. "Well, it seems my appetite has suddenly returned with a vengeance, and I was concerned I might not sleep at all if I didn't do something about it. I was looking for the kitchen, but if it's an imposition, I can forego."

"Come." He set his hand to the small of her back, and taking the lamp from her, held it aloft while he guided her along the hallway. "I've been known to sneak in at night on occasion, myself."

Oh, his touch! So hot it seared through the silk of her dressing gown and chased after the tingling that refused to abate.

She should run.

Her stomach growled again.

A low chuckle reverberated through his chest. "We need to take care of that hunger, or you'll be pacing the floor until breakfast."

By the time they reached the kitchen, Sarah was a bundle of nerves, from the top of her head to her bare feet. Oh, no! Please don't let him notice she'd not bothered with slippers. Or the havoc his nearness provoked. She eased away from his hand.

He didn't seem to notice her maneuver. He set the lamp down and pulled a chair to a large wooden table. "Sit. I know where to look."

A quick survey of the paraphernalia in front of her produced a few bowls nesting inside one another, a couple of pots holding heaven knew what, a tray holding various and sundry items, and a large knife that appeared to be exceedingly sharp. The cook's preparation table.

Eastleigh returned with a platter holding a hunk of bread, cheese, and a jar of fruit. He set them on the table and pulled a chair next to her. "I found some excellent Stilton.

Don't know if you like morello cherries, but I brought them just in case. Cook hides all she can from Mum, or they end up in her liquor cabinet as a cordial."

Lord, he sat far too close for comfort. She could barely think.

He sawed on the bread and tossed her a crooked grin. "I won't bite if that's what has you looking so concerned."

She shifted in her seat. "I'm only wondering if this is at all proper."

"What? Stealing into my own kitchen?" He speared a thin slice of Stilton on the end of the knife and lifted it to her lips. "Eat."

For pity's sake, she'd never done anything so unmannerly as to take food off a carving knife.

At her hesitation, he leaned closer and tugged at her chin until her lips parted. He slid the piece of cheese into her mouth. The rich, creamy texture nearly caused her to moan.

"That's it. Good girl." The timbre of his voice deepened, while at the same time, it took on a smoky quality. And his eyes—no mistaking the hunger in them. He speared another slice, popped it into his own mouth, and chewed slowly.

Oh, why was he looking at her like that? She wanted to say something clever to lighten the moment, but her frazzled brain came up with nothing.

"More?"

She nodded.

He carved a few slices, set the knife down, and proceeded to feed her by hand. "This is the first time we've been alone since our arrival."

His words, low in his throat, came as a seductive breeze across her cheek. As his fingers left her mouth, they made a light sweep along her bottom lip. Her throat tightened. Had he done that on purpose, or was it merely her imagination?

"Indeed," was all she could manage.

"There has always been someone around to inhibit my knocking upon your chamber door. I suspect on purpose. But what do you know, here we are in the kitchen." He blinked, slow and lazily. "I rather like it. Do you?"

She dared not respond lest her voice not function. Instead, she watched him pick up the jar of cherries, and with the tip of the knife, remove the beeswax off the top. He set the blade down, his actions slow and deliberate.

Not bothering with a spoon or fork, he dipped his fingers straight into the jar, lifted out one of the dark cherries, and gave it a little shake. He was going to feed her again, and she wouldn't stop him. Didn't think she could. She didn't want to.

"You have the most beautiful, kissable mouth I have ever seen." His eyes darkened, and he leaned closer. "Now open."

Heart pounding, she complied. Her eyelids drifted nearly shut as he slid the syrupy morsel past her lips. A drop of liquid pooled at the corner of her mouth. Before she could do anything about it, he swept up the juice with his thumb, and then licked the tip. "That should have been my tongue taking care of removing such sweetness."

A ribbon of heat unfurled in her belly. Oh, Lord! Her eyes shot wide, and she stood so fast the chair fell back with a clatter. She gulped, swallowing the cherry whole.

"What?" He examined his stained thumb and licked it again. He looked at her with a sultry grin. "Do you have any idea how long I have wanted to kiss you?"

She reached for the lantern, hoping her trembling

fingers could hang onto it. "I had better remove myself to my chamber."

"I'll see you there." He stood.

"No, I had best make my way alone."

"If you wish." He picked up a candle sitting in a small pewter holder, and lighting it off the lamp, set the candle down. "Can I ask you a question before you take your leave?"

She was so lightheaded she was afraid to respond.

"Never mind, I'll ask anyway." He leaned a hip on the table and folded his arms over his chest. "Have you wondered what a shared kiss might be like?"

Oh, she had, but she wouldn't dare admit it! "Lord Eastleigh, I do need to go."

"Yet you haven't moved an inch, your eyes just dropped to my mouth, and your cheeks are the color of the cherry you just swallowed. Whole, I'll bet."

His gaze swept the length of her and back up. "Let me tell you how it is—you do want to know, but you find yourself in a predicament. You are alone with me in your night clothes. And you are afraid."

He unfolded his arms and leaned back, his palms against the table. "You're safe with me. I would never hurt you or push you to do anything against your will. But it's written all over you—you want that kiss."

He tossed her a little grin. "You'll get it, and we'll both be happier for having done so. But I'll make certain you're in a place you feel safe and where nothing further can occur but a simple kiss. Now, good night."

• • •

Sarah stood in the middle of the flower garden, her face to the sun, and breathed in the fresh, sweetly scented air. Doctor Hemphill had been right—keeping a journal was imperative. If she hadn't snatched up the pen upon awakening her very first morning here, the vague memory of a spring garden filled with a riot of colors might have escaped her. At this rate of recovery, perhaps she would be home—wherever that was—in no time.

An orange and black butterfly flitted from one bright flower to another. *Such a beautiful thing.* The thought sent a wave of pleasure washing through her. She stepped around Daisy, who lay curled at her feet. "Look here, Mr. Jenkins, a painted lady."

The gardener, bent on one knee checking cabbage roses for mites, glanced her way. "Other than Lady Willamette Malvern, I've not met anyone who knows so much about flowers and bugs, Miss Marks."

"Can you believe that's the third species of Lepidoptera I've caught sight of this morning? I'm going to need something other than a pen for my sketches."

"Then you shall have whatever you require, madam," came Eastleigh's familiar, deep voice.

Startled, Sarah turned, and there he stood, leaning a shoulder against one of the thick pillars supporting the covered terrace, one long leg crossed casually over the other at the ankle, tea cup in hand. Her throat thickened, and heat scored her insides. He was dressed in shirtsleeves again, and a cream-colored waistcoat covered his flat stomach. She spied his dark superfine jacket hanging on the back of a chair. How long had he been watching her? The rakish way he grinned melted her bones.

Shading her eyes with her hand, she called out. "What a marvelous garden you have, Eastleigh. I feel as though I've come home."

His smile widened, dazzling her. "I do believe you're quite at ease amidst a blaze of flowers. Which I find most tantalizing. Three species of what, you say?" He set his cup down, stepped from the terrace, and approached her, moving with a lazy grace.

She swallowed hard, ignoring the way her heartbeat kicked up. Oh, please don't let him mention the other night in the kitchen!

Gathering her scattered thoughts, she motioned around the garden. "Lepidoptera. Look here, a common blue." She pointed to a small, periwinkle-colored butterfly perched on a flower and fanning its wings at about the same rate as her breath fluttered in her breast. "Although why it gets the lowly name of common, I hardly know, since it is quite the loveliest of flying things."

"Ouch!" The gardener sucked on his finger. "Beg pardon, I cut myself."

"Wash it thoroughly and dab it with honey," Sarah replied. "Then wrap it in a clean cloth to prevent infection." Her pulse tripped a beat. "Oh! How did I know that?"

"I don't have a clue." Eastleigh continued moving toward her, slow and easy. "But it seems you do, don't you?" His gaze remained fixed on her. "Jenkins, make your way to the kitchens. Cook will provide the honey."

"Yes, sir." The gardener stood and hastened toward the servants' entrance.

Something powerful shifted in Eastleigh, redefining the space between them. Sarah dizzied at his purposeful approach, wrought now with a kind of feral energy. If it was a species they spoke of, here was a magnificent human specimen. His shirt, crisp and white beneath his waistcoat, lay open at the neck. The black riding breeches tucked into glossy black boots could be called indecent the way they hugged slim hips that rolled when he moved.

Her heart left her chest and jumped into her throat. "Take care with the path you're on, sir or you might trample the seedlings."

"Oh, I'm clearly on the right path." The intensity of his gaze deepened, sending a little shiver through her. "It seems that I find myself thinking of you to the point of distraction. Especially these past two days." He paused in front of her and set his fingers to the stem of a pale blue graceful deutzia, as if meaning to pluck it.

"Oh, no!" She reached out to stop him. "I mean…" She froze when she realized what she had done, and that his hand beneath hers held more fire than the sun overhead. "What I meant was…was that it's far too fragile a flower to be snapped off at the stalk like that."

Slowly, he turned his hand under hers until their palms met, one pulsating against the other. "You look beautiful this morning," he said. "But then, I don't find my assessment particularly unusual."

The timbre of his voice vibrated through her as though a deep chord had been struck. And then, except for a small movement of his thumb, stillness came over him. She stared at the way he caressed her skin in soft, supple strokes. Her thoughts slowed until they only mimicked what had been, until a brief moment ago, a decently intelligent mind. His fingers were long and strong, his nails clean and trimmed, his palm broad. And that wonderful musk surrounding him.

She drew in a shallow breath. "Please, stop." She didn't mean a word. Not at all. The sense of freedom that had soared through her when she'd earlier stepped into the garden cried for greater release. *Touch me more.* She tried for another breath, only to have it escape her lungs in a quiver.

"You'll have to be the one to pull free." His voice came low in his chest, raw and husky. "For I cannot seem to let you go."

She watched the slow swirling of his thumb.

He took a small step closer. He was so near, the heat of his body penetrated her more deeply than the sun's rays. "We are in the garden now, in full view of whatever spectator might wander by, so you are in a safe place."

"So I realize," she uttered, continuing to contemplate his gentle caress as if it were a magnet—finding and capturing every fiber she possessed. Oh, her ears were ringing.

"And all they would encounter is me standing before you with your hand in mine." He was so close, his words tumbled onto her mouth. "Innocent enough, wouldn't they think?"

"I...I would suppose so," she said calmly, but the quick inrush of her breath told another story.

A low sound left his throat. His other hand came up and tucked a loose curl behind her ear, sending a thousand shivers running through her. "They'd not have any way of knowing the simple act convolutes your insides, would they?"

"Oh, dear."

"Nor would they know that I have hungered for such a moment as this."

Tearing her gaze from his hand, she peered up at him. Lord, he was about to kiss her. And there was nothing she could—or would—do to stop him for she, too, had been thoroughly distracted by thoughts of him ever since that night in the kitchen.

"Eastleigh," she whispered, and closing her eyes, swayed into him.

His supple mouth found hers and gently shaped it against his own. He kissed her with a slow hunger until she grew weak. His arm went around her, holding her upright— cradling her. His free hand found her cheek, and his fingers traced a warm, sensuous trail, like sunbeams washing across her face. He released her lips long enough to murmur against her mouth, things she couldn't make out, soothing endearments. And then, with a low moan, his kiss deepened, and his tongue parted her lips, sweeping inside.

"Ho, there!" Doctor Hemphill called out, rounding the corner of the house.

They both stepped back, but the harsh expression on the physician's face told Sarah he'd seen plenty. She turned her head in embarrassment.

Eastleigh put his back to her, shielding her, and fisted his hands on his hips. "What the devil do you want?"

Hemphill halted. "You've family arriving."

"Bloody hell. How many?"

"Three carriages, five uniformed outriders, and two gentlemen on horseback, most likely Ridley and Thomas since Sebastian prefers holding court inside a conveyance."

Eastleigh headed for the terrace. "Brilliant. The whole lot of them."

She heard the noise then—the rattle of carriages, the

pounding of hoofs. Fear gripped her insides.

He glanced over his shoulder. "Go the back way up to your chamber. There's no need to join us until you're ready." He grabbed his jacket and headed toward the front of the house shooting her a mischievous grin. "Which could be next week, if it suits you."

Sarah lifted her skirts and hurried past the doctor. "If you'll excuse me."

"Miss Marks," Hemphill called out.

She already had one foot inside the doorway, but she paused. "Sir?"

He stepped onto the terrace, deep lines furrowing his brow. "Again, I must remind you to take care, and that you are not my only patient."

"And might I remind you that I have two very prominent goals, one of which is to regain my memory, and the other is to return home, which I cannot get to without the other. You offend me, Doctor Hemphill."

Something in the man softened, but only a little. "And what if your memory returns and you find home is not a place you wish to return to? What would you do then, Miss Marks? Would you endeavor to remain here?"

Something dark flashed through her brain, and foreboding washed behind it. Wherever home was, it was not a pleasant place. Not at all. She turned and hurried into the house and up the stairs, a sinking feeling in the pit of her stomach.

She entered her bedchamber, locked the door, and promptly ran into a fleshy, mob-capped maid. She stumbled backward. "Oh!"

"Beg pardon, Miss Marks. Tildy's me name, and I'm to be yer permanent chambermaid. I was off to see me mum when ye arrived, so Sally saw to yer needs, meantime."

"Oh, Tildy, please help me. I'm soiled from the garden. And my hair."

The maid helped Sarah out of her gown, and then went to the wardrobe where she dug around and removed a pink frock. She shook it out with a snap of her wrist. "Will this do?"

A great roar sounded from below.

"What in heaven's name was that?" Sarah stepped into the gown, giving no heed to the design.

"That would be the Malverns having at it. But not to worry, Miss Marks, they's just playing sport with one another. Now, if'n ye'll sit, I'll see to yer hair."

Moving to the boudoir table, Sarah slid onto the blue velvet-covered bench and proceeded to nervously tap her foot while Tildy combed the loose tendrils in place. The idea of remaining in her lovely chambers drew a sigh from Sarah. What was to dislike in here, while who knew *what* awaited her below?

"His lordship did up this room," Tildy said, watching Sarah through the mirror.

"You mean he chose everything in here?"

Tildy nodded. "Except for Mum's quarters, he done the choosing on everything in the house. Planned the outside, as well. A right talented gentleman, he is."

Stunned, Sarah regarded her chambers from a new perspective. Like the gardens outside, everything in here was balanced to perfection. The white background of the wallpaper lent the room a sense of airy springtime. And if it weren't for the soft blue of the counterpane, the bulky four-poster would have overwhelmed all else. So, he'd plucked the lovely, soft color off the breasts of those small birds dotting the wallpaper, and used it as accents, right down to the velvet chaise in the corner, the bench she sat upon, and the curtains covering the double doors leading to the balcony. "Amazing."

Tildy nodded and smiled at Sarah through the mirror. "Did it while he healed. No one knew he had it in him."

When Tildy finished the toilette, Sarah stood to make her exit. The maid swung the door open, and Sarah paused at the cacophony drifting up from below. There went her nerves. "Would you ready a walking dress for me should I feel a need to escape the Malvern frivolity?"

Tildy giggled. "Indeed, Miss Marks."

Sarah made her way down the stairs and stepped into the noisy parlor, the taste of Eastleigh's kiss still embarrassingly fresh on her lips. Every head turned her way, and conversation ceased. They were a beautiful and handsome lot, five men and three ladies. No…wait…didn't Eastleigh say there were four brothers and four sisters? It only took seconds to pick out Lady Willamette, or Will, as he'd called her. She stood amongst the men, her hair in a like-style and dressed in men's clothing.

Eastleigh stepped to Sarah's side, but before he could speak, Doctor Hemphill came forward. "I'd like to introduce you to Mum's ward, Miss Sarah Marks, he said.

She worked up the courage to speak. "I'm terribly sorry to be late. I was in the garden tending the flowers. I do so love them." Oh, dear. They simply stared. What did they know about her? Had Mum told them of her amnesia? Had Eastleigh?

Lady Willamette scowled and made a beeline for Sarah,

her long, panted legs swallowing up the carpet. "What did you say her name was?"

Sarah stiffened. She could darn well speak for herself. "I'm Miss Sarah Marks, and I take it you are Lady Willamette?"

Eastleigh frowned and took a step closer to Sarah. "What the devil, Will? Don't start with your incessant pestering."

Will ignored Eastleigh's order. "You are partial to flowers, are you, Miss Marks? I'm rather proud of mine. Read every book I can get my hands on regarding the art of the English garden. Do you read as well?"

A bit of panic rose in Sarah's throat at Will's aggressiveness. She looked to Eastleigh.

"I've told them of your accident and loss of memory." He turned to his sister. "Go easy on her, Will."

Sarah tried to relax, but something made her wary of Eastleigh's sister. Relief swept through her when he escorted her around the room and introduced her to the others. Ridley, a year younger than Eastleigh, was as tall and quite handsome, as were the lot of them.

"How are you getting along with Mum?" Ridley grinned. Unlike Eastleigh, his front teeth were even and unbroken, but not so, his nose. That had taken a beating at some point in his life, for there was a decided hitch near the bridge. Thomas stepped forward, friendly and full of easy laughter. But when it came to Sebastian, youngest of the four, he was wildly flirtatious, the kiss he settled on the back of Sarah's hand far too lengthy. She thought it rather humorous that Eastleigh stepped between them and waltzed her over to visit with Lily, Rose, and Iris.

Will sat in a settee with her attention focused on Sarah all the while, a glass of champagne dangling between her fingers.

Each of Eastleigh's brothers and sisters took a turn in conversation, one trying to outdo the other with wild tales of their youth. She thanked Rose for the use of her clothing and made the rounds until, reluctantly, she came face to face with Will once more.

Will patted the settee beside her. "Come, let's talk of gardens."

Sarah sat, not trusting the woman, but for the life of her, not knowing why.

Will lazily took a sip of champagne and went back to dangling the flute between her fingers. "Tell me what you know of the mignonette."

"Well," Sarah promptly replied. "If one is to grow a handsome tree, then one should never allow a single seed to ripen. One must assiduously remove the seedpods as soon as sighted." *Now, that came out rather efficiently.*

Will crossed a leg in a manly way and set her foot pumping. "And the Indian pink?"

"Only the most popular flower in today's garden," Sarah responded without hesitation. "If one were to sow them in a frame and set them out in May, then one would enjoy blooms the entire summer."

"Excellent, Miss Marks." Will stood. "Eastleigh, a word in the library in ten." She left the room.

At Eastleigh's approach, Sarah stood as well. "Would you mind terribly if I saw myself to my chambers? I feel as though I've had enough excitement for a bit." She rubbed her temples.

Eastleigh's brows knit together. "A headache?"

"I feel one coming on. If you don't mind…"

"I'll see you to your room."

"No, please. I'm fine, and the others are watching. It wouldn't do to have us exit together. Where's your mother?"

"My father is unable to leave home, so she remains with him."

"And Mum? Where is she?"

"Oh, she won't show herself until high tea. See you then?"

· · ·

Eastleigh made certain Hemphill was in the library when Will entered. By the aggressive manner in which his sister had addressed Sarah, this must be about her.

Will walked over and tossed a book atop the desk where Eastleigh was seated. He glanced at the title and felt the color drain from his face. "Where'd you get this?"

She leaned over the desk. "It's mine, Eastleigh. A favorite I take everywhere with me. Read the title."

"I just did." He shot a speaking glance at Hemphill.

"Try page one hundred twenty-six," she said.

Eastleigh shook his head and tried to swallow the cotton in his throat. That pulsating, familiar pain rolled through his head. Not another bloody headache.

She grabbed up the book. "Then I will. First the title, if you please. It's called *A Treatise on the English Garden,* by none other than Miss Sarah Marks."

Her lip curled at Hemphill's fast approach. She flipped open the book. "Oh, and here's the page of which I spoke. It's regarding the mignonette—*If one is to grow a handsome tree, then one should never allow a single seed to ripen. One must assiduously remove the seedpods as soon as sighted.*"

She slapped the tome back onto the desk. "Sound familiar? It should since it is verbatim the very words *your* Miss Marks spoke. I was in London not a fortnight ago attending a lecture by the *real* Miss Marks. I can assure you, the woman you harbor is a fake."

Doctor Hemphill stepped to the desk and flipped through the well-worn pages. "Lady Willamette, I beg your confidence in this matter. The lady of whom we speak suffers amnesia. With her love of gardening, it is likely she owns a copy of this very book, and has it as worn through as yours. When asked her name after the accident, she mayhap responded with whatever her damaged mind could pull up. And if you knew exactly which page she quoted, what makes you think her brain doesn't know the same? Have you forgotten your brother's first response when asked his name was to give us that of his horse?"

Will snorted. "I don't happen to agree with your method of keeping information from an amnesiac so as to allow one's memory to return on its own. Why don't we try it my way and wave this book under her nose? I'm not convinced she isn't a liar."

A muscle in Hemphill's jaw twitched. "Lady Willamette. Should we accuse our guest of anything right now, we may well lose her permanently."

Chapter Eight

Sarah inspected the serviceable-looking walking dress with its blue and brown striped skirt, solid blue sleeves, and brown laced bodice. Upon closer examination, she found the cambric to be finely woven and the tailoring exquisite. "This will certainly do, Tildy. Thank you."

The maid helped Sarah into the outfit. "Miss Marks?"

"Yes?" Sarah twirled in front of the mirror. *A perfect fit.*

"Best not wander onto Sir Crocodile's land whilst yer out an' about."

Sarah shot Tildy a questioning frown. "Sir *Crocodile*?"

Tildy laughed. "Sir Robert Garreck. Knighted by the Queen, he was. Everyone calls him that 'cause he'll snap yer head clean off if'n ye step so much as a toe on his land. Shot at the gamekeeper fer gettin' after a loose sheep once. Heard Sir Crocodile ate the poor thing."

"Oh, dear. How will I know when I'm on his property?"

Tildy handed her the matching bonnet. "Except for the

statues of the horses' arses alongside the road, he marks what's his with a low stone wall."

"Then this snapping *Sir Crocodile* would be Lord Eastleigh's cousin?"

A slow grin captured Tildy's mouth. "A handful, that one. In more ways than I'd care t'count."

. . .

The wild cherry tree Sarah sat beneath was in full bloom. Blossoms, loosened now and then by puffs of wind from the heavens, fell about her like scented snow. Across the small stream lay a field of bluebells looking like azure velvet against Mother Nature's lush green carpet. Lord, but she loved the outdoors. There was freedom here. No one to tell her yea or nay. *Hmm.* She jotted a note in that regard alongside one of her floral sketches. She'd be certain to apprise Doctor Hemphill of her revelation upon her return.

Now, to find a way across the stream to the bluebells without soaking her boots. Tucking her drawings inside the pouch, she stood, removed her bonnet, and strolled upstream until she spied a small footbridge. She'd have to backtrack. But first, there was a low stone wall to climb over in order to reach the bridge. Heavens, how was there suddenly this barrier?

She glanced about. *Which way to go from here?* Where had the sun gone? And when had the sky turned a stormy gray? She followed the stream, hoping to be headed in the right direction. The distinct *chink-chink-chink* of metal hammering against metal caught her attention. *A smithy.* So, she was near the stables? How had she got so turned around?

As the building came into view, the steady, heavy rhythm of the smithy's pounding grew louder. She rounded the stable's corner.

And froze in her tracks at the sight of a half-naked man.

She was certain she'd never before seen a man in such a state. The sight made her a bit dizzy. He stood with his back to her, shirtless and wearing nothing more than dirty buckskins over lean hips, a leather apron, and gloves. Dust-covered boots swathed his long legs. Ebony hair hung in a riot of curls and stuck to the perspiration along his neck. His thick arms and broad back glistened with sweat while his muscles bunched and released with every strike of the hammer against glowing metal.

God in heaven! She twitched at every smack of the mallet. She should get away fast. Which way to go? A lump caught in her throat, but she couldn't move.

He paused, hammer in mid-air, head bent to the side as if listening for a sound behind him.

Oh, dear Lord. Run!

He turned, his face a mask of fury. And then his countenance transformed—softened as his crude regard traveled her length. The arm holding the hammer lowered, and a slow smile loosened his generous mouth. Setting down the mallet, he removed his heavy gloves, tossed them aside, and lifted the leather apron over his head, exposing a flat, muscled stomach and broad chest.

Sarah caught herself staring at a garish scar marring the left side of his body and averted her attention over his shoulder. He grabbed a towel hanging on a hook and took his time wiping perspiration from his face and arms. "Who are you, and did you fall from the sky?" His deep voice split the air between them.

Thankful her skirts hid her shaking knees, she stiffened, shot her chin in the air, and found her voice. "I am Miss Sarah Marks, sir. I've got turned around. If you will respectfully direct me toward Easton Park, I'll be on my way."

He cocked a brow. "Respectfully? *Humph*. I respect nothing belonging to Eastleigh."

The nerve. "I'll have you know, I am Mum's ward, sir."

A chuckle rumbled through his chest. "That's a rich one. Now I *know* you fell from the sky. And landed on your head." He reached to another hook, removed a white shirt, and yanked it over his head, leaving it to hang loose.

Lucifer himself wouldn't have looked so devilish.

"I'll be off now," she said. "I'll find my own way if you choose not to be a gentleman and direct me." She went to shove her leather pouch under her arm and realized it was the bonnet she held. Oh, dear, she'd left her sketches and journal under the tree. Things weren't going well at all.

"You just turned pale." He moved forward with a quizzical frown.

She stepped back.

"I won't hurt you." His voice softened, reminding Sarah of how Eastleigh had spoken those very words.

"I...I really must be going now, but I left something under a tree, and I'm afraid I shan't find it again."

"You followed the stream?" He strolled toward her, his gait easy and relaxed.

She nodded.

Taking her by the elbow, he turned her around. "Come along, then."

She yanked her arm away.

He chuckled and dropped his hand. "I'm merely showing you the way. Don't be a dolt."

Dolt? How dare he. "I am nothing of the sort, merely lost." She scurried to catch up with him, aware that it took her two steps to his long one to maintain his easy pace. Just like Eastleigh. She sized him up. About the same height as well.

He regarded her with amusement. No wonder Tildy said he was a handful. What she wouldn't give to know what had caused the two cousins to be at odds. Surely it couldn't be over a fifteen-foot-wide strip of land? "May I inquire as to what you were creating when I happened by?"

A mischievous smile tipped the corners of his mouth. "Do you like my statues at the entry to my property?" They passed a tree, and he casually reached up for a handful of leaves, tearing and tossing them as he strolled along. "I'll take your silence as a no."

"I don't think your purpose in putting them there was because you were especially proud of them."

"Do tell." He tossed the remaining leaves in the air and walked under the rain of green. "I thought them rather clever." He pointed to the pouch propped beneath the cherry tree. "Is that what you're after?"

She turned in a circle. "Yes, but how did we get onto this side of the wall again?"

"Ah, there's a tricky bit up a ways where there's a gap in the wall just as the stream turns."

"Which you've designed on purpose."

His hand splayed over his heart. "Would thee so wound me with vile accusations, milady?"

When she only glared at him, he shot her a wicked half-smile. "Your pardon while I gather the packet, Miss Marks, and then I'll point the way for you."

She watched him retrieve the pouch and return, his gait lazy beneath his thin cambric shirt. Why, he wasn't frightening at all. "You can't be what they say—"

"Sir Crocodile?" Humor lit his eyes. "The very one."

"You know of your nickname?"

He shrugged. "Who doesn't? You fell out of the sky back there, and already you know what they call me." He turned his head. "I believe we have company."

The drumming of hoof beats reached Sarah's ears. Eastleigh raced into view atop a fine-looking brown beast with a black tail and mane, the ground quaking. He pulled the horse to a halt so hard the animal danced in a circle, clods of grass and dirt flying about. He eyed his cousin's disheveled appearance, then gave Sarah a thorough once-over, his scowl besting the one Sir Crocodile had given her when first he'd caught sight of her. "Are you all right?"

"Of course."

"Get off my property, Eastleigh." Whatever emanated from Sir Robert Garreck just then was powerful, malevolent, and shot right through Sarah like a swallow of acrid vinegar. A chill slithered down her spine.

"I've come to get what's mine," Eastleigh responded.

What? Sarah's back went up. "Yours? I'm Mum's ward, in case you forgot."

Laughter, deep and hearty rolled out of Garreck. "She's Mum's ward, Augie. Ain't that something?"

"Shut it, Rob. Come, madam." He held a hand out to her and glanced upward. "We'll be fortunate to make it back to the stables before the skies open."

Sarah didn't know why, but she suddenly wanted away from this man standing beside her. She scurried to the safety of Eastleigh but halted, and took a step back. Up close, the sheer size of the beast he rode was daunting.

He extended his hand. "Commodore won't hurt you. Come, step on my boot."

"You're certain?"

"Indeed. Hurry, the weather is about to turn."

She took a cautious step forward and grabbed Eastleigh's hand.

He swung her up so easily, she was straddled behind him before she had time to think, her skirts skimming the tops of her walking boots. The horse danced a half-circle and back. Sarah yipped and clasped the sides of Eastleigh's jacket, her heart jumping to her throat. Sitting atop a horse didn't feel natural. Not at all!

"Steady," Eastleigh murmured to the horse. "Put your hands around my waist, madam, and hold tight."

She scooted forward until she was up against his back and could clasp her hands against his hard stomach. His scent caught between her body and his. *Oh, my.* If it weren't for her bunched skirts, her thighs would be fitted directly against his hips!

Sir Robert's piercing gaze followed her every move. "Off my property, Eastleigh. Now." He turned, then paused and glanced over his shoulder with a puckish grin. "But as for you, Miss Marks, you are welcome anytime. And bring Mum along. I haven't seen my grandmother since her last delivery of apple cider."

Chapter Nine

The horse took a step forward. Sarah gripped the front of Eastleigh's shirt and let out a pitiful squeak. No, she definitely did not ride by habit.

Eastleigh halted the beast and slid his gloved hand over hers. "Are you certain you're all right?"

"The only thing I'm fair…fairly certain of, is that I must have led my father's horses to the smithy and never rode a one. Furthermore, I feel as though I'm ten feet off the ground and about to tumble beneath this monster's great hooves, where I shall surely meet my demise. I don't care for this one bit, Eastleigh."

"Then you need to ride in front. Sit tight." Before she knew what he was about, he threw a leg over the neck of the horse and slid to the ground with graceful ease. She slipped a bit in the saddle, and terror washed through her anew.

"Easy, now." He righted her. "Lean over and grip the pommel." He stepped to the horse's head, stroking and murmuring in soothing tones. "Ease yourself all the way forward, then adjust your skirts while I have my back to you."

After she did as she was told, he mounted behind her in one smooth motion. This time it was *he* who set *his* body against *hers*. It was *his* thighs cradling *her* hips. Oh, my. His one hand slid around her waist, tucking her close to him. He took the reins with the other. She swallowed hard against the tide of emotion washing through her and searched for a decent breath.

"I've got hold of you," he said. "But grab a handful of the horse's mane. Doing so will help you maintain your balance. There's a storm nearly upon us, so we'd best pick up speed. Ready?"

She grasped a hank of black mane with both hands and nodded. His words of encouragement were warm and husky in her ear, his hand splayed over her stomach comforting, yet sending shockwaves of…of *pleasure* through her. A squeeze of his legs against the horse, and the beast eased into a walk, then a trot, and soon, a canter. All the while, Sarah bumped about in the saddle.

"Let your hips relax, and you won't bounce so." He gripped the side of her waist, and with strong fingers, urged her hips into a back and forth motion that matched the horse's movements—along with Eastleigh's. Not only was the difference in the ride immediate, but oh, dear, the graceful cadence of the horse set her and Eastleigh moving together in a manner that one could call provocative. Could he be aware of what she was thinking? Or feeling? Or was this movement so common she would be considered a prig to make note of it?

"That's it," he murmured, his words throaty in her ear. "You've got things right now. Feel how smooth and natural the three of us move together." He slid his hand back to her belly. "Settle in and enjoy the ride, I've got you."

But the intimacy of Eastleigh's hips rolling in cadence with hers did more than allow her to enjoy the ride. Something began to tingle inside her. God help her, she wanted to ride forever in his arms, wanted to delve deep into the erotic feelings shooting through her. She leaned the back of her head against his chest and closed her eyes to everything that was not *him*.

His arm tightened around her, and his breath, hot against her ear, grew heavier. Not at all proper, this, but so inviting, so comforting—and something else so very wicked, she dared not let her mind settle on where such waywardness could lead. What she did have the courage to do, was allow her focus to remain on him. As she let go of all restraint, exquisite currents passed from him into her until she felt as though the two of them were one.

The farther they rode along in silence, the more helpless she became to control what rolled through her. She gave in to the pleasure of their bodies moving in unison to a steady rhythm, gave in to his heady scent surrounding her, to his heated breath against her cheek. A fat raindrop hit her. And then another. "Oh!" She let go of the horse's mane with one hand and swiped at her cheeks, but the action rocked her in the saddle and she let out a yip.

"Careful." Eastleigh readjusted his hold, pulling her even closer.

She grabbed at a hank of the beast's hair again. No amount of wet was worth such a fright. She was nearly crushed against Eastleigh now, he held her so close. More drops assaulted her. Oh, they couldn't reach the stables fast enough to suit her. She leaned her head against his chest and settled fully into him.

"We'll not make tea, I'm afraid." His words, deep in his throat had taken on a raw, primitive tone. "You'll soon be soaked through since the storm is coming straight at us and not from behind where my body might protect you. Sorry."

And then the skies opened up.

Sarah tried to blink away the pelting rain, but to no avail. She relented and kept her eyes closed, loving how doing so increased her sensitivity to his penetrating presence. Who would have thought riding atop a horse with a man like Eastleigh could send one's senses reeling?

Did he just plant a light kiss atop her head? Raw, visceral emotion throbbed down her belly and begged for release.

"Finally, the stables," he said.

She opened her eyes, just as Eastleigh halted in front of the entry. "Not a moment too soon. I'm soaked through and feeling chilled to the bone."

"Stay in the saddle, I'll walk you in." He slid off the horse while Sarah continued to cling to the animal's mane.

Once inside, Eastleigh closed the doors to the storm and held his arms open to her. "Let go, I'll catch you."

She fell into him, and he scowled. "As I thought. You're soaked whilst I sat behind you and had your body for protection. Here, put this on."

He pulled off his coat and tossed it over the rail of an empty stall. Shedding his jacket, he set it over her shoulders. "At least the family will be gathered for tea, so you can slip into the house with them unawares."

Making short work of his cravat and waistcoat, he whipped off his shirt and began to towel off her face and hair.

Which left him naked from the waist up!

And here she was, mere inches away. Oh, her heart pounded so—surely he must be able to hear it. She closed her eyes in an attempt to obliterate the image of bare skin and rippling muscles while he rubbed his shirt through her hair—hair that had fallen loose at some point.

Nearly naked. Just like Sir Garreck. While the two bodies were not dissimilar, shock at seeing a half-clad Garreck was one thing, but with Eastleigh? What this man's near-nudity did to her was an entirely different matter. How she wanted to step into him, desperately wanted to touch his skin.

Wanted him to kiss her.

Helpless to do otherwise, she opened her eyes, and a shockwave rippled through her. There were scars. Multiple scars. Some seemed as though he'd been gouged, while others looked as if he'd been sliced at. She reached out and touched him. "You've been hurt," she whispered.

He sucked in his breath, his skin quivering where her fingers skimmed along his flesh. "My family will be leaving in the morning, and then we need to talk—you, me, and Doctor Hemphill." His words were strained, hoarse in his throat.

She nodded, focused on her fingers trailing along his stomach and the thrill it gave her.

He paused with his bunched shirt against her cheek. And then he moved it again, this time slowly, as if in a caress.

Her fingers traced one scar, and then another. "From the war?" Her voice sounded as a mere whisper.

When he failed to respond, she glanced up into eyes filled with longing. No matter how naïve she might be, there was no mistaking his desire for her. He turned the shirt until it was the back of his fingers tracing her cheek and not the fabric. "Lord, but you're beautiful."

He studied her for a long moment, and then his lips parted, and she knew what was coming. She lifted her chin in silent acquiescence.

His warm lips touched hers, just a brush. "God help me, I should not do this," he murmured, but it was too late, for his mouth settled on hers, and his arms went around her.

A small groan fell into her mouth. "Forgive me, I cannot stop."

She pulled away from his kiss and touched her lips to his chest. She licked his heated skin. She heard a soft moan, thinking it was his, but perhaps not?

"Eastleigh," she whispered and lifted her mouth to his again in a near frantic urge to have him…to have him where? She wound her arms around his neck. His hand found her breast and this time she was certain it was his moan she heard. And then his mouth settled on hers again, and when his tongue found hers and probed, a flame ignited in her so hot it burned.

Suddenly a memory.

An awful memory.

Of a sharp pain between her legs. Of her whimpering, then begging…not wanting to be touched again. By…by her husband.

Her husband!

She jumped back in horror. "Don't touch me!"

He stepped forward with a quizzical frown, but she

managed to wave him off before one of her hands covered her mouth and the other clutched at the pain gripping her stomach. "Oh, dear God, Eastleigh. I am a married woman. We cannot do this."

He reached out and grabbed her shoulders, his face ashen. "Tell me what you remember?"

She shrugged off his hands and backed away. "Please, no."

Shivering, she lifted his coat from over the rail and wrapped it around her shoulders. "Leave me be," she cried. "I cannot. I am married."

He grabbed her by the shoulders again. "To whom?"

"I…I don't know. I cannot see him in my mind's eye. I only know he is cruel."

"Cruel? How so?"

"Let me go!"

He was shaking her now, a scowl distorting his features. "Tell me, damn it!"

Twisting free from his grasp, she sped from the stable and into the house, ignoring the shocked stares of servants.

As she ran up the stairs to her chamber, Hemphill's shouts at Eastleigh fell on her ears, a jumble of words to which she paid no heed. Stumbling into her room and locking the door behind her, she leaned back against the hard panel and wept.

Oh God, oh God, why couldn't she remember anything more? What did he look like, this husband of hers? Had she imagined things? No, she was certain she was married…for how else would an intimate encounter take place with… with someone she knew…but didn't know?

Could she have been attacked by someone? No. In the flash of memory, when she'd recalled the pain, somehow she *knew* it had been a husband who had done the inflicting. For the first time since she'd awoken in that strange inn beside Eastleigh, she didn't just weep, she sobbed, great heaping sobs that tore through her with a vengeance until she was spent.

She opened her eyes, expecting to see the maid standing in a corner, watching the spectacle. But she was alone. She spied what looked to be a book lying in the middle of the bed with a note atop. Wiping her eyes, she moved to the four-poster where she read the large letters scrawled across the page.

"Thought you might find this of particular interest. Will."

Sarah lifted the piece of paper off the book, and seeing the title, gasped.

A Treatise on the English Garden, by Miss Sarah Marks.

Fingers trembling, she lifted the book off the counterpane. Slowly, she turned the pages. And then she pressed the book to her breast and slumped to the floor.

She knew this book. Knew it well. It was her bible — not the Good Book, from which her father forced her to recite every day, but the dearest book she owned, one where she could find any information she needed in order to tend to her beloved garden. Written by one Sarah Marks.

No, she was not the author. She remembered who she was now.

Her name was Lilith Stokes.

And she was a vicar's daughter.

A very married vicar's daughter.

Chapter Ten

A familiar scratching at the door told Lilith that Tildy had come to see to her needs. When Lilith turned the key in the lock, she found the ashen-faced maid wringing her hands. "His lordship and the good doctor ask your permission to enter your chambers, miss."

She couldn't possibly face Eastleigh after what had sinfully transpired between them. Not ever. "Please inform Lord Eastleigh that I respectfully decline, and that as soon as this storm let's up, I would be grateful if he would provide me with transportation to my parents' home in Aylesham." Her mother and father would lead her to a husband she had obviously run away from. Whatever it was that had caused her to flee, she was now prepared to face the issue head-on.

"Yes, ma'am." Tildy backed away, chewing her bottom lip. "After I've delivered the message, should I return and see to yer needs?"

Lilith shook her head. "Since there is nothing to pack,

I'll be fine tending to myself."

Tildy glanced over Lilith's shoulder to the wardrobe. "But what of all yer lovely things…"

"They aren't mine. I'll be leaving them behind." Oh, she desperately needed to be alone. "Please, Tildy, leave me."

The maid nodded and turned toward the servants' stairway. The book in Lilith's hand grew suddenly heavy. "Wait. Give this to Lord Eastleigh, and inform him there is a note inside. Tell him if he fails to understand its meaning, he can ask Lady Willamette to kindly explain."

Lilith closed the door, wrapped her arms around herself, and stepped out onto the covered balcony. She watched the rain fall in great, heavy sheets. No doubt she would have to wait until morning the way this weather kept up. She grew weary trying to think. What had happened to her still lay scattered about in her mind like so many pieces of a jigsaw puzzle. No matter how hard she tried, she couldn't manage to find all of the pieces and fit them together into any kind of rational order. She didn't know how long she'd stood there, trying to remember more of her life, when Tildy called out.

"I'm sorry to enter, miss, but you didn't seem to hear me scratching on the door. The doctor sent me back with a note." She handed the folded scrap of paper to Lilith. "Should I wait in case there's a reply?"

Lilith nodded and opened the missive. So, he insisted on accompanying her to her parents' home. She hadn't thought that far ahead, but he was right—she couldn't very well travel alone. And who else was there to go along, Tildy? That wouldn't do. He'd made no mention of Eastleigh. But why should he? And why would Eastleigh care to respond to a married woman? Oh, Lord, help her.

She swiped her hand across her forehead. "Tell Doctor Hemphill I'll be eager to travel as soon as the weather cooperates. If it is clear in the morning, we should leave first thing."

"Yes, miss. Will that be all?" She fidgeted as though she'd something else to say.

Lilith regarded the chambermaid. "Why are you suddenly acting so queerly?"

Tildy shrugged. "I shouldn't be telling tales lest I be let go, miss."

A small laugh choked Lilith. "Since I'll be keeping to my room, and depart when the storm abates, who pray tell would I gossip with?" And why was she so suddenly curious? What should anything having to do with Easton Park matter?

"Well, 'tis his lordship, miss. He's very upset after the argument he had with the doctor, and he's come down with one of his terrible headaches. He's locked away in his chambers, and there's been a lot of noise behind his doors, like things breaking. Big things. Perhaps if you went to him…"

"I…I wouldn't know what to say, Tildy." Mindful of the pain lancing her chest, Lilith shuddered involuntarily and rubbed her arms as if she'd taken a chill. "I'm sorry for Lord Eastleigh, I truly am, but there is nothing I can do."

A great sadness swept over Tildy's countenance. "I'll see to bringing your meals, then. Ring if you need me, miss."

She opened the door to exit, and there stood Mum, looking sorrowful, and with a bottle in her hand. Not waiting for an invitation, she stepped inside, and excusing the maid, set the vessel on a side table holding a porcelain tea set. "I brought some of my good cider to take along. Just in case you won't be back for apple season. 'Tis a shame you have to leave us so soon. It's near time to make my cherry cordial. We would've had a time of it, you and me."

Tears popped out of nowhere, but Lilith laughed through them. "Oh, Mum, how I will miss you."

"Then don't go. You have yet to see my collections. And I've many more stories to tell."

"But I must, Mum."

Mum opened the bottle of apple cider and splashed the amber liquid into two of the tea cups, apparently forgetting she'd brought it as a gift. She handed one to Lilith and took up the other one. "Hemphill and Augie had a terrible tiff."

Lilith started to say she knew, but clamped her mouth shut.

"Something about the doctor seeing you home," Mum said. "Gave Augie a terrible megrim, I'm afraid. But don't take his condition as a sign of weakness. He's stronger than all of us put together for having come through his troubles thus far. Ridley's gone to see what the terrible racket is. They're close as twins."

Lilith closed her eyes briefly to shut out more tears. Why, oh, why, did it break her heart to hear about this clan? Could it be that despite their odd ways, they were close-knit? Unlike her family? The sudden realization that she was an only child and had lived a cold, isolated existence struck her like a heavy blow. Some memories, it would seem, weren't worth salvaging.

• • •

Lilith leaned her head against the red velvet squabs of Eastleigh's expensive carriage and studied Doctor Hemphill.

After five days on the road, bluntness was just the thing, she decided, since he'd been so insistent upon accompanying her to her parents' home.

Her hand swept lightly over Daisy, who lay curled asleep in her lap. "I've come to realize these past few days that I do not care much for my father, Doctor Hemphill."

Unperturbed, he said, "And why is that, Miss Stokes?"

She brushed at her gown and gave him a set-down glare. "Please, call me Lilith. At least until my parents can inform us of my married name."

Hemphill gave a little nod of acquiescence. "Then tell me, Lilith, why do you not care much for your father?"

"Because he is the most self-absorbed man one would ever chance to meet. He is a pitiable vicar, in my estimation. Perhaps half the village is of the same opinion. I cannot recall at present."

"And what makes him self-absorbed and poor at his position—in your estimation, of course."

She leaned forward in challenge. "Ask him when the last time was that he actually wrote a sermon for the good people of Aylesham." She sat back, smug. "He purchases a year's worth of sermons from some chap in London and delivers them on a Sunday in the exact order in which they arrive, the devil with what the parishioners might require to feed their souls."

She no longer smoothed the wrinkles in her skirt— she flicked at them as though they irritated her skin. "His only interest is land-grabbing. Buys it on the cheap when some poor fellow comes to him in dire straits. Ever so kindly, and with ever so much élan, he relieves the beggar of his despicable problem by purchasing his land. With little cash. Very little. Then he rents the land or farm back to the unsuspecting fool. Little by little, my father is eating up the area—like a mouse after an entire wheel of cheese, slowly, steadily until he has it all. He won't rest until he owns more than his titled eldest brother. Which will never happen, and so he is a miserable cur for whom I have little respect."

"You're so very angry, Lilith. Mightn't you be taking some of your rage out on your father? In case you haven't noticed, the closer we get to Aylesham, the curter you become."

She gave him a spiteful grin. "I do hope you are around when the good vicar decides to have a go at showing his temper." She gave a flick of her hand. "Never mind. He only displays that in private—when the day servants are gone, and the live-ins are tucked away in their tiny little beds, in the farthest corner of the attic."

Doctor Hemphill sighed. "Those are rather strong words coming from a vicar's daughter who has displayed a fine upbringing, good moral character, and high intellect at every turn."

She lifted a brow. "Perhaps there is another layer to me that went unexposed 'til now, Doctor Hemphill?"

He shook his head. "We all have a dark side when pushed to our limit. You are likely merely frightened of what lies ahead because you have a spouse you cannot put a name or face to but are certain he mistreats you. Set aside your fears, if you will, for you'll not be placed in the home of one who will abuse you. I'll see to it."

Her laughter came harsh and abrupt. "Then our destination is not my father's home, after all?"

Hemphill pinched the bridge of his nose. "Your father mistreats you?"

"In all ways, I do not recall. I am only certain he does. He didn't want me, you see. He desired a son. Which is why he named me Lilith."

Puzzlement swept over Hemphill's countenance. "Forgive me, but I don't grasp the connection."

She laughed again, this time lighter, pleased she knew something the good doctor, with all his education, did not. "Why, Doctor Hemphill, you must attend one of my father's sermons. He makes it ever so clear that Lilith was Adam's first wife. She was made of the same mud and earth as was he, but she was rebellious and independent and would not mind him, so Adam divorced her and cast her out. Then, while he slept, God took Adam's rib and made Eve, a woman meant to be obedient."

She grinned. "Oh, dear. Eve did go and take that nasty little bite that cast the two of them out of Eden, didn't she?"

At last, Lilith was enjoying herself. "I think I shall become an apple biter."

. . .

Four days living in her father's home and he'd yet to speak to Lilith, let alone look her in the eye. And her mother, pale and withdrawn, refused to discuss Lilith's husband. The most she would say was that she didn't know the man since he was not from the village surround, and that Lilith had run off and married him without first letting her parents know.

When Lilith learned Doctor Hemphill had sent a note ahead of their arrival telling her parents that Lilith must discover her husband's identity on her own, she grew livid. "I don't care that Lady Willamette had no business leaving Miss

Marks' gardening book in my room," she said, fitting flowers, one by one, into a crystal vase. "Shocking as the event was, it gave me back my name and most of my memory, did it not?"

Doctor Hemphill shrugged. "Another bit of it, at least, but we could have lost you, entirely, Lilith. I've seen this occur with too many others when given a terrible shock." He scrubbed his hand through his hair. "Please, bear with me. I know what I'm about. You weren't around when Eastleigh had a setback. It's quite destructive to one's system to remember a few things only to have everything swept away again by a single, foolish act."

"What foolish act? Eastleigh did something to cause a relapse?"

Hemphill waved her off. "It's of little importance now."

Something sorrowful swept through her at the mention of Eastleigh's name. Quickly, she dismissed it. "Speaking of whom. What kind of man would cast his own sister out because she didn't follow his orders to keep the gardening book to herself?"

"Those were my orders, Lilith, not his. And I am not in the least concerned about Eastleigh ordering Lady Willamette off his property. Those Malverns squabble like noisy geese, routinely send one or the other on their way, but within a fortnight, there they are, together again. One wouldn't know a cross word had ever passed between them."

He glanced at the clock and chuckled. "Will's likely having tea with Eastleigh and Mum, as we speak. They may be an unruly bunch, but the love they share is so full of passion as to be priceless. With them, one must be prepared to take the good with the bad. I rather enjoy their quirky ways."

At the remembrance of high tea with Mum and Eastleigh, a sharp pain swept through Lilith. Well, of all things—she missed him. And she missed Mum. For pity's sake, she even missed Easton Park and all that it represented. Tears clogged her throat.

When she spied Doctor Hemphill studying her, panic bit at her heels. It wouldn't do to have him guess her secret feelings. Shoving the remaining flowers into the vase, she pulled off her apron and hanging it on a hook, headed for the door. "I'll see to these later. I'm off for a walk."

"But not beyond the property," Hemphill said.

"Of course not." But she knew exactly where she was headed—not to stroll in the sunny grazing field, where she'd once found solace, nor to her garden full of flowers where peace abounded, but to the smithy. If anyone in this village knew of her husband, he would. She'd known Jonathan since they were children, her learning to walk the horses to be shod, him learning the trade. Everyone from these parts took their cattle to him. He was the best around since his father had passed over to the eternal side.

Picking up her pace, she tried, to no avail, to keep her mind off Eastleigh. That first morning when she'd awoken in that unpleasant inn, when he'd touched her head wound and told her he'd not harm her—was that when she'd begun to trust him? Was that when the attraction had set in? Her mind captured poignant vignettes—his winsome smile exposing that one chipped tooth, his warm and wonderful kisses that left her boneless. Of his heated body rolling provocatively against hers while they rode along on his horse.

Her breathing grew labored, but not in the least from the brisk pace she kept. Oh, she couldn't let herself think such sinful thoughts of him. She could not. Even if her husband was cruel, and she refused to live with him, he was still her spouse and would be for the rest of her days.

The memory of Eastleigh's kisses caught at the corners of her mind once again, sending her pulse racing and her mood plummeting.

As a man thinketh in his heart, so is he.

Those words her father preached had never meant much before. But now they took on a sorrowful depth that threatened to break her heart. She'd nearly sinned with Eastleigh. Or was she, a married woman, sinning even now—*as she thinketh*? Heaven help her, was she destined to suffer forever at the memory of him? Or would she soon forget him?

Time. She needed time.

"Jonathan," she called out on her approach to the smithy, desperately in need of diversion.

The burly man set the glowing metal he'd been working on into the fire. A wide grin split his round face in two. "Miss Lilith. A right pleasure to see you." He looked beyond her, suddenly appearing nervous, his smile evaporating. "Did yer father send you?"

"No horses today, I'm afraid. I was out for a stroll and heard your hammering, so I thought to stop by. What an unseasonably warm day, isn't it? You shouldn't be working in the hot sun."

Jonathan withdrew the piece of metal from the fire and went back to bending it into shape, saying nothing.

"Jonathan?"

"Miss Lilith, I'm right busy." He glanced up, but he must have noticed how she stared at him with her jaw dropped, because he quickly returned to his task, the blush to his cheeks deepening.

Good heavens, he was avoiding her. She cleared her throat. "How long since I last brought the horses? Any idea? I must keep track, or my father will have my neck."

Jonathan's face turned an even deeper red. He pounded harder on the hot metal. "Miss Lilith, yer father came by the other day and told me I wasn't to speak to you. Not even a hello. I've gone against him, and if I say anything more…"

He paused, the mallet in his hand resting on the hot piece of iron, pleading in his eyes. "Miss Lilith, I need my work. If yer father won't have nuthin' further to do with me, like he says, if'n I speak to you, well, I won't have no work once word gets around."

She let go his name with a whoosh. "Jonathan!"

"Please, Miss Lilith."

She lifted her hand and backed away. "Don't beg, Jonathan. Whatever you do in life, never beg."

She turned and ran away from the edge of the village, past the church, to the house and beyond, to the stream where over the years, she'd routinely watered her father's horses. She bent over and gulped in air, perspiration running down her face, her spine, and everywhere in between.

Swim, that's what she would do. Something her father had forbidden because she was a female. Like riding a horse. And dancing. Well, mayhap she didn't care much about riding a horse, but swim she would. A new strength blossomed in her. She was a married woman; she could do as she pleased—until she located her husband, at least. But no longer would her father be judge or jailer.

She couldn't shed her clothing fast enough. Maybe she'd

dance a little jig in the water while she was at it. Stripped to her chemise, she waded into the cool stream and closed her eyes, marveling at the calming effect the pure water flowing around her legs had on her. Deeper she went until she stood waist high. Minnows darted about, and in the shadows of the great willow tree, she spied a good-sized fish. She did not know she'd be able to see the bottom out here. Next, she'd try fishing, another act her father deemed for men alone. She took in a big gulp of a breath, bent at the knees and submerged herself. She came up sputtering and laughing.

And then she sobered at the sound of her father's harsh voice, at the sound of a whip snapping in the air, and at the sound of a series of grunts as Jonathan dashed past her and disappeared from sight. They had both followed her?

"Lilith, damn your whoring soul. Get out of there this minute!"

Neck-deep, she turned to face her father. No more. He no longer held any power over her. "Go away. I'm having a swim."

The whip cracked through the air over her head, its tip barely missing her face. "Father!"

When he raised the whip again, she held her breath and dipped beneath the surface once more. The next thing she knew, he was dragging her out of the water, her chemise wet and clinging to her like a second skin.

"You filthy harlot." The whip cracked across her wet back. Hot pain set her on fire. She fell to the ground, writhing in agony, unable to swallow her screams.

"Malcolm, no!" It was her mother doing the begging.

The whip cracked again.

Another scream tore from Lilith's throat.

"Cease your bloody cruelty!" Doctor Hemphill bellowed as he ran to her.

Something greater than calm suddenly pervaded Lilith. It was as though angels had swooped down and took her pain, held her father at bay while she turned, as if in slow motion, and grabbed the tip of the whip. Hand over hand, she worked her way up the leather cord until her grip rested a hand's breadth from his.

"Never again," she swore softly. "Never, ever again, will you treat me so cruelly, as you have done on so many occasions."

Hemphill's hand settled on the whip between them. "She's right. Never again."

He stood between them, but suddenly, another image flashed before her. The face of her husband overlaid that of her father's.

She blinked.

Memories of the man she married tumbled into her head like a kaleidoscope set in motion. No! How could she have married *him*? But in her heart, she knew that what her mind revealed was the truth. She dropped her hand from the whip and stepped away, leaving it to Hemphill and her father.

Hot fear gave way to cold anger. She turned to mother. "I remember everything now." Collecting her clothing, she covered herself as best she could and headed toward the house. "And I intend to kill him."

Her mother lurched forward. "You'll hang."

"Then so be it," Lilith called over her shoulder. "I've nothing left to lose."

By the time she'd packed her meager things and collected Daisy, Doctor Hemphill had the carriage pulled around to the front. "I'm going along."

She shook her head. Bitterness, frigid as the North Sea, flowed through her veins. "I'll see to this alone. And I'll not have you with me, Doctor Hemphill, so find another way home on your own. Your methods for recovery do not suit me."

"Try and stop me," he replied.

Her mother stepped out the front door with a carpet bag in hand, her face still pale as bleached linen. "I'm going along, as well."

Before Lilith could speak, her mother scurried to the carriage and handed her bag to Hemphill. With a scowl, she climbed into the conveyance and peered out at Lilith. "I intend to be present when you face your husband."

Lilith glanced from her mother, sitting rigid in the carriage, to Doctor Hemphill, who held his hand extended to her. She lifted her chin and let the sound of her words fracture the air like cracking ice. "Then don't either one of you speak to me, for I shall not utter a word to you."

• • •

True to her word, they rode the distance in silence, along a familiar road. Angry to the core, Lilith would see to a divorce if she hadn't the nerve to kill her husband. And if a divorce wasn't possible, she would leave for the Americas. She'd make a good governess.

It was storming when they drove up the drive she'd come to know well. How could all of this have escaped her? How could her disloyal memory have played so many tricks on her?

The carriage pulled to a halt. Not waiting for Doctor

Hemphill to help her down, she swung the door open, deposited Daisy onto the ground, and stomped past the footman and into the house, not caring that she was dripping wet and soaking the carpet. She knew right where she'd find her husband this time of day.

She marched to the library and flung the door wide. He sat behind his desk, a startled look on his face.

"Eastleigh, you beast!"

He stood, the shock on his face disintegrating. He squared his shoulders, and a corner of his mouth tipped up. "Welcome home, Lady Eastleigh."

Chapter Eleven

A bloody miracle if Eastleigh's frozen smile didn't shatter. How the hell was he supposed to handle this so Lilith wouldn't relapse or lose her memory altogether? And why had she called him a beast?

Hemphill stepped through the doorway.

Eastleigh heaved a sigh of relief and rubbed at the muscles pinching the back of his neck.

A woman sidled in alongside the doctor and stood in a corner of the room. Lilith's mother? She had to be for the uncanny resemblance. Bloody brilliant. As if he hadn't enough to deal with.

His forced smile faded. "Where do we go from here, Hemphill?"

"I suggest we all sit," the doctor responded. "Forgive my brief introductions—Mrs. Stokes, meet Lord Eastleigh, and vice versa."

Hemphill offered one of the two chairs in front of the

desk to Mrs. Stokes and held out the other for Lilith. When she stepped away, he said, "That would include you, as well, Lady Eastleigh."

Her chin rose and her arms swept around her waist. She paced in front of the window. "I prefer to stand."

Hemphill scowled. "I asked you to sit directly across from your husband for a reason, Lady—"

"Do *not* call me that." Lilith stalked to the chair and sat, shooting Eastleigh a glance so hateful he mentally winced. The doctor carried a chair from beside a reading table and situated himself between the two women.

Mrs. Stokes leaned forward, and looking past Hemphill, regarded her daughter. "You were part and parcel of this foolhardy marriage." She waved her hand about. "Or arrangement. Or whatever you wish to call this absurd folly. So unless Lord Eastleigh has abused you to within an inch of your life, such as your father was prone to do—"

Eastleigh's blood went cold. "Are you saying my wife was ill-treated by her father? A vicar?" *Devil take it, I'll call the man out!*

Mrs. Stokes' spine stiffened in the same manner he'd seen Lilith do a hundred times. "Spare the rod, spoil the child was her father's dictum."

Lilith laughed. Such a cold, humorless sound, that. "Oh, thy rod and thy staff they comfort me."

Those were the very words she'd used in response to Mum's idea that she loosen up a bit. He thought them clever back then. Good God, what a dour family she hailed from—a complete contradiction to his own.

A tight band settled about Eastleigh's head. Not another one of those headaches. Not now. Damn it, he'd run his life with great proficiency before going off to war, and as a military officer, he'd commanded his troops with the same organized expertise. But since sustaining his injuries, about the only thing he'd taken charge of was marrying a woman he'd not met in the flesh until their wedding day. Now look at the wretched mess he'd cooked up. Well, things were about to change.

Again, her mother leaned past the doctor and addressed her daughter. "Oh, do behave, Lilith. The journey here was tedious enough without you acting as if the world has wronged you when you were the one who initiated the goings-on. So please, a little decorum, if you will."

Puzzlement swept over Lilith's countenance. "Me? Doing the initiating?"

Eastleigh's heart stalled. Oh, hell, she didn't remember everything after all, such as Hemphill indicated in the note he'd sent ahead. He shot a worried glance at the doctor.

"So it would seem," Hemphill responded, reading Eastleigh's thoughts. "Tell us what you recollect, Lilith."

"I recall..." Her chin quivered. "I recall that he is my *husband,* and he has treated me in a beastly manner." She issued the word husband, as if it were poison to be spat out, rose from her chair, and moved to stand in front of the window.

A bone-chilling jolt ran through Eastleigh. He settled hard eyes on her and returned the disrespect. "How so, *wife?*"

Doctor Hemphill raised a hand to intervene. "Tell us what makes you call your husband a beast."

A flush crawled up her neck and swept over her face. Clasping her hands so tight the knuckles turned white, she lifted her chin and turned her face toward the window, leaving only her profile visible. "He knows very well of what I speak."

The burgeoning ache drumming through Eastleigh's head sent a thread of alarm weaving through him. Bloody hell. The discomfort had all the markings of what had confined him for several days after Lilith had hied off to Aylesham. He pinched the bridge of his nose, as if doing so might head off the pain. Suddenly weary, he struggled for his voice. "I wouldn't knowingly hurt you for the world, Lilith, so tell me—what have I done?"

Hemphill scowled. "You all right, Eastleigh? Not another one of those headaches coming on?"

A sudden realization struck him as to what Lilith could be referring. He regarded Hemphill and Mrs. Stokes. "Might Lilith and I have a moment to ourselves?"

The crease deepened in the doctor's brow, but then it was as if a shaft of understanding shot through his eyes. He stood. "If you insist, but I'll be right outside the door. Do you require your powders?"

Eastleigh waved him off. "Have them ready in my chambers."

Hemphill escorted Mrs. Stokes from the library. He paused at the threshold and glanced over his shoulder. "In the meantime, tread lightly, Eastleigh. For both your sakes."

Tread lightly? God forbid, he didn't want to lose Lilith. Even with her so obviously upset and presently acting cold as an ice queen, he knew for certain she was what he wanted in a wife. He'd caught glimpses of her tender side, of the passion that simmered beneath the surface. And there was her intellect. He'd seen promise in her—in them as a couple.

By now, he doubted he'd be much good without her. "Lilith, when I'd healed enough from my war injuries to take a wife…"

He pinched the cords on the back of his neck again, the headache worsening. "That didn't come out precisely as I meant. What I am trying to say is that not only did I need to marry, I *desired* a wife. But I wanted to find the right one."

He paused. If he was going to take charge, he may as well go all the way. He took in a deep breath and spilled out the rest. "I had grown quite lonely living here with only Mum, Hemphill, and the servants for company. The occasional visits from my family were not enough. Then my father fell ill, which left him bound to his home. I was given fair warning his days were numbered, which meant that at any time, I could inherit his title and all the responsibilities that went with it."

Spots danced before his eyes, and the light filtering through the windows hurt like the devil. But he was nearly finished with what he had to say, so he plodded on. "Despite my not being completely healed, my family churned out a constant dialogue that I seek a wife. Not only did I despise the thought of them interfering in something so important, I could not have withstood tramping about London as if in pursuit of my next horse. The din of the town alone would have done me in, not to mention the shallow women I would've had to wade through.

"I've changed a great deal since the war—since my injuries. Where once my trips to London were long and wicked celebrations, I can no longer abide anything of the sort. Truth be known, my boisterous family is about all I can tolerate. Even then, when they come to call, I need to disappear on occasion just to set my inner world to rights."

She turned. Those cornflower blue eyes settled on him, and his heart stumbled in his chest. Dare he say it? "I wanted more than a mere marriage of convenience, Lilith. I wanted someone who could live quietly in the countryside alongside me, someone educated enough to hold engaging conversations in the dead of winter, someone who shared a love of the outdoors, and resonated to the idea of rearing a family together—come what may. I desired someone…"

Oh, his head. He blinked, trying to ease the pain and obliterate the flashes of hideous scenes of war the headache had begun to spew forth. He ran a hand down his right leg, the injury a lesser pain now that the torture in his skull had taken over. Odd how that worked.

Her brows furrowed. "Are you ill?"

"My injuries produce a kind of megrim under tremendous stress. But we need to ignore my situation and get more important things settled." He took in another slow breath, part for courage and part in a futile attempt to ease the increasing ache. He was going to risk telling all, without Hemphill present. "I secured the services of a certain Mrs. Hazelthorpe."

At the mention of the woman, something odd flashed through Lilith's eyes.

He leaned forward. "Do you recognize the name?"

"Yes, but I cannot recall how I know of her." She tightened her arms around her waist and rubbed at them as if chilled.

"I procured her services in order to help me locate a woman such as the one I described. Mrs. Hazelthorpe runs a particular kind of confidential service. A matrimonial match-making service, to be exact."

Another flash of awareness settled in those blue eyes.

"You had retained the woman's services, as well," he said. "In fact, your letter of request, complete with a detailed description of yourself and your preference in a husband, landed on her desk a week before mine."

She paled. "And this woman thought us a good match?"

He nodded. "To use her words, she pronounced us *evenly yoked.* There was no one in your village or surroundings who suited you, and your father had grown quite adamant that you marry someone of his choosing. You and I corresponded for several months through this woman's service. Our communication was rather awkward at first, but as time passed, a friendship grew."

He offered a slight shrug. "At least, I construed it as amicable. We found we had similar roots, and at least in the missives, we seemed to have comparable likes and dislikes. Since your father is the third son of an earl and your mother the daughter of a viscount, I thought it a boon to find someone who, when the time came, could also meet the demands of an earl's wife, yet still prefer quiet, country living."

He reached into a drawer, pulled out a stack of letters bound by a neat ribbon, and shoved them her way. "I saved everything you sent me."

Then he removed a miniature of her and slid it across the desk. "You sent me this, as well."

She moved to the chair in front of him and sat. Ignoring the letters, she picked up the small, hand-painted portrait and studied it for a while. "But despite the fact I am of age, my father didn't approve of what I had decided. So before he could intervene and beat me bloody, I lit out on my own without an escort, leaving a note behind. Thus, I married a man I had never laid eyes on until the day of my wedding. Do I have this right?"

Eastleigh gave her a faint smile. "Dire as it sounds, at least you now recollect. Knowing your parents were against the marriage, and you were of age, we agreed to meet in the small village of Marsham, where I'd prearranged for the vicar to marry us. We spent our first wedded night in a decent inn there. The next morning, we headed toward the sea where a ship awaited to take us to the Continent for an extended tour. That's when we were waylaid by thieves."

She sat quietly, staring at the miniature with no expression. An odd fear seeped through the pain he struggled against. He set an elbow on the chair's arm and ran a thumb back and forth over his chipped tooth. "Might I add, the portrait doesn't do you justice?"

When she failed to respond, he regarded her for a long moment. If only she could cast off that mantle of ice she encased herself in, he could show her so much of what she had missed in life. "Even without your memory and in your fragile state, I thought we had become friends of late, if nothing else, so I held out hope."

She set the miniature down and placed her hands flat upon the desk, fingers splayed. "I…I wear no ring."

The familiar roar in his ears was beginning to take hold. It seemed he needed his powders after all—or next would come the shouts and screams inside his head, the bloody battle scenes playing out after that. But he couldn't break away just yet or he might never have another chance at reconciliation. "I planned to take you to a jeweler in Paris and have one designed. I wanted you to wear a ring like none other."

She glanced up, her eyes round. "You wore your boots to bed. On our wedding night?"

He shook his head and felt everything inside rattle. "As I said, we were at a decent inn our first night." He swiped at the perspiration now beading his brow. "We were set upon the next day and robbed. I carried you most of the way to the flea-bit inn where you slept the night through, only to awaken the next morning recalling nothing. That was when I slept with my boots on and the key in my pocket in case we were set upon again."

"You lied to me, Eastleigh. All this time, you lied to me."

"Think back, Lilith. I *never* lied to you. I was only very careful to leave things out because I thought it best to have a doctor direct your course of treatment. If you recall, I refused to call you Sarah Marks, even when you demanded I do so. Instead, I referred to you as madam. I nearly slipped up a few times. I was desperate to see you home so that I could gain Hemphill's expertise."

He was going to lose her, he could feel it coming. His brain knocked against the inside of his head, triggering flashes of light that nearly blinded him.

"Why didn't you correct me when I told you my name was Sarah Marks?"

He shifted in his seat and bent his head from side to side, trying to ease the wretched pulling of his neck muscles. Little good that did. "There was the worst of it, Lilith. When you gave me the name Sarah Marks, I grew sick at heart and nearly panicked. I knew I had to keep you calm or you could have been in great danger. Drat it all, when I was first injured, my brain couldn't manage to dredge up my own name for a full year. Whenever anyone would ask, I'd spit out the damnedest monikers. On several occasions, I even claimed the name of my horse as my Christian name, but never was I able to conjure up my own."

"Who knows about us? Is your family aware of the particulars? Is Mum?"

He started to shake his head, but the pain stopped him. He had to squint in order to see her clearly now. He set his fingers to his temple and pressed as inconspicuously as possible. "Only Doctor Hemphill knew you were my wife, and he was adamant no one else be informed lest they slip and harm you with no malice intended. For obvious reasons, I couldn't risk Mum knowing. I did send a missive off to your parents as soon as we arrived here explaining everything, but I told them to stay put under doctor's orders."

Her brows knit together. "You told no one else of your plans to marry me before you left Easton Park?"

"You've met my family. A rowdier bunch you'll likely never run across. They would have had opinions, badgered me to death. Hell, Ridley probably would have followed me. No, I planned on returning from the Continent with my wife in tow some three or four months into our marriage."

She stood. "Good. Then I wish for an annulment."

I knew it. Despite his head full of fire, a rueful laugh escaped him. "Impossible. The marriage was consummated."

She paled and pressed a knotted fist against her stomach. Then she straightened and settled a cold stare upon him. "Oh, I do recall that part. Which is why I called you a beast. You hurt me, Eastleigh."

He swept a hand across his forehead. "If I caused you pain, I am sorry. You indicated nothing of the sort, Lilith. Even when I inquired, you said not a word. Although I once dallied with half the young widows in London, I had never before been with an innocent. I was as careful as I could be under the circumstances. There shouldn't be any discomfort next time."

"Next time? Never!" Her voice rose with each word. "You nearly tore me asunder."

Oh hell.

Whatever reserves he had left dissipated like water through a sieve. Pressing the heels of his palms to his temples, he squeezed as if to exorcise the demons spearing his head and shouted. "For God's sake, Lilith, you lay there stiff as a goddamn board! I suggested we wait, but you insisted we 'get the deed done', and then you proceeded to set your rigid legs apart just enough for me to…to…"

Oh, hell.

"We made a mistake, Lilith. But at the time, I thought you might be right—get the wedding night over with, then enjoy a tour of the Continent while we—"

Damn his pounding head. He had to end this conversation in a hurry. "Let's discuss this on the morrow, after you've rested."

He paused and, locking his gaze with hers, softened his voice. "After you've had time to think about our kisses, about how you've responded to them in a way that tells both of us there's hope for a well-matched marriage. In every respect."

Her mouth dropped open at his words. She stared at him, as if she'd never connected one act with the other. Then her lips formed a pale white slit. "You lied easily enough before. Tell the courts the marriage was never consummated. You have the clout to do whatever might be needed to see that an annulment is granted."

"Why? So you can run back to your dear father and let him beat you to within an inch of your life? No. You are my wife and as such, you are under my protection. What if you are with child? Have you thought of that?"

She wheeled around and stomped to the window, her back to him. "I am certain I'm not with child, so if you refuse an annulment, then I ask you to have pity and grant me a settlement so I can live on my own."

He sat for a long while, staring at her stiff back, growing wearier by the moment. Damn it, he'd fought enough battles to consume several life times. The last thing he needed was to jump headlong into a war with his wife. *His wife.* What a bloody mess.

He hauled in a deep breath and, letting out a heavy sigh, pressed his fingers to his temples again. "I have an urgent need to end our discussion for today. A good deal of recollection has come your way. You need time to mull things over. Sleep on what you are asking of me, Lilith. If, on the morrow, you still wish an annulment, we will discuss it further."

She moved a bit closer to where he sat and lifted her chin. "And if, during the night, I should change my mind? What then?"

Derisive laughter spilled from his gut. "Perhaps by then my mind will have moved in the opposite direction, and I will want nothing further to do with you."

He paused, their gazes locked. And then something deep inside drew out his words like the Excalibur being drawn from the stone. "However, my dear wife, if it turns out you decide to fully commit to this marriage in every respect, then you had better damn well yank that rod out of your arse, move into the chambers next to mine, and leave the bloody door between us unlocked!"

He pushed back his chair and stood, nearly keeling over. He had to get out of there. Had to get to his rooms. Get his powders.

Too late.

A seed of hot pain, deep inside his brain, burst into a fiery vision of bloodied bodies strewn about, of dead and dying horses. Cannons roared above cries and screams, and the smell of acrid gun powder burnt his nostrils all over again. Layered beneath it all was the echo of a male's voice gasping his name, begging for help. Over and over, the mournful sound rolled through his head—and fell into his battered heart.

"G...get...Hemphill." Unable to focus, he attempted to make his way around the desk, but his boot snagged the corner. He tripped and pitched forward.

Chapter Twelve

"Eastleigh!" Lilith screamed.

In the seconds it took for the double doors to fly open and a small crowd to rush in, blood spilled from Eastleigh's scalp and pooled on the hardwood floor.

"Bloody hell!" Ridley bent to one side of his brother while Hemphill knelt near Eastleigh's head. Thomas and Sebastian gathered around them, both cursing.

Lilith's knees gave way. She sat with a hard jolt on the nearest chair and bit down on her knuckles to keep silent. Her mother sidled in. She stood off to the left, not bothering to so much as glance Lilith's way.

"A head wound can be shallow and still bleed vigorously," Hemphill said, examining Eastleigh's scalp. "So while I suggest you do not panic, someone get me a cloth. I'll need to put pressure on the injury to staunch the flow of blood before we make any attempt to move him."

Three pristine handkerchiefs shot out of breast pockets

like white flags waving. The brothers stuffed them into Hemphill's hand.

"He's out cold," Ridley said, his words filled with dark fury.

"That's the worry," Hemphill said, not looking up from the handful of linens he pressed against Eastleigh's wound. "No telling what another knock on the head has done to his memory. Someone ready three or four footmen to carry him to his chambers."

Sebastian stood. "We're his brothers." Shedding his tightly fitted jacket and tossing it aside without a glance as to where it landed, he rolled back his sleeves. "We'll see to him."

Thomas and Ridley stood and did the same. In the process of casting off his jacket, Ridley shot Lilith a glare so ominous her already queasy stomach nearly lost its contents.

"I don't know what the devil went on in here," he growled. "But when I return for my clothing, you had better have answers for me, because I intend to have them."

Lilith bit the inside of her lip in a vain attempt to hold her nerves steady. "He had a headache that had worsened, so he was attempting to leave when he tripped coming around his desk. I think he hit his head on the sharp corner of the chess table on the way down."

The contempt in Ridley's narrowed eyes could have cut steel. "If he didn't have a headache before you arrived, then he damn well has one now."

Lilith flinched. But then she recoiled from the wince and let the hurt settle inside her. Truth was truth. Ridley had every right to be angry with her. "What happened to your brother is entirely my fault."

"Enough!" Hemphill shouted. "Let's get him moving or call the footmen to do the deed."

At the sight of the dark stain eating up the pristine white cloths pressed to Eastleigh's head, a small moan escaped her lips.

Thomas kneeled next to the doctor. "I can manage to keep the handkerchiefs on him long enough to get him to his bed." He replaced Hemphill's hold with his own, slipped his other arm beneath Eastleigh's neck and shoulder area, then nodded to his brothers.

"Ready on three," Ridley said, and with a fluid motion that could not have been better orchestrated, the brothers lifted Eastleigh as though he weighed little more than a young boy and carried him off.

Hemphill started to trail behind but paused long enough to shoot a glance at Lilith. "I knew he had a megrim coming on when I left you two, but even you noticed his condition? I have a need to inquire so as to know best how to treat him."

She nodded. "He'd grown quite pale, and he kept scrubbing at his neck and pressing at his temples the entire short while that we conversed. I asked if he was all right, but he shook off my inquiry and kept on with the conversation. Finally, he said he had to discontinue the discussion, and after a few more words, he made to leave." She glanced at the blood stain and looked away, unable to bear the sight of what their argument had caused. "That's when it happened. The fall, I mean."

Hemphill settled an authoritative regard on her mother. "Mrs. Stokes, I would advise you to take heart and see to your daughter while I tend to her husband. Lilith, the chamber you used prior to your leaving has been made ready. Wait for me there, and I'll come to you as soon as I am able. Do not, under any circumstance, bid Ridley entry with his temper gone off the way it has."

He turned to exit and nearly ran into Mum, her eyes wide. "What's happened to my Augie?"

"He took a fall," Hemphill called out as he disappeared from sight. "See Lilith gets to her chambers, if you will."

Mum is to see me to my chambers? Had Hemphill lost his senses? But when Mum stretched out her hand in a compassionate, beckoning gesture, a kind of strength shone in the depths of her eyes that gave Lilith a sudden measure of comfort.

And the meek shall inherit the earth.

Lilith swallowed the bile in her throat and went to Mum, whose arms swept around her. Tildy stood outside the door, wringing her hands. "Would you tend to my mother, Tildy? Are there chambers ready for her?"

"Indeed, my lady. I'll be caring for the both of ye." Tildy gave a small bow of her head, and the sweep of her skirts told Lilith there had been a bend of the knee as well. How bittersweet—a show of respect for a short-lived lady of the manor.

"Mrs. Stokes," Mum said. "Would you care to join us for tea? Tildy will see to having it brought to your daughter's chambers since she's to remain there until the good doctor can see to her."

Lilith's mother swept past them and into the corridor, head down with her eyes cast to the floor. The color in her cheeks deepened. "I think not. Show me to my rooms, if you will, Tildy."

For the first time, Lilith became acutely aware of how

her mother had never come to her aid, no matter what her father had said or done. A familiar, hollow ache caught in the pit of her stomach. But for whatever reason, the feeling left her, replaced by an odd sense of compassion. Mother had been afraid all her married life. She still was.

No wonder her mother felt fear. It raced through Lilith's veins now, as well, right behind confusion and hurt. What a mess she'd made of things. And what if the fall had done damage to Eastleigh's memory again? Ridley was right— this was all her doing.

A squeeze of her hand, and Mum said, "Come, dear. We can wait this out over tea. You look as though you are about to expire on the spot."

"I feel as though I might, at that." With shaking fingers, she took Mum's bent elbow, as much to guide Mum as to steady herself. As they exited the library, two parlor maids rushed in, each carrying a bucket of steaming water, brushes, and cloths.

Lilith glanced back at them. They were already on their knees and leaning over the dark stain on the floor. That was Eastleigh's blood—blood that would not have been shed if not for her.

A sickening shockwave ran through her.

God in Heaven, what have I done?

The French mantel clock had barely chimed five times when a knock sounded. Lilith rose from where she sat at the table across from Mum and moved to the door, unlocking it once

Hemphill had announced himself.

Lilith had to swallow hard to get her throat to work. "How is Eastleigh?"

Doctor Hemphill entered and scrubbed his hand over his eyes. "Hard to say. I stitched up his head wound and filled him with laudanum, so he's still unconscious. We'll keep the treatment going for three to five days. From past experience, that is what was required when a megrim this bad set in. The danger is that if the brain swells, we won't know until it's too late, but if we withhold medication at this point, he could easily have a setback with the amnesia. The next twelve hours will tell us if there is any engorgement, but if that's not the case, we won't know whether he's had a relapse in memory until he awakens."

Lilith began to pace, biting her lip and rubbing at the chills running up and down her arms. Tears pricked the backs of her eyes. "Lord in heaven. If we lose him—"

"Get hold of yourself, Lilith. It does no good to consider those kinds of thoughts. I like to remember that we've pulled him through worse."

"Oh, dear," Mum said. "I'm going to go sit with him."

Hemphill turned to her. "He's sleeping, Mum."

"Well, that didn't stop me from holding vigil in the past, did it?" She was out the door in a flash.

Oh, how Lilith wanted to be the one rushing to his side, but his family was likely gathered around him. She would be the last person they'd want to see. She pressed her fingers to her lips and sucked in a breath through her nose to keep from weeping. Turning her back to Hemphill, she moved to the tall mantel and pressed her forehead against the marble, cool on her skin despite the fire burning in the hearth below.

"Will you keep me apprised of his condition?" Her words trembled when they left her mouth. She suddenly realized she cared about Eastleigh far more than she wanted to admit to herself.

"Of course. But you're his wife, you should be—"

She raised a hand. "Please. His family would have my head should I attempt to see him at this point. I ignored the obvious worsening of his condition and selfishly asked him for an annulment. I believe that's what sent him over the edge."

Hemphill's eyebrows shot up. "An annulment? But—"

"Since we three are the only ones aware the marriage was consummated—and I know for certain I am not with child—I asked him to cooperate."

"You mean you asked him to lie."

Her stomach did a flip at Hemphill's words. She took in another breath to try and release the tension in her chest. Little good that did. "And now look at the horrid situation I have created. I should leave the premises as soon as possible. I would not care to have Ridley toss me out on my behind."

"You are Lady Eastleigh, he cannot do that. Besides, I talked him out of confronting you. He and his brothers rode off to inform their parents of Eastleigh's accident."

"But they'll be back. Then there's that bully Will to deal with." Unable to hold back her tears, Lilith covered her face with her hands and wept.

Hemphill touched her shoulder.

She flinched and jumped back as if the contact burned her.

He dropped his hand and stepped away from her. "You act as though I was about to strike you." His brows stitched together. "Good God, Lilith. Is this the result of having spent years with an abusive father?"

"I'm sorry. I…I confess, I can be a bit alarmed by a man's touch. I had no business thinking I could manage a decent relationship with a man when they frighten me so. I have done Eastleigh a terrible injustice."

"Which is why you asked for the annulment, isn't it?"

Unable to face Hemphill's scrutiny, she stared over his shoulder at nothing, her chin quivering. "In all likelihood, you've got things right."

He reached toward her, but then, as if thinking better of it, dropped his hand. He moved to the door and opened it. "Eastleigh is in a deep sleep, but it might do you a bit of good to sit with him awhile. Mum is there with him, and I've chased the rest of the family from his room for the time being. You'll be safe."

Lilith wrapped her arms around herself against the sudden chill at the idea of stepping out into the corridor. God knew what kind of gossip was running rampant.

"You'll have your privacy. I'll see to it."

They made their way along the corridor to Eastleigh's chambers and entered the darkened room. Lilith paused a moment for her eyes to adjust. Then she stepped to the side of the bed. Eastleigh lay before her, deathly still, his face ashen. A white bandage was wound around his head. Dark blotches stained one side. She fisted her hand against her mouth to keep from crying out.

Hemphill brought a chair next to where Mum sat and motioned for Lilith to sit. Then he moved to the other side of the bed and carefully went about changing Eastleigh's bandage.

Mum reached out and covered Lilith's clenched hands with one of her own and whispered, "We've been through this before with his headaches."

"But not with a wound."

"Oh, dear. You should have seen him when he first arrived from the Crimean—"

Hemphill shook his head, quieting them. He came around to where Lilith sat. "You're still my patient," he said quietly. "You need your rest now."

"You're right. I'm enervated. I can see myself out." She stood and made for the door, but it opened before she reached it.

Will!

Lilith felt the blood drain from her face.

Hands on her hips, feet wide apart, Will blocked the doorway. "We're going to have a little talk, you and I."

Hemphill rushed around Lilith and boldly pushed Will back until they stood in the middle of the corridor. He glanced over his shoulder. "Lilith, stay in the room."

He turned back to Will. "You will not disrupt either of my patients. If you insist on badgering Lady Eastleigh," he growled, "I will have you tossed out. Do you understand?"

Lilith had only *thought* she'd endured Hemphill's sternness in the past. The severe tone of his voice had her standing at attention.

Will glared at Lilith over the doctor's shoulder, then marched along the corridor and stomped down the stairs. If looks were daggers, Lilith would be dead.

With the little dignity Lilith had left, she managed to make her way to her room without stumbling over her own feet. By the time she got there, she was weeping so hard she couldn't see to grasp the door's handle.

Hemphill opened it for her. "I suggest you allow me to administer a small dose of laudanum to help you rest. You've been through a terrible ordeal."

Chapter Thirteen

Lilith paced the floor, waiting for word on Eastleigh. Hemphill had finally given up trying to keep Will at bay and had told Lilith to remain in her room until he could escort her to Eastleigh.

She'd barely set eyes on him these past three days for all the laudanum Hemphill had insisted she take. And the few times he'd taken her to Eastleigh, her brain had been in such a fog, she could barely recall the visits.

Last night, she'd refused to be drugged, only to toss and turn until the wee hours, her nerves in a frazzle. Finally, she could stand it no longer and had made her way to Eastleigh's quarters. At least surly Will had gone to bed, leaving Lilith free to sit beside her husband's bed without concerning herself that she might be pounced upon at any moment. She'd remained with him until the break of dawn.

In the light of day, however, and with Will up and about, waiting for Hemphill to escort her seemed reasonable. Lilith doubted her fractured nerves could take much more of Will's assaults. Damn that woman and her vile tongue. Where was Hemphill, for heaven's sake?

What was she to do with herself until he showed up? She'd managed to drag out the completion of her toilette until the noon meal. But nearly three hours had passed since, with nothing to look forward to but high tea while awaiting word of Eastleigh's condition. Alone. She'd wandered onto the balcony three times. No sense going out there again just to stare at flower beds she wasn't about to dally in, not with Will down there digging around.

A light tapping sounded on her door. Distinctly Hemphill's coded knock. Thank the Lord, he could take her to Eastleigh. She rushed to the door and opened it.

"Ridley," was all she could manage with her breath freezing in her lungs.

He regarded her with that damnable penetrating gaze. He was much, much bigger than she remembered. But then she recalled he was a fraction smaller than Eastleigh. Perhaps it was the green jacket giving his shoulders a broader look or the fawn-colored breeches tucked into high-top, brown riding boots that made him appear taller. No matter—the truth of it was, the man created a formidable presence.

Daunted, she managed a breath and gathered courage. "What of Eastleigh?" How could her voice not be shaking? Her legs were.

"There's no change in him."

"Then why are you here?"

"I've brought your letters."

She glanced down at the packet in his hand. They were the missives she'd written to Eastleigh. He'd left them sitting on the corner of his desk. "Those belong to your brother. I can tell you so because I wrote them."

"Interesting letters, these."

"You read them?"

"Every word."

"How awful of you. Those were private."

"Were they, now?" He glanced over her shoulder. "We need to talk. And since there is no other place in this house by which to ensure we won't be overheard, you should invite me in."

He wished to invade her private space? "That wouldn't be at all proper."

A rueful smile touched his lips. He leaned a shoulder against the door frame and slowly slapped the letters against the palm of his other hand. "Does that mean you are perfectly at ease discussing your personal affairs with your door wide open for the servants to hear and pass on to every living relative?"

His piercing gaze trapped and held hers. Something inside her began to crumble. It would not do to let drop her well-bred mask—not in front of him, of all people. "I am not *personally fine* discussing any of my affairs with you, so please leave."

"Unless you wish to have me force my way in, you had better reconsider."

She stood in frank disbelief, staring at him. "You wouldn't."

His answering laughter tumbled along the corridor as he strolled inside.

Lilith stepped back until she stood nearly in the corridor. She glanced to her right just as a mob capped maid peeked out a bedroom door, then promptly disappeared.

The silence that followed strained her ears. She looked in the other direction and caught sight of a couple more servants peering. Oh, this simply would not do. Anger poured into all the places inside her that gave her courage. She stepped inside and quietly closed the door behind her.

Ridley sat in the center of a low, broad chair, the packet of letters balanced on one bent leg resting on the other knee.

Lilith moved to the open doors leading to the balcony. She kept her back to him. "You're a strange lot, you Malverns."

"And hopefully, we will remain as such."

Was there humor lacing his words? What in heaven's name was he up to? She clasped her hands together to cease their shaking.

"I wouldn't mind meeting a woman like the one in these letters," he said in a quiet voice.

She gave a start, and then strove for impassivity. "What are you getting at?"

"What I mean is, I understand why Eastleigh asked for your hand. He would've been quite taken with whoever wrote these."

She wheeled around, shock prickling her body. "Are you insinuating I hired someone to create those on my behalf? I can assure you it was I who wrote every word."

He studied her, slowly rubbing his thumb over his bottom lip, much as Eastleigh ran his over his chipped tooth. "I know that. But do you?"

The breath went out of her. She had no idea what he was getting at and wasn't so sure she wanted to be made aware. "You should go now."

"What are you so afraid of that you cannot let yourself be the delightful woman displayed in these letters? And why can you only be that person by using sheaves of paper as your shield?" He spread his arms wide, rested them in a lazy manner against the back of the chair, and regarded her through half-closed lids. "Tell me, Lilith."

She tried to swallow against her suddenly parched throat, but gave up and stared at him, the air hanging heavy between them. With his leg still crossed one over the other, his arms slung over the chair, and his eyes much softer, he suddenly appeared relaxed and friendly.

"I've a feeling you could be nice if you wanted to be," she said.

He lifted a brow. "Maybe I want to be."

His response made her chest ache. Eastleigh did the same thing—set his head just so and lifted a brow whenever he slipped into a clever mood. "I do not understand you at all, Ridley."

"Are you afraid of men?"

A shockwave jolted her. She swiped an unsteady hand across the thin film of perspiration forming on her brow. "You've been talking to Hemphill."

He nodded, his gazed locked with hers.

"Did he tell you what I requested of Eastleigh?"

Again he nodded. "I also had a long talk with your mother after I read your letters. Or should I say, I sat Mrs. Stokes down and insisted she give up the family secrets. You, Lilith, are frightened of anything to do with the male species. And you are afraid to trust anyone, especially since you are a vicar's daughter who feels even the Almighty God your cruel father yammers on about has betrayed you. You have little faith in anything or anyone. Yet you sought out a husband. Doesn't that tell you something?"

"Go away."

"No."

Fresh tears stung the backs of her eyes. She had to get rid of him. "What is your purpose in coming here, Ridley? To torture me?"

"I came to escort you to my brother," he said softly. "And I'll not allow Will to bully you should you cross paths."

Another something out of his mouth she hadn't expected. Sudden desperation threatened to overwhelm her. He couldn't know all of what had transpired between her and Eastleigh. Some words were better left unsaid. "That's not the only reason you've invaded my quarters, is it?"

"Hear me out, Lilith. Don't throw away what you two might build together because of some misguided notion he might treat you in a manner your father has."

"It seems the good doctor was rather loose-tongued with you." Her mind tracked back to her wedding night. And the pain. And then Eastleigh's gentle words before he'd fallen, that he thought the two of them could be quite compatible. A torrent of emotions rained through her. She blinked back tears. Lord, would they never cease?

Ridley stood and held out a hand to her. "Hemphill came to me because he knew I had the letters and that I'd changed my mind about you. He only wants to help. Now come along."

She stared at his open palm as conscious thought all but collapsed. His hand was broad and long fingered, with a signet ring on the smallest digit—so much like Eastleigh's, yet somehow different. She placed her shaky palm against his, and feeling the heat, the pulse, the very life force beating within him, she jerked back.

"What is it, Lilith?"

"I..." She turned away from him and wrapped her arms around her waist. "A man's hands can hurt."

"Eastleigh would not use his to hurt you. Neither would I." He took her by the shoulders and gently turned her to face him once again.

It was all she could do not to pull away.

"I gave you a fright the other day, and I am truly sorry. I've a bit of a temper that lands me in a fix now and then, but I would never strike you."

When she stood there, not thinking but embracing his words in ways she'd never done before, the small smile left his lips. "Seeing as how I got your mother to give up your past, you ought to be able to have your turn at me. Anything else you'd care to inquire of me?"

She paused for a moment. "Not about you at the moment, but I'm rather curious as to what happened between Sir Robert Garrick and Eastleigh for them to be at odds."

He lifted a brow. "You surprise me. I take it you've met my cousin?"

"Briefly." She saw no reason to tell Ridley what had occurred that day.

"I'm not aware of what took place between them," he said. "But since returning from the war, Rob will have nothing further to do with a Malvern. We were always close growing up. He was as much a brother to us as we four. It has something to do with Eastleigh, but we can't figure out what."

Eastleigh. She looked up at Ridley but then turned a cheek, not wanting him to see the tears clouding her eyes yet again. She had to hurry him along lest they fall.

"It's all right to weep in front of family, you know."

"Is that what you consider me, Ridley? Family?"

"If you'll let yourself be."

"But what if Eastleigh doesn't want me back after how I behaved? After what I demanded?"

"Then you'll have to talk with Mum and let her help you change Eastleigh's mind. If anyone can do it, she can."

"But what if he still doesn't want to make a life with me?"

"At this point, you have no guarantees of anything. If he doesn't want you back, or if you do not wish to remain, at least you can be certain of where you stand. At any rate, you both have a good deal to work out, but in the long run, how can you make any other choice?"

He stretched out his hand to her again. "Lilith, I am asking you to trust me. For just a moment, put your hand in mine."

She stared at it for a long moment. Then she opened hers, and he pressed his palm to it. "What's the first thing you feel?"

"Fear." She jerked away and wiped her hand on her skirt.

He watched her movements. "You feel no warmth? No secure sense of having a brotherly strength to lean on?"

She drew in a long breath. "I'm not sure."

"Then try again."

Once more, she reached out and placed her trembling hand in his. This time she forced it to remain until the shaking subsided. She felt the heat then, the warmth…and yes, a feeling he would not hurt her.

"There you go," he said in a mellow voice. "As long as you remain Lady Eastleigh, you'll not be alone. You've family now to keep you safe."

She stared at his hand as his fingers closed around hers. Unshed tears clogged her throat, and she cleared it to get her words out. "I'm not certain I would want this kind of thing to become a regular habit."

A corner of his mouth lifted. "Come Lilith. Your husband needs you."

• • •

"Lilith." Hemphill stood from where he sat in a chair and laid a book on the side table.

"Doctor." She barely glanced at him, her attention riveted on the bed. As her eyes adjusted to the darkened room, she could tell Eastleigh's color had returned. Her heart nearly broke loose from her ribcage. Even unconscious, he was a beautiful man. He was her husband. And it was her fault he lay so still.

Ridley gave Hemphill a nod. "You can take things from here. I'll see they're not disturbed."

The door closed behind Ridley, and Hemphill offered Lilith a brief smile. "Good to see you."

She gave a nod. "I've had a change of heart. I...I do hope Eastleigh will have one as well."

Pulse racing, she stepped to his bedside and watched the thin blanket covering his bare chest slowly move up and down with his every breath.

Wake up!

A small noise escaped her lips. Catching hold of herself, she swallowed against unspent tears. For pity's sake, could she have any left for all the weeping she'd done? Realizing her fists had balled, she released them and touched the back of her hand against the cool skin of Eastleigh's brow. Her fingers stroked lightly through his curls. So thick, yet silken, as she'd always suspected. She touched the bandage covering the cut from his fall, and her breath hitched.

Remembering Hemphill, she speared him with a look that begged for the response she prayed for. "Tell me he's going to be all right. Tell me he'll not have lost his memory again."

"I haven't administered any laudanum since morning, so the medication should be wearing off soon. Then we'll know where we stand as far as how his memory serves him. I'll leave you alone for now. Use the bell pull if he awakens, or if you should need anything. Since we are all on the alert, you'll get a quick response."

Chapter Fourteen

A familiar, beckoning fragrance—but of what?—invaded Eastleigh's jumbled senses. Supple fingers swept through his hair, slow and gentle.

Keep doing that.

His brain felt like slow moving sludge, but at least the bloody headache was gone. He'd been through this before. Many times. He drew a breath and waited for his mind to assemble.

A curious emotion pulled at him. Loneliness? No, he'd grown used to the hollowness such a feeling produced. His chest rose and fell in another long breath. What the devil had preceded his headache this time? He stilled his mind. It wouldn't do to try and force recollections. To push only produced chaos.

Did he just moan?

The fingers through his hair ceased their gentle stroking. Something shifted inside him. The wall barring his thoughts fell away.

Lilith.

The word acted like a catalyst, and his mind swirled into dizzying motion. God above. She wanted to leave him. And then everything came clear and the jagged pieces fell into place. All except for that one blasted part of his past that had yet to come forth. Anger bit into his gut. Nothing new, it always followed one of these sessions, yet it ran deeper this time. Because of her? Because he'd waited too long to take his powders and had done this to himself?

He managed to work his eyelids open. She sat in a chair at his bedside, hands folded in her lap. He studied her. She stared back, bold and guileless. And then she offered him a weak smile.

As he watched her, waiting for all his senses to fully awaken, a look of bewilderment washed over her countenance. The knuckles on her clasped hands turned white. Blankly, he surveyed the room, the silence intolerably heavy. The anger rolling through him wasn't completely related to her—but a good deal of it was.

She cleared her throat. Her gaze dropped to his mouth. "You've been asleep for nearly three days, what with the laudanum…"

What was she doing here? Did she still want the annulment? His gut wrenched at the idea.

What was it about her that he couldn't leave her alone? Why would he want such a stiff prude anyway? Confusion caused his throat to grow thick, and an attempt to swallow failed. He squinted. "Open the blasted curtains. I can't see a thing."

She rose, rounded the foot of the bed, and moved to the

balcony doors where she drew open the heavy blue fabric. "A rather cloudy day, I'm afraid, but there are flowers in the garden in full bloom. I'll see to having fresh ones brought in."

Her voice, light and cheery, fell on his ears, but he noted her shaking fingers as they paused briefly on the curtains. She dropped her hand and turned. He wanted to roar in defiance of her false, breezy tone.

Time slowed on her march back to him. As she neared the bed, his gaze settled on the sway of her hips, and his groin tightened. Odd, but she seemed more womanly than he remembered. She sat. It was as if he could feel her touching his skin. Heart racing, he refused to look away, his mouth a tight slit.

"Is the headache gone?"

"Completely."

Despite her intent to appear relaxed, tension tugged at the corners of her mouth. "I am sorry you've been so ill. Doctor Hemphill said the laudanum would wear off by tomorrow. In the meantime, you should remain abed."

With a rustle of the linens, he worked his way into a sitting position against the pillows, the bedcovers falling to his waist and exposing his bare upper body. She stared at his chest for a moment and then brought her gaze back up to meet his.

He raked his fingers through his hair. "If you're still of a mind, we should discuss the terms of the annulment."

A flicker of shock ran through her eyes. She turned a cheek to him for a brief moment, as if arranging her own thoughts. Then she held her head at a proud angle. "Really, sir, I'd rather we change the subject. At least for now. First off, we need to have Doctor Hemphill check you."

He cocked a brow. "I suggest we not ignore the topic any longer."

In the interminable silence that followed, their gazes locked. Derision rode wild in him, but nonetheless, disappointment at his own words seeped through him like water filling empty spaces between rocks.

Lilith sprang to her feet and moved to the wall holding the bell pull and gave it a good yank. Then she made her way to the door, her fingers grasping for the handle, reminding him of the day at the inn when she'd tried to escape the locked room. "I fear you are not up to a discussion at the moment. I need to fetch the doctor before we continue."

"One hour," he growled.

She made to step from the room but paused long enough to shoot him a sidelong glance. "Beg pardon?"

His harsh words would have undone anyone, but she held his gaze steady. "There's no sense stringing this out any longer, Lilith. One hour and we shall have our discussion."

Her chin lifted. "Don't try and browbeat me into submission."

"This is hardly the time to challenge me." His dark mood turned black. "Be back here in an hour."

"Or what?"

Despite her flippant response, she looked near tears. His head spun and the knot in his chest tightened to the point of suffocation.

She opened the door and hurried past Hemphill, who stepped inside.

"What the devil? She's changed."

"Indeed," Hemphill said. "I doubt she's in favor of the

annulment any longer, but she has to be the one to tell you, not me. She's having trouble expressing her feelings after having had a lifetime of being afraid to speak her mind, lest she be beaten. She is also filled with a great amount of guilt for what happened to you. She blames herself. You need to give her time. Don't forget how long it's taken you to heal."

Eastleigh focused on the gray sky beyond the windows, his heart heavy in his chest. "I still have a long way to go. Is this the way it is to be, Hemphill? A spat between husband and wife and I'm back in bed for days on end? Perhaps loneliness wasn't the lesser evil after all."

• • •

Lilith entered her chamber, pressed her back against the closed door, and shut her eyes. How she'd had to fight against the backlash of her own fears. "Well, that went swimmingly."

A rustling on the balcony brought her eyes open. "Mother?"

She stared at her mother's stiffened back, acutely aware of how she herself had adopted the same stance years ago. Now she knew full-well why—it happened whenever she was afraid or hadn't known what to expect. The deportment wasn't in the least becoming, nor did it send out a warm message. How had she never noticed this cold remoteness before?

A firm resolve settled in her bones. Whatever it took, she would change her stiff bearing once and for all.

Her mother turned to her. Lips pursed, she gave Lilith a scathing once-over—an all-too-familiar gesture indicating verbal arrows were about to be slung. "Your husband has improved?"

Lilith studied her mother for a moment, an even greater sense of freedom and empowerment filling her as she stood with fine posture, but not as her mother did, in that formidable manner meant to keep everyone at bay. It might take some time...she might falter now and then...but she'd have it right in the end.

"He's awake. The doctor is with him."

Ridley's words washed through her mind—*what are you afraid of*? Well, she intended to become exceedingly aware of what frightened her. And if those fears were dragons, she would slay them all—one by one. Entering Eastleigh's chambers had been the first. The second was at hand. She moved onto the balcony and peered at the gardens below. "Is that why you've helped yourself into my quarters—to inquire of Lord Eastleigh's health?"

Her mother moved to stand beside her. For a long, silent moment, she, too, regarded the flowers. Suddenly her back lost some of its stiffness, and the muscles in her face sagged. Unfolding her arms, she set her palms to the railing and leaned into it. "Were you aware that whenever you were beaten, if your father hadn't completely worked out his anger, he waited until you were asleep and then turned his hand on me?"

Chills rippled nonstop along Lilith's skin. "I...I thought I was the only one to bear the whip. When did he start with you?"

"Shortly after our nuptials."

Dear Lord! "Had there been any hint of this kind of behavior before you wed?"

Her mother shook her head. "Whilst courting, his

exemplary behavior would have put an angel to shame. He even wrote me sonnets." A wistful note fluttered through her voice but disappeared in a blink. "Being the impoverished, third son of an earl, he didn't want me so much as my father's money."

She gave a little huff and raised her chin. "A dowry—that's all I was good for."

For the first time, Lilith realized she shared not only some of her mother's mannerisms, but her life-long pain. How had Lilith missed this? Had she so encased herself in ice in order to survive that she had been ignorant of Mother's signals? "Why are you telling me this now?"

A look settled upon her mother's countenance that Lilith had not seen before. Was she seeing compassion? Inner pain? "Because I want you to commit to making a decent life for yourself here. And I hope you will tell Eastleigh so directly. He is a good man, of a kind you'll not likely encounter again."

A memory of the awful pain and embarrassment Lilith had endured during their wedding night gave her a shudder. Eastleigh had given her one hour. To do what? March back into his chamber and remove her clothing and climb into his bed? Even though both Mum and Hemphill had said Eastleigh would be a growling bear upon awakening, she'd had to fight for enough courage just to get up and walk out on him and his ferocious mood.

She shoved a loose curl behind her ear. "Truth be told, Mother, I have realized that he is a good man, but I have great doubts that I am fit for the likes of him." She rubbed harder at her arms and set to pacing. "Until today, I have not been able to let a man so much as offer his hand to escort me up a stair. Father—"

Her mother spread her arms wide as if tossing her emotions in the air. "Don't be foolish, Lilith. Soon, there will be nothing but faded memories of your father's cruelty. Look around you. This house vibrates with life and laughter. You will want for nothing here. And Eastleigh is a good man, the best you could ever hope for."

Lilith swallowed the lump in her throat. "Eastleigh deserves far better than what I have to offer. Thus far, I have been a miserable excuse for a spouse."

"Indeed, you have." Her mother's voice softened. "However, you can be the best wife he could ever hope to have if you set your mind to it."

Lilith shuddered at another recollection of their wedding night. *Not with regard to the physical.* Only a few moments ago, he'd awakened a surly man. The growling voice, the fury in his eyes—all aimed at her. Would he end up like her father and take everything out on her when she failed to please him? The determination she'd had when she'd set out for his chambers had quickly faded. "I…I don't know if I have what it takes to…to become what he desires in every sense of the word."

"Desires?" Her mother's piercing gaze held hers for a long moment. And then her shoulders sagged. "Oh, Lilith. I understand far more than you might think."

She dropped her hands to her sides, and her tone lost its harshness. "I'm afraid much of what is working against you is my fault. I failed you as a mother in…" She lifted her chin. "In rather delicate matters. I fear in that regard, I cannot help you even now because I have never experienced the kind of love or tenderness that one reads about. That I want for you. I am terribly sorry."

She straightened her shoulders and lifted her chin. "However, Mum is waiting for you. She'll have the information you require."

Lilith's brows scrunched together. "Mum? Information?"

Her mother turned her back to Lilith but not before she caught the flush to her mother's cheeks. "Despite her challenging my sensibilities, Mum can be a very wise woman when she so chooses. There are certain things you should know in order to become a...a decent wife. Things I cannot possibly explain since I have no experience of my own by which to relate. But Mum...well, she's even spent the night with a sheik or two and still smiles when she recounts her stories. In vivid detail."

A bubble of laughter worked its way up Lilith's throat. "She's told you such things?"

Her mother nodded. "Things I wish I would've known long ago." She spun on her heel, displaying a kind of brilliance in her eyes Lilith had never seen. Then a vague, little smile brushed across her mother's mouth, and she glanced over Lilith's shoulder with a faraway look in her eye. "Please, go to her."

Lilith backed out of the room and leaned against the corridor wall, quelling the emotion the strange conversation with her mother had produced. Then she swept down the hall to Mum's chambers where, upon tapping on the door, she was bid to enter.

The sight of Mum's room knocked Lilith near senseless. But why should she be surprised after her tales of the Middle East? There wasn't so much as a scrap of wallpaper to be found. The walls, painted a bright, cobalt blue, held all manner of esoteric art—from smartly patterned carpets to hammered gold platters. She nearly stumbled over a full tiger skin, head and all. A strange animal with horns twisting in spirals was mounted over the fireplace. Had Mum taken the beast to ground on her own? She wouldn't be surprised if that were true, not where this woman was concerned. Turning in a slow circle, she took in the myriad of colorful silks in pinks, oranges, and purples draping what passed for a bed and tenting the ceiling.

"Eastleigh's awake, Mum. His headache is gone, and he seems to know me and his surroundings." She decided to leave out the part about his terrible disposition and ultimatum.

Mum grinned. "Good enough, gel. Just make sure to keep out of his way for the next few hours. Even if he calls for you, hide out somewhere. He wakes up after one of these bouts in a frightful mood that would make Attila the Hun cower, but he's over it soon enough. Care for a bit of the hookah?"

Lilith spied a tall emerald green bottle, its top encased in fine filigreed silver, standing next to Mum's silk-covered chaise. A hose snaked from the glass container filled with water and smoke, then draped over Mum's arm where she held the golden tip between her fingers. She puffed on it, a twinkle in her eye.

"What's a hookah?"

"'Tis the thing to do in Turkey."

At the realization her spine had grown rigid, Lilith forced her shoulders and chin to relax. She would conquer that ridiculous stance if it killed her. "Do women there engage in this act as well?"

Mum shrugged and sucked on the end of the hose while her scrutiny of Lilith never faltered. "I care not a whit what women in the desert do with their lives. What I do concern myself with is the contentment of the Malvern family. And at the moment, one in particular. Prince Augie cares a great deal for you, don't you know?"

A frisson of trepidation skittered through Lilith. "Nothing like jumping right into the subject, is there?"

"Why waste time when he's about ready to hunt you down and take you into a new and delightful world? As soon as he's up and around, he'll be coming after you. Best if you time it right and seek him out first. Surprise him and give him a night he'll never forget."

Lilith's cheeks flamed. She pressed her hands to her blistering face.

Mum laughed. "His headache is gone, so if I were you, I'd go to him in a couple of hours. Let him know you not only approve of him as a husband, but you intend on making him prick-proud at every turn."

Lilith gasped. It took another couple of deep breaths before she could manage to speak. "There are certain things that are...well, that were quite..."

A spark flashed in Mum's eyes. "Ah, I am not thick-headed, gel, merely forgetful now and then. It won't hurt the next time." Mum's voice gentled. "And if you relax and give in to what's buried inside you, there's going to be a good many years of getting to know my fine prince in ways you never dreamed of. Your mother told me you were once a beautiful, high-spirited child, until your father beat the joy out of you. Believe me, there's magic to be had when two people are willing. You'll find the joy you lost, dear, wait and see."

Heat burned Lilith's cheeks, yet she couldn't help a foolish grin. "You speak rather intimately of your own grandson, Mum."

"Bah, I'm speaking of a man. Doesn't matter whose blood runs in his veins. You'll need to work at purging yourself of a few rigid moral codes, the likes of which serve no purpose other than to drive a man to a mistress and his wife into utter despair. Doesn't it tell you how wrong things are if the only way I could shed such inequities was to traipse around in men's clothing in strange countries where women get their noses cut off just for looking at another man?"

"Is that why you traveled far and wide with Lady Stanhope?"

"Now that I can set you to rights, you'll have no need to run off to a foreign country to discover that what is considered a natural instinct in males lies in the marrow of the female as well. We aren't meant to suffer in the marital bed. And the notion that only women of low character enjoy the physical act is sheer poppycock."

Mum studied Lilith with a purpose that set her heart thumping in her chest. "You're not so much afraid of the pain, but of your own feelings, gel. You don't think 'tis right to enjoy the pleasures a man can bestow upon you."

At the memory of Eastleigh's hands all over her that day in the stable, Lilith's face heated once again. "I confess to having little knowledge of...of such intimacies." She swallowed hard to keep from stumbling over her words again. "And how do you know he cares about me if I do not know that myself?"

Mum's eyes twinkled. She sucked on the pipe and gave a little shrug. "Mayhap it's the way he can't take his eyes off you when you are oblivious of his attention. Or the way he says your name—different from how he says any others— kind of rolls around in his mouth, as if he's tasting you at the same time."

Mum's risqué words sent Lilith's heart racing. "I am desperate to change my ways, Mum. And I need to do so quickly. I do not want to lose him."

The old woman chuckled and patted the settee. "Come, gel. Sit beside me. I've much to tell you."

Chapter Fifteen

By the time Lilith slipped back into Eastleigh's chambers, darkness was nearly upon them. The chair still sat next to his bed at the same angle as when she'd nearly knocked it over in her haste to exit the room. Quietly making her way over to where he lay with his eyes closed, she sat and studied him.

Her mother was right—he was a good man, a decent man, and she would protect him now as he'd protected her when she'd had no memory. Good Lord, to think Mrs. Hazelthorpe might have unknowingly matched her up with someone like her own father who'd been all sonnets and roses in the beginning.

Once Mum had delved into the mysterious secrets of intimacy with a man, a whole new world had been unveiled for Lilith. This, too, gave a new edge to her that left her feeling even more empowered. How bizarre to have a feisty old lady be the one to enlighten her of what magic could transpire between a man and a woman. And in terms filled with so much spice they belonged in a bawdy house. Wrestling a grin down to a tiny smile at her considerations, she folded her hands in her lap.

Eastleigh opened his eyes, and with no change in demeanor, focused on her. "If you've come to say goodbye, don't bother." His words came flat and without emotion, but gone was that fiery anger.

Had he thought she'd been packing when all this time she'd been following Mum's direction to stay away for a while? "I know my hour was up some time ago, but I had things to sort out. Now I've returned," she said quietly but with decided conviction. "And here I shall remain."

She stood and lit the lamp next to his bed. Expressionless, his dull gaze roved from her head to her toes and back again. Mum's words echoed in her head. *He can't take his eyes off you.*

Returning to her seat, she sat tall with her hands folded in her lap. She looked him square in the eye. "I've had my things moved into the chamber connecting with yours. I'm not going anywhere, so if you don't want me here, you'll have to toss me off the balcony."

He studied her for a long moment, and then a familiar sparkle touched his eyes. "I'll do that very thing. Straight away."

She wanted to laugh. And cry. So this was the reckless tide of emotion Mum spoke of. It washed through Lilith and made her mindless—made her want to shout out how utterly mad he drove her.

His hand slid to the edge of the bed, palm up in offering. While there was no mistaking the desire in his eyes, his act of offering his hand seemed born of pure and simple affection. She leaned forward and placed her hand in his. He squeezed. Somewhere in the warmth of their connection, his pulse beat faintly against her skin. The subtle scent of chamomile soap drifted her way. She caught her bottom lip between her teeth.

And then, as though they'd been merely discussing the weather, he lifted the covers and peered under them. "I'd remove myself from this bed, madam," he said in a lazy drawl, "but I am utterly naked."

She nearly expired on the spot. *That was it? That was all it was going to take to settle things between them?* She breathed a sigh of relief and smiled. "Indeed."

The covers dropped. "Was this your doing, wife?"

She shook her head. "Entirely your brothers. The scamps. They said you all sleep that way and insisted you be comfortable."

A corner of his mouth curled. "Entirely their doing?"

He was teasing her. And oh, how she liked it. "You grumbled and moaned that your bedclothes were twisting about until you felt tied and bound, so they removed them. At least, that's what I'd been told to expect when I came to you."

Amusement flashed through his eyes—along with something else she couldn't quite fathom. "It was them who took care of me?"

"Except for Doctor Hemphill checking on your progress and Mum hanging over his shoulder. Your brothers insisted on seeing to you all the while, including bathing you. Since I was heavily dosed with laudanum by that bully of a doctor, I could barely make it out of my room but a few times." She decided not to mention Will and her theatrics.

He bent his other arm and, sliding it behind his head,

settled deeper into the pillows. "And did you sleep well at night?" His voice had grown husky, and the warmth of his hand intensified.

She stole a glance at the large bed with its high, carved mahogany headboard and the stack of pillows beside his that she hoped to occupy.

A light of awareness flashed through his eyes, and it was as though his heated musk enveloped her completely. "Do you wish to be my wife in every sense of the word, Lilith?"

His words no longer resonated from his throat, but from somewhere deep in his chest, a low rumble that caused her every nerve to quake.

Oh, Lord, she had a lot to make up for. She slipped her hand from his, rose, and made her way across the room. Her back to him, she ran her shaky fingertips along the carved mahogany fireplace and over the curve of the ormolu clock. She had so much to say. If only she could find the right words.

She lifted her chin. "I…I have been a fool, and I am sorry I treated you badly. That wasn't right of me."

"You weren't ready," he said quietly.

"On the contrary. Whenever you happened to touch me…the very nearness of you, it…it did things to me that I did not understand, especially after our first night together. My thinking was corrupted by a lifetime of ill treatment, so I tried to cast you off at every turn lest I encounter something I could not tolerate. You were so far out of my shallow depths; I was like a frightened fish out of water."

"You think differently now?" His voice, a bare rasp fell in the air around her.

Feeling his gaze piercing her back, she nodded. "I once thought tears and emotions utterly useless in seeing one through life. Strength and courage were all that mattered. And self-discipline without folly. I was also taught to make a decision and once done, never question it or change my mind. I had no idea how such narrow thinking could scar a relationship. The effect you had on me was at the very pinnacle of challenging these skewed principles."

"But now?"

Her heart jumped into her throat. Oh, this was more difficult than she had anticipated. "The rarity of two people being matched as equally as us through a matrimonial service…well, think of the odds."

"So you think we might be evenly yoked?"

Her breath quivered. If only she was certain how he was taking this…this confession of sorts. "I believe there is promise in us, sir. What a pity I don't even know what to call you now."

"Anything but Augie will do." Humor wove through his deep tones.

She swept a hand over her brow. "I've been such a prudish bore. But I…I do believe I am quite redeemable if given the chance. I…I ask you to help me learn to relax a bit…help me uncover whatever might be buried in me….help me find joy and freedom in living a less restrictive life. What I am trying to say is… Oh, I guess Mum said it right all along—I have been fraught in many areas, and I'd be a lot better off without a rod up my arse."

He chuckled—laughter filled with kindness.

She ran her hand over the mantel, her fingers ceasing to tremble at the sound. Despite her nervousness, her sense of self and the feeling of liberation were growing by leaps and bounds. "I know the two of us are rather stubborn people, which hadn't been revealed in our exchange of letters, but nonetheless, I do believe we have possibility."

In the long silence that followed, she kept her back to him. What was he thinking? What would he want of her?

"Then you require lessons, Lilith," he finally said. "And if you will turn around, we can begin with lesson number one."

She turned.

And gasped.

He stood beside the bed wearing nothing but a sultry smile. "Your first lesson, dear wife, is to know what your husband looks like naked when not in a supine position."

Her fingers splayed over her breast.

"Go ahead, have your fill," he urged. "Start at the top of my head and work your way down. And…" His pause seemed a purposeful beat meant to envelop her in a space filled by him alone. "Take all the time you need."

Focusing on his brown curls tumbling over his forehead, pleasure washed through her. She'd run her fingers through those thick locks. Indeed, his hair was as silken and lush as she'd imagined.

A smile tugged at her lips. And then his eyes caught her attention. It was all there in his hungry look—he wanted to devour her. Lusty chills danced over her flesh.

As she worked her way to his mouth, cohesive thought left her brain. His roguish half-grin sent a thrill swimming through her blood. He must have known the effect he had on her, for the tip of his tongue scraped the edge of his chipped tooth, and a sensuous curve played about the edge of his enticing mouth.

Some primordial part of her took over—suddenly she

wanted *her* tongue in that little space. Truth be told, she wanted her tongue all over him.

He drew in a visible breath that seemed to steal the air from her lungs. She relinquished all willpower to slowly study his glorious form inch by inch as he'd instructed. Instead, like a lost soul coming off a parched desert, she drank him in all at once—from his broad shoulders and beautiful, sculpted chest, to his narrow hips and long legs. And then there was that part of him she'd once thought might split her in two. It thickened as she stared.

His quiet laugh startled her, and her cheeks scalded. How long had she been staring at that one particular spot? If the very sight of him corrupted her body, mind, and soul, what would their coming together, flesh to flesh do to her? Gracious, she suddenly had to will herself to stand upright. Was every bone in her body dissolving? And this excitement that rolled through her belly—it felt akin to being afraid, only deliciously so.

"Time for lesson number two, Lilith."

As if he'd reached through the ethers, his presence surrounded her. She drew in a shaky breath. "And my next lesson?"

"Come, my dear," he said, low and husky. "Come over here and touch me."

Chapter Sixteen

Lilith stepped forward, her breath catching in her throat. She moved closer. Eastleigh's eyes laughed into hers, yet there was power in him—restrained, measured—feral. Closer still, and the heat and musk emanating from his naked body clung to her skin like a midnight fog. His lids lowered, veiling his thoughts.

He knows what he does to me. And he'll make full use of this knowledge.

Her focus shifted to the heady pull of his dizzying energy. Her heartbeat stuttered, then made a great leap, as if it might pierce the surface of her skin. Oh, she wanted to touch every inch of him. "Would you consider me terribly ill-mannered if I did not ask your permission, but instead charted my own territory?"

"Ah, an excellent student." His ragged exhalation fell against her mouth. "Do take your time, though."

She reached up and traced the rich outline of his parted

lips, then slipped a fingertip between them. He scraped his teeth over its pad, sending a thousand sparks shooting through her. "Oh!"

She ignored his suggestion to touch him slowly, just as she'd disobeyed when he'd said to take her merry time ogling. Instead, she set her hands to the solid density of his chest. At her touch, his muscles bunched. Scars marked his skin. She bit her bottom lip and ran a finger over each one. "From the war?"

He nodded.

Heart drumming, her hands coasted along the hard planes of his belly. A tactile intensity shot through her fingers—like unleashed lightning—twisting her stomach into knots. Sheer ecstasy. As she set her mouth to his flesh, her eyes drifted shut. His hot skin tasted clean, hinting of salt. She licked, and a small moan escaped him.

He settled a curled fist beneath her chin and nudged it upward. "Eyes open, darling. Closing them is part of the next lesson. Go on—keep touching me while you look your fill."

She turned her attention to the bed, and then back onto him. "I doubt I can stand upright much longer."

Amusement broke over his countenance. He shook his head. "The bed belongs in lesson number three—we're only on the second one."

"Well, then." She began a slow descent with her fingers, tracing the fine line of hair that swirled around his navel and trailed down to the part of him that had once frightened her but now entranced her. Blood quickening, the back of her hand brushed against his hard arousal.

He hissed, and for a moment, his eyes lost their focus. "Witch."

"You said I could chart my own territory," she murmured. "But in any case, you had better take hold of my hips because my knees are about to lose their bones."

A deep breath escaped him, and with one hand, he complied. With the other, he freed her pinned hair, shook it loose, and began working the buttons on the back of her gown.

Undiluted lust gripped her. She closed her fingers around his arousal, amazed that skin could remain so soft and supple, yet cloak such hardness. Her thumb traced the plump head and found a slick bead of liquid. Spreading it about the tip, she squeezed his shaft, and then slowly moved her hand up and down, the action sending a thrill running through her. A low sound left her lips, and she clutched the hard curve of his flexed buttock with her other hand, digging into his flesh.

"Sweet Christ!" His gaze followed the slow slide of her fingers, a fever shadowing his eyes.

Oh, she could be wicked after all! Throaty laughter escaped her lungs.

He pushed her dress off her shoulders and effortlessly worked the garment to the floor. Sweeping his arms around her, he pulled her to his naked body. His mouth settled soft and warm against her lips. And then his tongue slipped inside, and the kiss deepened, drawing her into a pleasure so intense she had to grab his shoulders for support.

How had he managed to dispense with the rest of her clothing? She did not know, but suddenly they were skin to skin. She ran her hands over his shoulders, along his back, raked her fingers through his hair. Had his hold on her been any less firm, she would have sunk to the floor.

He eased away and lifted his head, studying her for a long moment, his chest heaving. She could not read his expression. And then, without letting go, he leaned over and drew back the covers. Straightening, he lifted her in his arms. "We did things your way on our wedding night, and it wasn't so pleasant, was it?"

She shook her head.

He planted light kisses along her forehead, across her cheek, and along the curve of her neck. "Now we do things my way. Time for lesson number three."

His movements were smooth and graceful as he laid her gently on the bed and slid in alongside her. Cupping her bottom in his hands, he pulled her against him, the long length of his erection pressing into her belly.

She could no longer think at all, could only feel and react as though she had fallen into a dizzying trance. He ran the back of his hand, feather soft, across her cheek. "You'll share my bed all night long. But I suppose you already guessed as much."

His gaze skated up and down her body, and then he buried his face in the curve of her neck. "Dear God, but I want to possess you." His voice reverberated low and seductive across her skin. "Help me to be strong against this terrible urge to have all of you at once."

Dear angels in heaven! Blood thundered in her ears. "I cannot help you since I am nothing but greedy myself."

His tongue touched hers, warm and wet, and his hand moved to her breast. She shivered as his thumb and forefinger rolled the taut peak. But then he leaned down, took it in his mouth, and swirled his tongue around it with a groan. He used his teeth then, turning insignificant pain into unbearable pleasure. Her pounding heart sped up. She'd been raised on shame, and this had to be pure sin whipping through her, but oh, the gods were so very wrong—this was nothing short of glorious pleasure.

Aching with need, she cried out his name and clutched his shoulders. "Fill me up," she said breathlessly. "Oh, please, I need you."

His fingers gripped her bare hips, and he rolled her under him, his erection pulsing between them. That frantic need to have him inside her made her writhe with want, made her limbs spread wide to take him in.

"Sweet. So sweet, but oh, so wild," he whispered hoarsely as he planted kisses all over her skin. "I knew from the first there was great passion in you."

He worked his way down her body until his mouth touched the inside of her thigh. He trailed kisses along her calf to her foot. And then to the other, his lips scorching her skin, working upward until he found the apex of her thighs.

He set his tongue there.

The clamorous beat of her heart nearly drowned her own whimpers. She hadn't known…hadn't a clue such an act existed!

"I've wanted to explore you in every way." His tongue found her recesses. "For a very long time."

She could no longer feel the bed beneath them. She became his entirely—his world to map of his own accord.

Something far beyond her control suddenly took over. Her body stiffened. With a helpless cry, she set herself free from all restraint. Magic exploded within her, so powerful and astonishing it overtook her body until she quivered from head to toe. And then liquid pleasure rolled through her. She gasped his name.

He moved up against her and kissed the side of her throat. "I'm not finished."

Spreading her legs wider, he poised over her like a graceful cat. "I could lose my mind over you."

His low, rough voice skimming over her skin shot another hungry pang of lust through her. "Now. I need you now. Oh, please."

"As you wish." Reaching down with one hand, he fitted the tip of himself against her and slowly slid inside, withdrawing and easing in, little by little. And again. Her flesh closed about him, and at his groan, she clasped his hips and lifted her own to meet his. And drew him into her, stretching her, filling her.

Oh, God, this was her husband inside her—huge and hot.

"Lilith." A husky moan slipped past his lips as he stilled, hovering over her. "Are you all right?"

"How could I not be? You feel so good."

He looked down into her eyes and slowly withdrew, nearly out of her, and then back in. "Does that feel better?"

She could only moan in response.

"Wrap your legs around my back." He began a slow slide in and out, his weight resting on his arms, his head back, watching her. And then gradually, he moved faster, stroking her insides in a timeless rhythm. "You're so beautiful...so hot and slick...so..."

He grunted and penetrated deeper. Harder. "So everything."

She rocked her hips in rhythm with his and dug her fingers into his back. A pressure started deep in her inner core, but this time she knew what was coming and held nothing back. It intensified and then radiated outward, seizing her soul and leaving her helpless to do anything other than cry out his name.

His hands gripped her hips, and he set his face to the curve of her neck, nipping and sucking on her skin. With a deep groan, he buried himself to the hilt.

He stilled. A great shudder swept through him, and she felt him pulsate inside her.

Breath escaped him, and then his lips traced a line of kisses from along her cheek to her mouth. And then his kiss turned rough, filled with...with what? She couldn't name the emotion that radiated from him and into her. He drew back, enough to press his brow to hers.

Suddenly, he stilled.

A fragmented sound left his throat.

"My God, Lilith." With a low moan, he rolled off her and collapsed, his hands clenched to his head.

"What is it?"

"The megrim. It's back. Hemphill. Get him."

Chapter Seventeen

Eastleigh opened his eyes to a darkened room, his back to the edge of the bed. He knew full-well someone sat in a chair behind him, watching over him.

As usual.

Disgust rolled through him, then mingled with his foul disposition—yet another awful, black mood he'd have to endure over the next several hours. Was it the megrim or the laudanum causing the problem?

"Call for Hemphill," he said, not bothering to find out who sat watch.

"I am here," Hemphill said. "I'm giving Lilith a break."

Eastleigh rolled onto his back and rubbed at his eyes. "Christ, I think my condition has worsened."

"What brings you to that conclusion?"

"Isn't it obvious? These episodes are becoming more frequent and more intense. I had an attack when Lilith ran off to her parents' home, another when she returned, and now this after…"

"After conjugal relations? Lilith told me."

Eastleigh shoved the pillows behind him and worked his way into a sitting position. "Now it seems I cannot even perform husbandly duties without having to spend days in bed as a result." He shot Hemphill a dour glare. "If this is what's going to happen every time I climb into bed with my wife, it's not worth the kind of pain and misery I'd have to endure."

Hemphill lifted his hands, palms up, as if in defeat. "I honestly don't know what to tell you. I've not run into this kind of problem before. However, both you and Lilith have been under a great deal of pressure with the way things have played out since the two of you were wed. Like it or not, she's still healing, as well. She's worried about you, by the way, and hasn't left your side but for a few moments at a time. She's taken her meals in here as well."

Eastleigh slowly bent his head back and forth, working out the kinks. "How long have I been out this time?"

Hemphill reached for his tea. "Four days."

"Bloody hell! Count the number of days I've been incapacitated of late, and this illness, from which there seems no end, is taking up half my life." He rubbed at the bristle on his jaw. "I cannot keep this up, Hemphill. The attacks are more frequent than when I returned from the war."

He gave a wave of his hand. "Open the damn curtains, will you? I cannot tell you how weary I am of the darkness."

Without a word, Hemphill complied.

Eastleigh squinted at the bright light spilling into the room. Blue skies. Had there been decent weather all these days and he'd slept through it?

"What the devil time is it?"

"Nearly noon." Hemphill returned to his chair and to his cup of tea. "I would advise you to refrain from marital relations until you can manage a couple of weeks without one of your episodes."

Eastleigh glanced at the other side of the bed, at an indentation in the pillow. He brought it to his face. Lilith's scent—that enticing, clean, spring-like essence. A fist gripped his heart. She had slept beside him, and he hadn't even been aware of her presence? What kind of life was he offering her if he was to be incapacitated for most of it? What kind of misery was he setting himself up for?

He cursed under his breath. "This is hardly fair to Lilith."

The door opened, and she walked in. "You're awake."

"I am." He dropped his gaze to the foot of the bed. God, what did she think of him making passionate love to her only to keel over and lie comatose for days?

She glanced back and forth between him and Hemphill. "Am I interrupting?"

Hemphill shot Eastleigh a speaking glance. "Your husband might need a few hours to collect himself, which always seems to be the case after one of these episodes."

Foul mood or not, Eastleigh knew what he had to do. "Would you excuse us, Hemphill? There's something I wish to discuss with Lilith."

The doctor frowned. "If you are entertaining the idea of discussing anything of a serious nature, I highly recommend you delay a few hours. Better yet, a day or two."

"Damn it, Hemphill. Leave us."

"As you wish." He picked up his teacup and saucer, and bidding Lilith good day, exited the room.

She frowned and moved toward the bed. "You worry me, Eastleigh. What's wrong?"

He couldn't bear to look at her with what he had to say. All he knew was that his condition had turned him into half a man, and he could no longer live this way. Nor could he tolerate many more episodes. He wanted back his predictable, slow-paced life. To hell with concerns about loneliness. "How long before you'll know if you are with child?"

She clasped her hands together as if struggling for composure. "As of yesterday, I can tell you with certainty that I am not."

"You recently asked for an annulment —"

Her eyes widened. "That was in the past. We've moved beyond that miserable subject."

He shook his head. God, was it beginning to ache again, or was he only feeling the pressure from what he had to say? "I've come to the conclusion that we are not so evenly yoked after all."

She plopped down in the chair, her face ashen. "I did not please you when we were intimate?"

Tossing cold water on him couldn't have stunned him more. She wanted to blame herself? The thought hadn't crossed his mind. "God, Lilith. You pleased me more than you can know. But as a result, I had to spend yet another four days in bed."

She stiffened in that way he now knew to be a form of self-preservation. Those lovely blue eyes of hers stared at him. Unwavering. Piercing his very soul.

"I've endured one episode after another since we wed, and they seem to be worsening instead of diminishing. I cannot bear suffering through this affliction much more. I need peace and quiet—a rather boring life, actually."

She dropped her gaze to her clasped hands. "If you're not blaming me directly, then you blame our untenable situation?"

The fist gripping his heart tightened. "More that I blame this despicable illness."

"But we've recently consummated the marriage. We cannot—"

"Oh, for God's sake, Lilith. We consummated it the day we married. What's the difference if we lie through our teeth about one time or two?"

"It's no longer a matter of the three of us knowing, Eastleigh. There must be others in the household who are aware I spent time in your bed."

"Tildy is the only other person who knows. Believe me, she values her station here far more than she would be willing to dispense with a bit of gossip."

Lilith unclasped her hands and took to picking imaginary lint off her lap in rapid little movements. "I am quite aware that you awaken in a foul mood after one of these episodes. Perhaps Hemphill is right. We should discuss this on the morrow."

He drew a long breath into his lungs, then heaved a sigh. "Tomorrow won't make a bit of difference. You cannot possibly know what it's like to have endured what has finally become the unendurable. Sometimes the pain is so bad I continually vomit until I feel as though my insides might spill right out of my mouth. And if you recall, I am not fully recovered. There are pieces of my memory still missing."

Closing his eyes, he paused for a long moment. "Something happened while I was at war, Lilith. Something so terrible that I can only catch glimpses of it during my darkest hours."

"I am willing to see you through those times," she said.

"It's not fair for you to have to suffer along with me."

"But I want to." Her voice had gone soft as a baby's breath. "I...I wouldn't want to miss out on any part of you. I want to share the good times as well as the bad. Isn't that what marriage is supposed to be about, seeing one another through thick and thin?"

He opened his eyes.

And wished he hadn't.

He was going to miss her. He was going to miss those soulful eyes the color of cornflowers, her silken skin, even her voice. And he was going to miss a lifetime of making love to a woman filled with more passion than a man could ever hope for. But that could well be part of the problem. He'd taken her to his bed and ended up worse off than before.

Had it been the unbridled passion that had triggered a relapse? Was he to forego living like a normal man? The idea of an annulment, then taking another wife because his station in life required an heir, revolted him. His brothers would have offspring that would continue the lineage. That would have to do.

"Don't make this harder, Lilith. I simply cannot go on this way."

"So much for love."

"What did you say?"

Her gaze connected to his. This time it was filled with a hard glint, but it was gone in a flash. "Nothing. Please, go on."

"There's a dower house on my parents' property an hour from here. You can move in there while I see to the annulment."

A small noise left her throat. "You wish to abandon me

to an outlier house on land I've never stepped foot on, and without my say-so?"

He shoved a handful of curls off his brow, his fingers feeling more like knives slicing through his skull. "It wouldn't work to have us wandering around in the same house."

"Yes, of course." Her lips formed a thin line. "Perfectly understandable." Her arms tightened about her waist. "However, I would be utterly miserable having to reside on your father's estate on a permanent basis. After all, you'll inherit one day."

She made a wide sweep with her hand. "And this is the home you built for yourself. Obviously, I don't know the whole of it, but you'll likely inherit other properties farther away that you wouldn't be interested in visiting. I would do well alone on one of them, tending to my gardens. I cannot possibly return to my father."

The confusion in her eyes nearly undid him.

"I don't know where I might ultimately go—"

"You may remain in the dower house for a month while you decide where you want to reside. If it is your wish, you can choose anywhere to live *other* than Malvern property. You can build a cottage by the sea, for all I care. I owe you that much for having put you through this debacle."

"I see." She studied him for a long moment, then folded her hands in her lap and raised her chin. Her face was devoid of expression, her actions graceful. She was masterful at hiding her emotions. She had to be strung tight as a violin string.

She stood. "Then I will be gone in the morning. Goodbye, Eastleigh."

Chapter Eighteen

Barely able to see through the aqueous haze blurring her vision, Lilith wiped at her tears and peered through the carriage window at the imposing limestone mansion. If this was the dower house, what in heaven's name did the main estate look like? Despite its traditional Palladian architecture, the three-story structure somehow managed to appear stark and unfriendly. And then it dawned on her—the building sat amidst several acres of nothing but plain grass spiked with a few unremarkable trees.

Nary a flower in sight.

She was to live in this isolated place for an entire month? A pox on Mother for remaining behind.

Behind the structure and extending to the right in a half-moon shape stood a foreboding woodland. One could get lost wandering around alone in there.

Alone.

Her heart did a strange flip. Her mood dropped another

notch. It hadn't taken her long sitting at Eastleigh's bedside, listening to his excuses, to know he was likely right—their relationship had been volatile. It lacked harmony, and they were not suited. He deserved someone who caused him fewer headaches—literally. Good that she'd ignored the terrible urge to refuse to leave.

Her stomach growled. Sick at heart, she'd not been able to manage a bite before leaving Easton Park. Even now, the idea of food repulsed her. She gathered Daisy onto her lap and hugged her. The trip was only an hour's drive, she'd been told, so it couldn't be more than half past ten, yet it seemed as though she'd been on the road for days.

The coachman guided the carriage through tall iron gates and headed down a straight driveway. Boxwood lined either side of the entrance, clipped low and precise—as if a gardener, lacking flowers to tend, had nothing better to do. Gravel crunched beneath the slow moving wheels, resonating loudly within the silent carriage. She doubted entering through prison gates would feel much different.

The place appeared vacant. Another glance toward the dense woods edging the lawns and she pulled her cape tight about her shoulders. The driver hadn't even let her off, and already loneliness twined through her insides like a poisonous vine.

A steady pressure exerted itself inside her head. She rubbed her temples. Lord, but exhaustion was about to do her in. This must have something to do with her low mood— along with her stay at Easton Park ending in a fireball of hell.

Eastleigh.

Had she done the right thing by quietly leaving without

any goodbyes? Her resolve wavered. Should she have defied his orders and paid him her farewells this morning? Tried one more time to get him to change his mind? That would have been a thick-headed and shallow thing to have done. Let him come to her if he changes his mind.

She should never have engaged Mrs. Hazelthorpe's matchmaking services. Someone as eligible as Eastleigh would easily have found the right person to wed in no time. She pressed the back of her head against the squabs, her chest so tight she had to force her breaths.

The carriage pulled into a small, circular drive in front of the house. The coachman jumped from his perch, opened the door, and offered his hand.

"Thank you," Lilith said, exiting the carriage. Daisy tumbled after her and began running in wide circles, sniffing about. Suddenly, the air seemed quite scarce. She fought for breath. "It doesn't appear as though anyone is here."

"A rider was sent ahead to give notice of your arrival, so someone's sure to be about, milady. I'll see to your trunks."

The front door opened, and a short, rather plump woman stepped forth. She smoothed a white apron against a black dress and touched the bun at the back of her neck as if to make certain she was presentable. "Welcome to Penrose Cottage, milady."

Cottage? That was a laugh.

"I'm Mrs. Ackerman. Beggin' your pardon, but I'm the only one could be spared today, seeing as how the entire family is in residence." Her cheeks flushed. "Except for Lord Eastleigh. And…and you, of course. You'll have a right proper staff on the morrow, Lady Eastleigh."

Lilith nearly groaned. Apparently, word traveled fast. So

she was to be called Lady Eastleigh even with an annulment forthcoming? Oh, dear. If Eastleigh were to perish, she'd become his widow—and remain Lady Eastleigh forevermore. A blot on a good man's name, she'd be. She drew her teeth over her bottom lip and pressed a hand against her stomach.

Mrs. Ackerman's brows knit together. "Are you all right, milady? You've grown quite pale." She motioned toward the interior of the house. "Please, come in."

Lilith moved to the entry and stepped inside. "I've had a rather tiring few days. Would you please show me to my chambers?"

"Of course, milady."

The hollow click of Lilith's heels on the stone floor reverberated straight through her. An urge to rush back to the carriage nearly overtook her. But where to go from here? Certainly not back to Father. Nor to Easton Park where she was no longer welcome. What in the world was to become of her?

Mrs. Ackerman and the coachman exchanged words Lilith couldn't give a fig about hearing. The coachman bid his good-byes and departed. At the sound of harnesses rattling and retreating hoof beats, panic bit at her frail composure.

"Would you care to have me show you around, milady? Lady Ardmore's mother was the last person in residence before she moved to Easton Park. Having lived in the foreign countries, she acquired rather unusual tastes."

"Actually, I've been confined to the carriage for over an hour, so a bit of morning air might be just the thing." Lilith was wound so tight, she doubted she could manage a tour. Not to mention that her heart had been shattered and trying to make small talk with a servant was beyond her.

"Seeing as how there ain't nuthin' but the drive and road

out front, I'll show you to the rear entrance, milady."

"Thank you." Good, a garden out back where she might sit awhile.

Mrs. Ackerman led Lilith from the vestibule and along what should have been a wide corridor with doors leading to rooms on either side. To Lilith's amazement, no doors were to be seen. Nor did anything passing for walls face the hallway. Instead, a series of widely spaced white pillars etched in gold lined each side of the passageway.

A faint smile touched Mrs. Ackerman's mouth. "Mum couldn't abide being shut up inside dreary rooms, so she had the doors removed along with as many walls facing the corridor as was possible."

The interior of the house with its open, airy and colorful rooms stood in stark contrast to the cold, limestone exterior. And the furnishings were completely unrelated to the oppressive, dark and heavy furniture Lilith had grown up with. So why was she suddenly near tears? It seemed as if the inside of the house begged to lift her spirits, while her heart refused the invitation.

She didn't belong here.

Then where do I belong, for pity's sake?

She tucked a loose tendril behind her ear, as if the gesture might soothe her. "Gracious, I may as well be in a foreign land, but I rather like it."

"And you have yet to see the upper floors."

"Please, I require a bit of fresh air."

"Of course, milady, beg pardon." Mrs. Ackerman swept a hand to the double doors at the end of the straight corridor — or whatever one might name this unusual space.

Lilith exited onto a covered terrace, and her heart sank.

Not a flower in sight. Only more lawn and the dense forest turning to haze in the distance. Clipped boxwood lined empty flower beds, looking as forlorn as she felt. "Oh, dear."

Mrs. Ackerman stepped forward. "Mum used to have a spectacular rose garden here, but she took her prized bushes with her to Easton Park. If you'd like something planted, I can have the gardener discuss it with Lady Willamette. She oversees anything to do with the outdoors."

God, no! Will was the last person she'd want to run into. "I'm quite fine with the way it is, thank you."

Again, her stomach growled. "Would you mind seeing to a cup of tea and perhaps some toast or a crumpet?"

"At once, milady." Mrs. Ackerman disappeared inside, leaving the double doors open.

Lilith seated herself in the single wrought iron chair beside a table made from the same cold metal. An ache settled around her heart. She was having feelings never before experienced, but she didn't know what they were or what to do with them. She let out a sigh, the only sound in the morning air.

Come the morrow, there'd be no Eastleigh to greet her with his lazy grin. No speaking to her in a voice that grew husky whenever he regarded her a bit too long. There'd be no forgetting his wonderful scent or the heat emanating from him when he had the audacity to stand a fraction too close. And then there had been their first *real* lovemaking, when a firestorm had roared through her.

Visions of his blood staining the floor tracked through her mind like a muddy beast, obliterating the good memories. Her hunger dissipated, replaced by a hollow ache.

Hoof beats shook the earth, and the sound drew nearer.

Oh, no! Those Malvern men. She sprang from her seat, but before she was able to disappear, the horses rounded the corner of the house.

"Lilith!"

Not Malvern men, but Malvern women—Iris, Rose, and Violet—all three mounted atop magnificent beasts, and all three dressed in men's riding gear.

Rose's horse danced in a circle around the other two. "I know what you are thinking, Lilith. We dress like this whenever we ride on our own property. Which is often."

"Will's the only one who takes dressing like a man to the extreme," Iris said.

"Oh." Lilith took a step back from Rose's horse that refused to stop prancing.

"You're to come with us," Violet said. "Mama doesn't want you alone your first night here."

Good Lord, not with Will and the brothers on hand! "Please thank Lady Ardmore for me, but I am utterly exhausted."

Rose shook her head, the chestnut braid hanging over her shoulder flipping about. "We dare not return without you."

"Please, you've your entire family in residence. I would only be in the way."

"Our brothers raided the kitchens and left for Easton Park. Will tagged along. You should hurry since we mustn't miss the noon meal."

Rose moved her horse closer and looked down at Lilith. "Come, ride with me."

Lilith took a couple quick steps back. "I…I don't ride."

Iris shot Violet a speaking glance. "Mum left a small

curricle in the stable," Violet said. "We'll hitch one of our horses to it."

With that, she eased her mount right through the open door of the house and proceeded along the corridor. "Ackerman!" she hollered. "Lady Eastleigh is to spend the night with us. Collect some of her things and come along if you don't wish to be here alone."

Mrs. Ackerman opened the front doors and stood aside. Violet walked her horse right out the front entrance.

Lilith pressed her hand to her breast. "I do not believe what I just saw."

Rose shrugged. "Learned it from our brothers, she did. Meet us out front."

. . .

Eastleigh finished tying his cravat, then dropped into a chair. Why bother taking himself downstairs? He could just as easily have a tray sent up. Not that he had any appetite to speak of.

He closed his eyes and pinched the bridge of his nose. He'd never relished the days following an episode, but today, he may as well be walking knee-deep in mud with no relief in sight. He'd come to expect the black moods that followed an episode, the sense of not being quite present until the laudanum wore completely off. At least the duration of his infirmary had decreased in direct proportion to how much he recovered his memory. Today, however, things were different. In addition to everything else he'd endured, he'd been struck with a doleful sense that his soul had been hollowed out, that he no longer possessed a life with any purpose.

Lilith.

Blast it all, he couldn't stop thinking of her. And there was the rub. The decision he'd made regarding his marriage, difficult as it had been, was the right one. The marriage would soon be over and done with. No sense looking back. No sense doubting his own judgment.

Slapping his hands against his thighs as if to confirm his thoughts, he pushed himself to a standing position and exited his chambers. Too late for breakfast, but Mum would likely be on the terrace having tea on what had turned into a sunny day. He could use the company after being cooped up in his chambers for what seemed an eternity.

As he descended the stairs, the quirky notes of a piano solo surrounded him. Will? What was she doing here? And attempting to play that same Chopin Mazurska again. When in bloody hell would she figure out she had neither the sensitivity nor the patience to master anything that man had produced?

He slipped past the open doors to the parlor and out back to the terrace overlooking the gardens without her catching sight of him.

"Eastleigh." Ridley sat at the table with Mum and Sebastien, his face bereft of expression.

His back to Eastleigh, Sebastien glanced over his shoulder. "Join us?"

What the devil? Mum sat facing him, her usually bright smile blatantly missing, the twinkle in her eyes gone. "Do sit with us, Augie. We've been waiting for my ward, but she is nowhere to be found."

Ridley frowned. "Mum."

She pursed her lips and shot a scowl right back at Ridley. "If Augie's going to play games, why shouldn't we?" She turned to Eastleigh. "Sit."

He complied, but not without lifting a brow. "What's got into you?"

"Lilith left us without so much as a farewell."

Eastleigh's jaw clamped shut so tight it hurt. He drew in a breath while he forced his mouth to relax. "She's gone to the dower house already, has she? I had hoped to explain the situation first."

"Indeed," Mum said. "Now tell us why you tossed your good wife out on her arse."

"Good God, Mum." Eastleigh looked to the terrace ceiling while he collected his thoughts. "You know nothing about what occurred. I—"

"Like hell, I don't," she said. "Tildy did the packing, and as soon as the carriage rolled out the drive, she ran straight to me. Told me everything she knew. Shame on you."

Her eyes narrowed, and her face took on a heated flush.

Lord, he'd never seen Mum like this. As far back as he could recall, she'd always championed him, always treated him with an even temper filled with a bit of mischief and joy. Whenever he'd blundered in his youth, she had been the one who'd shown him how to learn from his mistakes. Never had she shamed him.

Whatever rolled around in his chest and knocked against his heart was fast gaining strength. He glanced around the table at his somber-faced brothers. At Mum, whose skin had flushed even deeper.

Suddenly, his cravat felt too tight. He tugged at it. "All of you know what I've suffered these past few years. You know how the headaches sicken me for days. You're well aware that it takes a good week out of my life every time I'm struck down. I won't go into particulars, but in my condition, suffice it to say, I have come to realize that I made a terrible mistake in taking a wife. I am not meant to be a husband to anyone. Thus, I have taken steps to seek an annulment."

Ridley and Sebastien stared at him as if turned to stone. Mum took a swallow of tea and set the cup down with a hard *clink*. "Nonsense. You have heirs to produce. Straighten yourself out and go after your wife. You'll find none better."

The pain was starting at the back of his head again. He rubbed at it. "I don't think it is wise to continue this conversation. Already, I feel the beginnings of another megrim."

Mum glanced at the maid standing off to the side. "Fetch Hemphill. Eastleigh needs his powders."

She turned back to her three grandsons. "Do you know what I consider a gentleman to be?"

Sebastien snorted.

Mum shot him a scowl. "I happen to be speaking to the three of you now, so hush. You might learn a thing or two."

Judging by the severity of Mum's disposition, now seemed a prudent time to pay careful attention. Eastleigh leaned back in his chair and focused on her.

She took another sip of tea and held the cup in her hand. "To the devil with titles and how much land or coin a man might possess. The definition of a true gentleman is one who serves himself second. You, Augie, served yourself first by making a life-changing decision without bothering to find out whether or not you and Lilith could adjust to the problems within your relationship. How very unfair of you."

She looked from one grandson to another. "Remember

what I am about to say because I will only say it once—a man gives up his true feelings while he is in a mood. He can say things he doesn't mean. He can do things he will come to regret. The result is that he's played havoc with his and others' lives."

Eastleigh fought the urge to squirm in his seat. Ridley shifted about in his. Sebastien swigged his coffee and kept his gaze fixed on the inside of the cup.

Mum wasn't finished. "Do you think the easy relationship your mother and father share simply happened on its own? I learned a thing or two in my day, and I passed the knowledge on to her. I intended to do the same with each of your wives, but in Augie's case, he didn't' give me a chance."

She paused once again to look each one in the eye. "Your mother learned how to handle your father's moods when he himself hadn't a clue. Think about that."

The flush to her cheeks deepened.

Eastleigh frowned. "Mum, are you all right?"

"I've lost my good temper, that's how I am. I have one last thing to say, and then I will take my leave and set it to rights. Imagine if your father had never married. With or without a family, he'd still have his title, his lands, and his coin. But he'd be living in that big house by himself, where he'd likely still have landed face down in the library one day. Imagine what his life would be like now, all crippled up, lying in that bed all day long with only dispassionate servants to care for him."

A chill shot through Eastleigh at the thought. He stood. He'd be damned if he'd go through another episode. He was going after his powders. He glanced at Ridley. "I've had enough of this. Since you're second in line, you find the wife.

You produce the Malvern heirs. I'm done with it all."

Ridley stood so fast his chair toppled over with a crash. "You blasted fool!" he yelled. "Hemphill told me what happened. Why don't you try keeping your lascivious nature in check while you work on things gradually? Mum's right. This isn't all about you. There are two people in your marriage, in case you haven't noticed. You tossed a good woman to the wolves."

Eastleigh's fists clenched and unclenched. He took a step toward Ridley. "You had better watch your tongue, brother. You're not exactly an all-knowing saint when it comes to women."

Sebastien stood and, with a groan, loosened his cravat. "Don't tell me I have to step into this ridiculous fracas."

Hemphill came around the corner of the house. "Stop this at once. I could have heard you all the way to London, for God's sake."

Mum stood as well, her face an even deeper shade of red. "As if a brawl is going to settle things. I'm taking to my room." She made to walk away, but stumbled, her hand gripping her chest. Something garbled left her throat.

Ridley and Sebastien, closest to her, grabbed her before she fell.

"Mum!"

Eastleigh shot around the table and took part in helping her into a chair.

Hemphill took one look at her and at her face, that had gone from red to ashen, and ordered them to take her upstairs.

"I'll carry her," Eastleigh said.

Hemphill rushed inside, calling out for Tildy to get Eastleigh's powders.

Eastleigh rushed up the stairs with Ridley and Sebastien on his heels.

Inside Mum's room, Ridley yanked the covers back. Gently, Eastleigh laid Mum on the bed. She held out a hand to him.

His heart hammering in his chest, he took it and leaned over her. "What is it, Mum?"

"You had best send for the family," she muttered. "Bring Lilith back with them."

Ridley stepped forward. "I'll go, Eastleigh. You should remain here and take your powders. It wouldn't do for you to have an episode along the way."

"He's right," Hemphill said. "Tildy's bringing your medication."

Frustrated, Eastleigh looked from Mum, to his brothers, to Hemphill. A feeling as though he'd failed everyone swept over him. "I'm sorry. I don't know what I was thinking losing my temper."

"I lost mine first," Ridley said heading for the door. "The apology is mine. I'll be back soon."

"Stay with me, Augie." Mum muttered. "I need you."

He swallowed a catch in his throat. God, the world couldn't lose Mum now. He turned to Ridley. "Go. And bring Lilith back with you. For Mum's sake."

• • •

The sun was nearly overhead by the time Lilith arrived at Eastleigh's childhood home. Sharp sunlight glanced off windows of an estate so large its silhouette dissected the blue sky and swallowed the horizon. She wasn't shocked at the size, not after Penrose Cottage.

Once inside, she came face to face with Eastleigh's mother. She hadn't known what to expect, other than remembering Hemphill's comment about Lady Ardmore being the sensible parent. While Lilith suspected the woman might prove to be a beauty, what with the attractive children she'd produced, what Lilith hadn't expected was someone so uncommonly nice, given her rank. There was no mistaking the strength in the woman, though.

"Please, call me Millicent," she said and clapped her hands at her daughters. "Never mind changing your clothing. Your father is fast fading, so don't dally. And Rose, take her bag to Eastleigh's old room. She'll be staying there."

The girls scampered up the wide staircase, now chattering away in French.

Lilith gulped. Eastleigh's room? How much did Lady Ardmore know of her son's plans to seek an annulment? She had to know something of why Lilith was housed at Penrose. Well, she couldn't very well inquire. Not yet, at least.

"Please, call me Lilith."

"Good." She slipped her arm through Lilith's and swept her hand toward the staircase. "Shall we take ourselves to the table?"

"The dining room is upstairs?" Lilith couldn't help hazarding a glance down one of the widest and longest corridors she'd ever seen. Had Eastleigh or his brothers ridden horses through here? The Queen's brigade could do so with room to spare.

Millicent laughed softly. "Lord Ardmore is confined to his chambers, so we dine with him whenever he's up to it."

Lilith gathered her wits. "Yes, of course."

They climbed the stairs with Lilith taking in as much of her surroundings as possible while trying to mind her etiquette.

A great deal of noise arose from an open door at the end of the upper corridor. "You are hearing Lord Ardmore's daughters greeting him. One moment he was healthy and robust, and the next, he was found unconscious in the library. He's paralyzed on his left side and both legs, but his mind is still clever, and he still has a great sense of humor. By the way, we have not spoken to him of Eastleigh's recent accident. Why distress a frail man?"

They entered Ardmore's chambers. *Good heavens.* Lilith nearly stumbled over the threshold. Rose sat beside her father with a large open book resting upon her bent knees. Iris and Violet sprawled across the foot of the bed. Amidst the three, propped on several bed pillows and with bedding tucked to beneath his arms, sat their father, pale and drawn, but smiling.

Millicent crossed the room and took up her husband's good hand. She signaled for Lilith to come forward. "Dear, I'd like you to meet Eastleigh's wife, Lilith."

He studied her for a moment through wizened eyes. And then his head gave a small nod. "You'll do."

Lilith smiled. Even though his thin words barely reached her ears, the powerful force in his eyes reached across the room and struck her inner core. No sense letting on that she would soon be the former Lady Eastleigh. "I suppose I will, at that."

Millicent gave his hand a squeeze. "We're having creamed peas and roast goose, dear." She spoke as if cooked fowl and a simple vegetable were exceptional fare.

Soft laughter left his lips. "My favorite."

Violet laughed. "Everything's your favorite, Papa."

Lilith shot a quick glance around the room—at the cozy fire, the wine-colored velvet curtains, the massive, masculine furniture. And books scattered about as if half the library had been hauled in. At a nearby table set for five, candles flickered. She nearly wept at the warm and wonderful scene. To have so much as sat on a bed in her father's house would have meant a good strapping. One never sat on such a contraption. One slept in it—and only at night.

The girls scrambled off the bed and joined Lilith and their mother at the table. One of the servants filled a plate then made her way to Ardmore's bed and proceeded to feed him.

Amidst the noisy chatter and the girls' interplay with their father throughout the meal, Lady Ardmore turned to Lilith. "We do know how to properly behave when it's required of us, but we choose to celebrate every day he is with us in a manner he relishes. We try not to diminish the zestful life he lived just because he's taken ill."

Lilith knew nothing of a close family like this. What an empty shell of a life she'd lived. Each day the same. Every meal a dreary repeat of the day prior. And in a house so quiet, the clock in the parlor could be heard ticking throughout the gloomy place. Thinking back, she'd known something had been very wrong in the way they lived, but pretense while outside the home was as important as Bible verse to her father, so she had ceded to his control, as had her mother. No wonder Lilith had loved her garden. Gently coaxing anything to life that gave her even a modicum of joy had quenched her parched soul.

Heavy footsteps sounded along the corridor.

Lady Ardmore set her serviette beside her plate and stood. "Ridley? What causes you to return so soon?"

"It's Mum. She's taken ill."

"What kind of ill?"

"She was holding her chest and turning pale before Sebastien and I grabbed her," he said. "Hemphill's with her."

Millicent turned to her husband.

"Go," he said in his thin voice. "You'll never forgive yourself otherwise."

"Stay here with your Papa," their mother ordered the girls. "Lilith, we need to leave at once."

"But I've been banned—"

Ridley took her by the elbow. "She's asked for you."

"Has Eastleigh been made aware of her request?"

"He knows and approves."

Lilith and Millicent hurried down the corridor, side by side. "Was she conscious when you left her?"

"Yes. But she's pale as a maid's apron and her mouth was twisted up like she was in a good deal of pain."

Chapter Nineteen

Lilith and Ridley stepped into the entry at Easton Park behind Millicent, who hurried up the stairs. Will bore down on them like a fire-breathing dragon.

Lilith's spine went rigid.

Ridley placed a hand at the small of her back. "Remember the strong woman who wrote those letters to my brother."

"Thank you. I shall." She took in a breath and exhaled slowly. No longer would she allow fear to dominate her life. No longer would she be ground beneath another's heel.

Will came to a halt in front of Lilith, her eyes blazing. "My, you weren't gone long."

The woman didn't bother to hide her condescending manner. Perhaps she did so with purpose, hoping to intimidate Lilith. But something must have shown in her demeanor, because the flames banked in Will's eyes, and a kind of wary scrutiny filtered in. "You barely managed an entire day at Penrose."

"Actually, Lady Willamette, I never even accomplished that much. Your mother was most gracious and insisted I spend time with her. A pity you weren't there."

Will lifted a brow, but the small white blotches appearing on each cheek gave her away. "Really?"

Wasn't it peculiar how dispensing with the abject fear that had controlled her lifelong actions suddenly managed to smooth out her hard edges and offered her a new kind of strength?

"Indeed." Lilith mirrored Will and hiked a brow right back. "I was invited to spend the night." A delightful brazenness crept through Lilith.

Ridley dropped his hand from her back, retreated a step, and folded his arms over his chest.

"I was given Eastleigh's old quarters." She couldn't help her smile.

She paused a brief moment and watched as the spots on Will's cheeks blossomed. "I daresay, once I return to Penrose, I should like to take your mother up on her kind offer and spend the night with your family."

Will's eyes narrowed, but for the first time since meeting her, Lilith swore the woman was at a loss for words.

Lilith turned and headed for the stairs. "If you'll excuse me, I believe Mum asked for me." Halting halfway up, she regarded Will. "But if it's not entirely too late, and I can see to taking a break, perhaps we might meet up for a bit in the garden for tea and a chat?"

She climbed the remaining steps only to find Thomas and Sebastian standing at the top.

"Brilliant," Thomas muttered.

"Brava," Sebastian whispered and, shoving a tumble of

curls off his brow, took up her hand. "She's been years late in getting a set-down from someone other than us."

"Oh. Well, that wasn't my objective. I merely intended to set my own boundaries with her. She can be a terrible bully. Why aren't you with Mum?"

"We're taking shifts." Sebastian lifted Lilith's hand to his lips. "She's asked for you."

"I know." She withdrew her hand. Now, if that had been Eastleigh's mouth pressed just so…

At the thought of Eastleigh, Lilith's heart jumped. She looked over their shoulders and to the entry of Mum's chamber. Surely he was at his grandmother's bedside. Oh, dear. "I wish to see Mum. Would you take me to her?"

"I'll escort her."

Both men stepped aside for Ridley, who took her arm.

"Lady Eastleigh," Sebastian said.

She halted, the name still at odds with her heart. "Yes?"

For once, he appeared quite serious. "I'm glad you returned. I do hope it's to be something permanent."

"I, as well," Thomas said. For a brief moment, he held her gaze with a unique force of his own. And then he made his way down the stairs.

Don't let there be tears. Not now.

"Despite his somewhat hedonistic past, he's rather tame now," Sebastian said. "Eastleigh, I mean. I do hope for the best."

He had a wild streak? "I've not had a glimpse of that side of him."

"Have you not?" Sebastian trotted down the stairs. "Then don't let on that I tipped you off. I shan't need another fist to my gut."

"He wouldn't."

Sebastian looked up at her. "It's been a few years, but I wouldn't place a wager."

She peered over the balcony rail in time to see Thomas disappear. Where Will had gone off to, Lilith didn't know. Fortifying herself with a deep breath, she took Ridley's arm and stepped inside Mum's chamber.

Eastleigh stood with an elbow leaning on the fireplace mantel, his thumb caressing that chipped tooth of his.

Their gazes locked.

The beat of her heart quickened.

His hand dropped from his mouth.

There it was again, that powerful force that passed between them like a shimmer of heat lightning. What was it that made her want to rush to him despite his dismissal of her? Truth be told, the connection now frightened her because there would be nothing to come of it.

She forced herself to look away, to where Mum lay. "Oh, dear." *How frail she looks. Please don't die.*

"Mum." Lilith crossed the room to the bed and leaned her hip on the mattress opposite the side where Lady Ardmore sat in a chair. Lilith took Mum's hand. "You're going to be fine. Just fine."

When Mum failed to respond, Lilith didn't know why, but she added, "Eastleigh's headache is gone, Mum. And... and, I think he's going to enjoy good health from here on out."

Mum's eyelids fluttered. She squeezed Lilith's hand, and the grimace on her lips shifted.

"Oh, Mum. I was to go with you to see your other grandson today. I'm so sorry the way things turned out." Again, Eastleigh's grandmother squeezed Lilith's hand, but this time her lips moved as if trying to say something. "What is it, Mum?"

Eastleigh moved to beside his mother, pulled up a chair, and took Mum's hand, his face a tight mask.

She squeezed Eastleigh's hand this time—Lilith could see the bony fingers moving on his. Oh, the tears were ready to fall, but not now. Mum needed hope and encouragement, not her blasted wailing. Unable to help herself, she slid her gaze to Eastleigh.

Slowly, he turned his head her way. Immobilized, she stared into those fathomless brown eyes as if he'd cast a spell. The fine hairs on the back of her neck tingled. Her throat tightened, trapping the air in her lungs.

Time stood still as he stared back, saying nothing.

The door swung open and Hemphill entered the room, fracturing the hypnotic moment. Tildy and Sally were right behind him. Tildy carried a tray holding a glass filled with a grayish liquid.

"I'll be lifting your head for you to drink a potion, Mum," the doctor said. "It's willow bark mixed with a tincture of foxglove to steady your heart, so it's important you cooperate."

Lilith let go of Mum's hand and, rising from the bed, stepped away, leaving Eastleigh and Hemphill to tend to her. Tildy and Sally stood at the doctor's ready while Lady Ardmore sat quietly in her chair. Ridley leaned against a wall, his arms folded across his chest, watching everyone.

Lilith glanced around the room and was struck numb. In one way or another, these people were family, every one of them. Tildy had been with the Malverns since Eastleigh was a child. Even Sally, with her face as red as a beet and swiping at tears running down her cheeks, was family. She'd been born on the earl's premises and followed her parents here after Eastleigh built his home. Her mother was Cook, and her father was John Coachman. They were servants, yes, but they were still a part of the closely-knit unit that made up Eastleigh's life. From the moment Lilith had stepped into this house, with no memory to serve her, she had sensed there was a vast difference in how these people lived than from whence she came. She didn't belong here.

Her mother slipped silently into the room and came to stand beside her. That's when it dawned on Lilith—she grew up in a cold home where wife, child, and servants were treated no better than the cows that were milked or the hens that laid. Everyone and everything performed a duty, silently. Her father, head of the family, was so very different from the head of this family—her husband.

Some kind of alteration had taken place in her mother since arriving. Would remaining here have transformed her, just as Lilith herself had been changed?

Doctor Hemphill stepped away from the bed. "She'll rest now, but she shouldn't be left alone, so we'll need to take shifts."

"I'll take the first," Eastleigh said.

The doctor raised a brow. "Are you up to it?"

"I'm fine." He sent a speaking glance Lilith's way. "In fact, I'm very fine."

"I'll sit with you," the doctor said. "Would someone bring me a cup of tea? Earl Grey, if you please. Anyone else?"

When everyone agreed, Sally and Tildy headed for the door.

As the doctor sat, he glanced at Eastleigh. "I'll take my same chamber as usual. Wouldn't do for me to leave."

He hadn't requested a room. In no uncertain terms, he'd stated which one was his. Even the good doctor was considered family. Every cell in Lilith's body shouted to her that she was no longer a part of the Malvern clan. But someone was missing, someone who had been absent from both Mum's and Eastleigh's life long enough.

What if Mum weren't to make it through the night?

At that moment, Lilith knew exactly what she had to do before she returned to Penrose. "I'll take a shift, but I am desperate for a bit of fresh air."

Eastleigh glanced out the window and frowned. "Don't wander. The weather is turning, and with the wind coming from the north, it could blow in a storm and send the rivers overflowing their banks before you'll know what's happening."

Lilith nodded. "I'll take care." She turned on her heel and upon exiting Mum's chamber, ran into Tildy, nearly upending the tea tray she carried.

The maid visibly paled. "Milady, I heard what you said to Mum about her other grandson. If ye've a mind to seek out Sir Crocodile—"

"Cease your chattering, Tildy." Lilith shot the maid a stern look meant to scare her into silence. "You will say nothing as to where I have gone off to. Do you understand?"

• • •

The moment Lilith entered Mum's room, a knot of confusion inside Eastleigh unraveled. He hadn't even been aware he carried such feelings. At the sight of her, he'd had to lock his knees to continue standing. Had to lean on the mantel to hold himself up. Had to use every ounce of discipline he possessed to keep from rushing to her when her focus needed to be on Mum. He was through being selfish and thinking only of his needs.

God, he'd missed Lilith.

He'd made a terrible mistake sending her off the way he had. Mum was right—no one should make any kind of decision when not in the right frame of mind, especially one as critical as a marriage. Heaven help him, he was like two different people when those episodes hit—a decent man and a fool. He'd allowed the fool in him to make a terrible choice, and then that fool depended on the integrity of the decent man to stick to his principles, to not look back, to abide the fool's dictates.

She'd sat across from him, holding Mum's hand, and when those startling blue eyes of hers locked with his, that hollowness, that sense of having no purpose in life, evaporated. It had been all he could do to remain focused on Mum and not ask Lilith to take him back right then and there. He'd ask her when she returned from her walk. He'd make things up to her. He would.

A pulsing urgency pounded through his veins. He wanted Lilith by his side. He wanted children with her. He wanted the kind of life he knew they both had in them. He'd give her time to adjust to him, to his life here at Easton Park. Whatever was required of him, he'd see to it that she would be the recipient of a more generous spirit on his part. He'd show her he was a man who could be trusted and respected. He'd do whatever it took to make sure they ended up a balanced couple so if his condition never improved, they could still live a decent and contented life together.

He leaned over and brushed his thumb across the top of

his grandmother's hand. "Mum, can you hear me?"

She gave a slight nod.

"Good, because I have something to say."

She squeezed his hand.

"I've come to the conclusion that men are years behind women in comprehending the nature of love. But for the first time in my life, I'm beginning to understand. I know I'm the one who sent Lilith away, but do you think she'll forgive me and take me back?"

A small smile tipped the corners of Mum's mouth.

"You like that taking me back part, don't you?"

She gave another squeeze to his hand.

"Then I need you to get better, Mum, because I have a special favor to ask of you."

Chapter Twenty

A fat raindrop splattered on Lilith's nose. Another on her cheek. Then more. She picked up her pace. How could she have forgotten an umbrella? Oh well, it probably would've ended up inside out, what with her on the dash and the blustery winds offering little in the way of good favor.

A streak of lightning zigzagged through the sky and hit a tree with a *craaack* that spewed sparks. Fierce thunder shook the ground. Lilith jumped and squealed. The scent of acrid smoke filled her nostrils. She took off running in earnest, the effort leaving her lungs ragged. And then the sky opened up in a torrent. Wind and rain pummeled her.

She ran for an eternity, but she was nearly there—at least she hoped she remembered the way. She just had to catch that jog in the stone wall. The storm worsened and the rain blew in sheets until she could barely see her hand in front of her. A sudden, sharp stitch ran through her right side. Oh, dear. She shoved a fist into it and kept running.

There—the stable!

Rounding the corner, she leaned against the closed doors and heaved in breaths, rubbing at the pain in her side. The place looked deserted. Where the devil was Rob?

Squinting through the rain, she spied a wide footpath. That had to lead to the house...to *his* home. Fog rolling in obscured the walkway. Barely able to see in front of her toes, she trudged up an incline, through a wooded copse, and across an expanse of lawn until she nearly tripped on the three steps leading to a terrace. A large stone house loomed before her, austere-looking in the downpour and mist. This couldn't be the front of the house, not at all.

She stepped onto the terrace and knocked on a nondescript door. Nothing. Finding it unlocked, she eased it open, her breath coming in great gulps, the pain in her side easing. A black Mackintosh, still dripping, hung on a hook while tall boots caked with mud stood beside it.

"Sir Robert," she called, startled by the weak volume to her voice. She paid no heed to what her soaked clothing might be doing to the stone floor.

She moved down the corridor. Opening another door, she found herself in what looked to be a central hall. A wide staircase led upward to another level. "Sir Robert Garreck, please come."

She bent over in an attempt to draw more air into her heaving lungs. Didn't he retain any servants? "Would someone please answer me?"

Double doors to the left of the stairs stood open. She hurried inside only to stumble to a halt at the unexpected opulence. She ventured further inside, step by step, feeling more the intruder than a messenger.

It took only seconds to see that Rob was not there, but she couldn't help the pull the room had on her. Like Easton Park, his home held the distinct mark of an artist with a flair for mixing unusual pieces that fit together rather splendidly. He must have traveled a great deal, what with the array of exotic wall hangings and furnishings.

She moved to the stone fireplace and ran her trembling fingers over a tall, three-tiered iron candelabrum he'd likely forged, its branches filled with spent candle wax. Next to it stood an easel holding an unfinished portrait of a hauntingly beautiful, dark-haired woman. Only half of her face had been completed while the other half remained a sketch. Impassioned eyes seeming to peer into the artist's soul looked to be filled with…with what? Desire? Or was that allurement? Rob had painted a subtle haze over the entire image, lending the woman an even greater sense of mystery. Was she real or only imagined?

Directly opposite the painting sat a large leather chair, its well-worn and sagging seat having received more than its fair share of use. An empty wine bottle and glass stood haphazardly on a table next to the chair.

A chill ran down Lilith's spine. She made a hasty exit, feeling as though she'd invaded exceedingly private territory.

"Rob?"

Oh, where the devil was he? She eyed the stairs with its plush, blue and gold runner. Dismissing the notion of climbing them, she called out again. "Sir Robert!"

But then she noticed the wet spots on the floor leading to the steps and the damp spots deepening the color of the carpet all the way to the upper landing. Oh, lovely—he'd likely gone to his chambers to change into something dry and couldn't hear her. Well, this was no proper social call—Mum was in a grave state. Grabbing hold of the elaborately carved banister, she climbed the stairs, her already strained lungs heaving again. "Sir Robert!"

Silence.

"Sir Crocodile, you blasted, ornery…where are you?" What if he wasn't here? No, he had to be. The Mackintosh was wet. If it was his.

The boots next to it were his, though—she recognized them from before. Reaching the top of the stairs, she glanced each way, and spying the only set of double doors, she rushed down the carpeted hallway and pounded with her fists.

"Sir Robert?"

Anger-filled alarm shot through her at the silence. She wanted to cry, to scream. What if Mum had worsened during all this wasted time? A fierce strength of will welled up in her and she gave the latch a swift turn. The door flew open and she nearly tumbled in. Her heart pounded at the sense she'd really crossed into forbidden territory this time.

The scene before her resembled a knight's lair of old. A fur throw lay across the foot of a wide accoutrement bed swathed in blue velvet trimmed in gold. Turkish carpets overlaid one another at various angles, blanketing the dark, wood-planked floor. Two large, tufted leather chairs flanked a roaring fire. A haphazard stack of books on a commode next to one chair looked as though they might topple at any moment.

"Sir Robert!"

He came from behind, turning her and sliding his arms around her so fast she didn't have time to react. Too stunned to utter a sound, she stared up at him, into dark, piercing eyes flashing danger.

"Welcome." He cupped the back of her head, and with his other, drew her tight to his length.

Before she could react, his mouth came down on hers. *Oh, God!* She struggled, trying to push him away. He was as strong as her husband, and her effort was as futile as trying to push a stubborn mule aside.

She bit down.

"Damn!" He let her go and backed up, swiping his hand across his mouth. "If you aren't here for sport, then what the hell are you doing in my bedchamber besides looking like a drowned rat?"

"How dare you! I am your cousin's wife, you licentious beast."

His jaw dropped. "Married? To Augie?"

Eyeing the door, she slipped past him and scampered down the hall. She glanced over her shoulder as she ran. "I came because of Mum. She's taken a bad turn, and everyone is being called to Easton Park. She'd want you there."

He could have stopped her, could have caught her in a flash, but he stood with his bare feet planted wide and his arms folded over his broad chest, the far-reaching length of his gaze penetrating her.

Practically tumbling down the stairs, she was out the front door and into the storm again. *Heaven help me.*

Knowing only one way back, she darted to the side of the house, found the path leading through the copse to the stables, and took off on the run. Oh, her lungs stung like the dickens, and her pounding heart was near to exiting her chest. What had she been thinking? No, she mustn't berate herself for going after him—she'd done this for Mum's sake.

Rounding the side of the stable, she gasped at the rise of water. What had been a fast-flowing stream when she'd arrived was now a raging river. Skirting the edge of the roaring, muddy water, she kept moving, the stitch in her side back again and nearly doubling her over.

Had someone called out her name? If so, it could only have come from *him*. Far be it for her to wait around to find out if Sir Crocodile gave a damn about his grandmother or not. Apt name, that.

She didn't have any idea how long she'd been running, but she could no longer feel her legs, and the sky had grown so dark she could barely see at all. A leafy branch, flung by the howling wind, slapped her in the face with a powerful, wet sting. Odd, was that thunder shaking the ground when she hadn't seen lightning? A bolt lit the sky and she saw the source of the quaking—the huge oak that had been struck by lightning when she first passed this way was falling over, its giant roots tearing loose from the ground with a mighty wrenching.

Too late. She couldn't get out of the away. The tree crashed to the ground in front of her, the leafy branches knocking her sideways.

Into the raging river.

Under she went, a sharp pain piercing her leg. Buried beneath twisted branches and a thick blanket of leaves, she tried forcing the weight from atop her, but nothing budged. Her lungs strained for air. She couldn't see, couldn't feel, and worst of all, she couldn't move her leg.

Dear God, she was pinned.

And about to drown!

A hand came under her, forcing her upper body to the

surface. She gasped for air.

"I've got you!"

It was Garreck. She didn't care who it was, she needed saving. Her head was finally above water—but barely. "I...I can't move my leg," she cried.

"Not at all?" His deep voice resonated in her ear.

"No." Between the rush of cold water and the panic gripping her, she gulped for more air. "Oh, Lord in heaven, get me out of here."

"Can you reach the branch to your right and hold your head up long enough for me to dive under and set you free?"

"I...I think so." She stretched her arm out and managed to grab hold of the smallest of the branches. "Oh, do hurry. I...I think the water's rising."

Taking a huge gulp of air, Garreck disappeared beneath the surface. Lilith felt a tugging on her leg. No pain, but every tug threatened to drag her under. She grappled for his shoulder and yanked on his shirt to get his attention.

He came to the surface sputtering. "Your left leg," he gasped, spraying water from his mouth. "A broken branch speared through your upper thigh. I can't seem to set it free."

A rush of water washed over her and her head dipped beneath the surface. Garreck pushed her upward. She coughed and spit, struggling to keep her chin and nose out of the water. "Oh, God, Rob, save me!"

• • •

Eastleigh eyed the mantel clock over Mum's fireplace and glanced around the room. What had happened to Lilith? It had been far too long since she'd left for a bit of fresh air.

She couldn't possibly be out in this horrid weather.

"Where's Lady Eastleigh?"

Tildy ducked her head and sidled out the door.

Foreboding crawled along Eastleigh's neck and snaked along his arms. He rose from Mum's bedside and lit out after the maid, anger quickening his stride. Stepping into the corridor, he caught sight of her scampering down the stairs. "Tildy!"

His booted heels pounded the carpet in loud thuds. "God damn it, when I call you, don't run from me!"

The maid stopped mid-stairs, her knuckles white against the banister, her shoulders scrunched to her ears.

A sickening ball formed in his stomach. "You had better turn around and start talking."

Tildy faced him, her chin quivering. "Lady Eastleigh went to fetch Sir Crocodile. For Mum, sir."

Had he heard right? "In this storm?"

"Weather hadn't turned until after she left, sir." Tildy's shaky fingers smoothed her apron in fitful strokes. "And when my lady told Mum what she intended to do fer her, Mum's lips moved into a yes that even I could make out clear as day."

The maid's hands dropped her apron and wrung together. "Lady Eastleigh ought to have been back by now, sir. Especially if'n yer cousin took his horse. Seein' as how she's not got back, I was settin' out after her."

"Good Christ!" Eastleigh raced down the stairs, calling to a footman. "See to it my horse is saddled at once." He glanced up at Hemphill, who stood at the balcony rail. "I'm going after Lilith. If anything happens to her, that son of a bitch…"

Hemphill raised his hand in a gesture that stopped Eastleigh mid-sentence and responded in a low, calm voice. "It looks to be only a mild attack for Mum. I'll stay with her while you fetch your wife."

His eyes narrowed, grew hard, and penetrated Eastleigh like light through water. "It wouldn't do to run about blaming anyone for anything. Especially since that missing piece of your past has yet to catch up with you."

Chapter Twenty-one

Despite soggy ground that threatened to bury hooves and break a leg, Eastleigh's gelding steadfastly obeyed every command and raced onward. Occasional bursts of thunder rolled through the distant sky, signaling the storm was at last finding another place to play havoc.

"Bloody hell," Eastleigh muttered at the sight of the rampant river spilling over its banks and forming a shallow lake in front of him. The trunk and heavy limbs of a downed oak blocked the flow.

He squinted.

A head bobbed in the river amongst broken branches thick with sodden leaves.

"Lilith?"

She cried out and waved with one hand. And then she grasped the branches again, her face pale.

"Hold on, I'm coming!" He scrambled off his horse and rushed into the icy river.

Coherent thought left him. Reacting on instinct, he grabbed at branches hand-over-fist trying to reach her. The rushing current slammed his ribs against the wild tangle of debris. He grunted and clutched a leaf-sodden limb. The tree snagged his clothing, yanked him around as if it were alive and intent on dragging him under.

A wave of murky water washed over Lilith's face. She came up sputtering and coughing. "Hurry! I...I can't hold on much longer."

He reached her, and she let go, clawing at him. He started for shore, but she yelped and her body held fast. "My leg, it's caught and..."

"Hold onto something while I set you free." He grabbed her under the shoulders, lifting her head above water, nausea twisting his gut.

A man's head popped out of the river, spewing water and gasping for air.

"Rob?" Eastleigh jerked in surprise. "What the hell are you doing here?"

"Attempting to save your wife, Augie. Got a knife?"

They stared at each other for a beat of silence before Rob scrubbed a hand over his face and shoved his hair from his eyes. "A branch speared her left leg clear through."

"Oh, bloody hell!" Eastleigh shoved a hand inside his boot and extracted a long blade. Hooking his foot into the crotch of an underwater limb, he prepared to dive.

"Hand it over, Augie."

Rob's utter calmness turned the world around Eastleigh into a bizarre backdrop that slowed and sped up all at once.

"Since she's my wife, I'll see to it." He slid an arm under Lilith—only to meet Rob's fingers holding onto her.

A brutal pain lanced through Eastleigh's head.

The image of a battlefield flashed through his mind. A dreadful vision of his sword penetrating flesh—Rob's flesh.

And then everything came back to him in a sickening rush—of Rob inside a tent, a dark stain growing on the right side of his otherwise immaculate red uniform jacket, his eyes wide in disbelief.

"Christ, Rob. I tried to kill you!"

A stretch of seconds ticked off as they stared at one another. And then Rob stretched out his hand. "I know right where to go, and since there's no time to waste, hand me the goddamn knife."

Lilith sputtered.

Eastleigh lifted her head a little higher. "I've got you."

"Hold onto her while I dive under and try to saw off the branch." Rob's eyes flashed dark with conviction. "It's a tangled mess down there. I got caught in it once, and nearly drowned. If I don't come up in a reasonable amount of time, and I haven't managed to cut her loose, you're going to have to yank her leg from where it's caught, or she'll not make it out of here."

More ugly images flashed through Eastleigh's brain, colliding one after another like a trail of dominoes. Months upon months of a bloody war where the two had fought side by side. They'd been family, watching each other's backs, and all the while, Rob had been a turncoat. A bloody spy for the Russians.

An agonized cry tore from Lilith's lips. "Let me go and save yourselves. Please, oh, please. If either of you—"

Another wave washed over her face. She coughed and spat. Eastleigh and Rob's hands clashed again as they propped up her head.

Raw emotion painted a grim face on Rob. "Think about it. She's your wife, and she needs you. Do you think I could bloody well live with myself if we did things the other way?"

A new realization gripped Eastleigh. In Rob's own way, he was saying good bye—just in case. Dear God, could things get any worse?

Rob held out his hand. "You know I'm right."

Eastleigh closed his eyes for a brief moment. It didn't matter that Rob had betrayed his country. The war was over. He shouldn't die. Not here. Not now.

"Damn it, Augie, give me the blasted knife! The water's still rising, and if the tree shifts, we're all doomed."

"Do something!" Lilith choked on another rush of water. "Don't let us all drown!"

God Almighty. Eastleigh handed over the knife. "You better damn well get the job done and get your sorry arse back to the surface. How do you think I could live with myself if you don't?"

A look passed between them.

"If anyone can accomplish this, Rob, it's you."

With a small nod, Rob curled his fingers around the hilt. "Like I said, if I can't cut her loose, you're going to have to tear her leg off the branch."

Which was the last thing Eastleigh wanted to do. No telling what kind of damage that might cause. Lilith could be left a cripple. Or bleed to death. "Damn it, man!"

Rob let go of Lilith, but his eyes held steady on Eastleigh. "For what it's worth, I was never a bloody turncoat."

Before Eastleigh could question what Rob meant, his cousin gulped a deep breath and disappeared beneath the choppy surface.

Time slowed.

Lilith's body bobbed as Rob worked at setting her free, and Eastleigh fought to hold her steady. Her ears were under water, and he doubted she could hear him, but he spoke to her anyway, trying to soothe her, and in talking, attempted to alleviate his own dread, as well.

Seconds ticked by. He couldn't lose her. He couldn't because…damn it, he loved her. *And Rob…Jesus God, don't let him get tangled down there and drown.*

Bits and strips of white fabric floated to the surface and caught amidst the debris, fluttering like so many tails on kites. Petticoats?

Lilith's body gave and she became buoyant. "My leg's free!"

She sputtered and clutched at him while she peered into the choppy water. "Where's Rob? Why isn't he coming up?"

Heaven help him, he didn't know. He grasped Lilith under her arms and headed toward the riverbank. "I've got to get you to shore, and then I'll go after him."

"Ouch!" she cried. "There's still the stick in my leg, and it's catching on things. Oh, help, it hurts. Pull it out."

"Can't. The branch acts like a plug and keeps you from bleeding out." He pushed away from the debris with his boot and pulled her through the water until he found solid footing. "Stop struggling, and let me do the work."

He tried to lift her with a hand under her knees, but he snagged the protruding piece of branch.

She screamed.

He turned her sideways and, holding her under her arms, lifted her to shore, where he carried her beyond the rushing water and laid her on her side.

Emotion he didn't have time to ponder sank into him like the talons of a great hawk. "Rob hasn't surfaced. I've got to go back for him. You're at least an inch deep in water here, so prop your head on your arm."

She waved her free hand at him. "Hurry!"

He glanced at the ugly piece of branch protruding from her thigh, laid bare by her torn dress and petticoats. With a sickening lurch to his stomach, he turned and ran back to the river.

He spied Rob clinging with one hand to the tree on the opposite side of where he'd dived under. Anyone with half a brain could see he was sapped of strength and losing his grip on the slippery tree.

Eastleigh splashed into the water and swam, his fit muscles nonetheless straining against the treacherous current trying to roll him under. Just as he reached Rob, his cousin's hands slipped from the branch and he disappeared from sight.

"Rob! No!" Eastleigh gulped a breath and dove under. Unable to see past his nose in the murky waters, he dragged himself along the submerged tree. *Damn it, not now. I can't fail Rob now. Where the hell is he?*

Eastleigh's chest burned, and his lungs screamed for air. Had Rob been swept away? His fingers snagged fabric. And then connected with a body, kicking and struggling.

He grabbed for Rob and met his fingers. Rob grasped Eastleigh's hand and gave a shove downward to his boot. Damn, Rob's foot was caught in the crook of a branch and twisted.

Eastleigh's lungs were giving out, so Rob had to be close to drowning. Eastleigh couldn't give up—couldn't let Rob die. Another hard yank, and Rob's foot sprang free. They both shot to the surface, holding onto the same branch for dear life and gulping in air.

"Let's go." Eastleigh grabbed Rob before he could slip away again. Together, they made it to shore. Stumbling to the soggy ground, they rolled onto their backs and collapsed, coughing, chests heaving.

"Let me get a bit more air," Rob said. "And then we'll see to getting your wife back to the house."

My wife! God help him, a wife he'd nearly cast from his life. Eastleigh staggered to his feet and loped over to where Lilith lay trembling from the cold. Good God! She was so pale her skin looked translucent. "Lilith, I can't carry you alone with that stick in your leg, and you can't walk. Rob's all right, and as soon as he gains some strength, we'll figure out a way to get you back to the house where Hemphill can see to you."

He eyed his horse, but with the way the branch protruded from Lilith's leg front to back, there was no way she—an especially poor rider—could manage.

An idea struck him.

Grabbing her skirt, he tore a strip from her dress and another from what remained of her tattered petticoats. "This is going to hurt like hell, but I need to get a bit of blood on the fabric."

She only winced when he bunched bits of cloth around the exit point of the branch and pressed down, just enough to release a thin flow of blood. She bit her bottom lip and fisted her hands but remained silent.

"You're a strong woman, darling. Not many could manage what you've been through. And I mean that in every sense of the word. Will you forgive me for being such a bumbling fool? It's been hell ever since you left, Lilith. I don't care how many megrims I have to suffer through, I want you by my side. Until the end of my days. I'm simply no good without you."

She began to sob and laugh at the same time. "Whatever happens in our lives, we go through it together?"

"Well said, darling." He kissed her forehead and rose. He tied the bloody strips of fabric to the saddle, and then slapped Commodore on the rump. The beast bolted. Kicking up chunks of muddy earth with its hooves, the horse disappeared into a gray landscape.

He returned to Lilith. "He'll be back to the stables in no time. As soon as the groomsman sees what's tied to the saddle, we'll have an entourage out after us. At least the path Commodore's tearing up will be easy to follow."

Rob, his breathing steady, strode to Eastleigh's side. "If you'll grasp her along her back and shoulders, I can take hold under her knees and ankles. If we can manage to walk in rhythm with one another, she'll be that much closer to help when it arrives."

Eastleigh nodded. "That's what I figured as well."

As Rob bent down in tandem with Eastleigh, something indefinable crossed Rob's features. "We once marched together rather smartly, didn't we? Think we can manage a decent go of it again?"

A corner of his mouth made a wry upturn. "Mayhap this time for a better reason than a bloody, worthless war, Augie? You count off."

Eastleigh swept muddied hair off Lilith's cheek. "Relax as much as you can, love, and let us do the work." He spoke softly, in hopes of soothing her. "We've carried the wounded before. We know what to do."

"Do what you must." Her words left her mouth in little more than a weak exhale. She gave them each a glance and then closed her eyes.

Eastleigh and Rob positioned themselves as they'd once done a hundred times over. At the count of three, they lifted Lilith as if she weighed nothing more than a bird in hand. Still, she grimaced, and it was as though her pain shot right into Eastleigh, becoming his. "So sorry, darling."

At another count of three, he and Rob stepped forward in unison, their steps an even, practiced cadence that had not been forgotten.

"Please talk," Lilith said, her eyes still closed. "If I have something to distract me, it might blunt the discomfort."

So the pain had set in. He'd wondered when that would occur. He regarded Lilith's leg and the ugly stick that had been sawed from the tree. God forbid she should end up with an infection and lose the leg…or worse. He and Rob gave one another a knowing glance.

"We've about a twenty minute walk," Eastleigh said, not knowing quite what else to say.

"At least the storm's let up," Rob replied.

Lilith groaned. "I can manage to figure out the weather and distance on my own, thank you very much. Your nonsense is doing nothing to distract me. There are things that need to be said between the two of you. I cannot think of a better time to do so than when your hands are full, which will make it impossible to pummel each other."

Rob grunted. "Makes me appreciate bachelorhood, she does."

"So you say," Lilith muttered.

Eastleigh had expected simplicity in his life once he wed. As if marriage would place some kind of finality to all the hell that had gone before. She was right. There were things that had to be cleared away, especially if he was ever to attain peace. "What do you mean you weren't a turncoat? I saw you inside the tent of that Russian Colonel. The lamplight cast your silhouettes against the canvas plain as day. You reached into your uniform jacket and pulled out a packet of papers I'd seen you stuff in there earlier. Then he handed you a stack of currency. I watched you count it. And that wasn't the first time, Rob."

Rob shot him a sideways glance. "I was a double agent. The secrets I turned over to the Russians were worth little, just enough to keep them believing I was on their side. I'm sorry you had to see certain things take place."

"I didn't know!" Eastleigh roared. "I thought you…the way you turned on me…"

A miserable little grin swiped Rob's mouth. "Looks like we nearly did each other in, hey, Augie?"

They walked along for a while longer with Lilith in their arms and her with her eyes closed, silent as death. And Eastleigh filled with the pain of having remembered everything.

"I'm sorry," he said. "I think war destroys any sense of who we are when we are trained to fight the enemy. In my mind, you being a turncoat was the worst of the lot. I'd lost too many of my men to your kind—or what I thought was your kind."

A grimness washed through Rob's eyes and meshed with something Eastleigh could not discern. "I'm afraid I left you in a rather bad way, as well, Cousin."

"You were only defending yourself."

Rob set his focus over Eastleigh's shoulder. "That's not what I'm trying to apologize for."

A shiver raced along Eastleigh's spine. "Then what the hell for?"

"After your sword went through me, and you turned away, the Russian colonel slipped in behind you. I struck you, intending to merely knock you out long enough for him to think I'd done you in so he'd let his guard down and I could get a shot at him."

"What are you saying?"

"I didn't mean to cause you so much damage, Augie."

Rob had caused his amnesia? Shock tore through him. He stumbled.

Lilith whimpered.

He shook his head to clear it and fell right back into step with Rob. "What the hell did you use on me?"

"A silver candelabrum the arrogant bastard insisted on carrying with him wherever he went."

"Who rescued you?"

"You mean who rescued *us*? Hemphill. He came along just in time, or we both likely would've bled out—you with a split skull and me having been run through."

Anger snaked through Eastleigh. "Then the *good* doctor knew everything all along."

"He is a good doctor. He saved the both of us, didn't he?"

"And said nothing to me all this while. The bloody bastard."

Rob shrugged. "You know Hemphill's theories. I agreed not to say anything to anyone, including your family. Had to let you despise me, even though your memory didn't allow you to reason why."

Eastleigh stared straight ahead, trying to sort out his feelings. "Is this why you've stayed away from our entire family all this while? From Mum?"

Rob gave him a rueful smile. "She can be a clever one at figuring things out, can't she?"

They rounded a copse, and Eastleigh spied a mass of figures heading their way. "Here they come."

Rob snorted. "Hemphill's with them. Still so pitiful in the saddle, one can spot him a mile off."

"Thank heavens," Lilith said. "I doubt I could've stood the two of you much longer."

Chapter Twenty-two

Lilith did not die on the dining room table while Hemphill operated on her as she'd feared. After Tildy washed her body and cleaned her hair, Doctor Hemphill placed a tea strainer over her nose and mouth and layered a cloth over the top where he dripped a smelly concoction he referred to as diethyl ether.

One moment she was awake, staring up at the lighted chandelier overhead, and the next thing she knew, she was lying in a big, comfortable bed in a room full of Malverns. The curtains were drawn wide, exposing a clear, blue sky.

"Look, she's opened her eyes," someone said, and the low din in the room quieted.

"There they went closed again. Someone get Hemphill."

Was that a moan? Coming from her? Oh, she didn't know. Or care. A heavy weight made the mattress sag, and a familiar hand touched her brow. Next thing, a kiss brushed her cheek, and that wonderful, deep voice she so loved to hear whispered in her ear. "You'll be all right, darling."

"Darling?" She struggled to respond, but couldn't manage whatever it was she'd meant to say. Anyway, she'd forgotten already and drifted off.

A dull, thudding pain wrapped around her thigh, pinched her muscles, and drew her awake. Her eyelids fluttered open. Where had the day gone? In a room lit by a single candle, sat Eastleigh, handsome but so serious looking, with deep shadows smudged beneath his eyes. One elbow was propped on the chair's arm, his thumb working at his chipped tooth. He wore his red silk banyan and dark slippers.

She glanced about the room. "I'm in your bed."

He leaned over and gently tucked a stray lock behind her ear. "If you do not yet have all your faculties, let me remind you there was a certain discussion before the ether was applied, whereby you demanded to end up nowhere else."

She took a long moment looking around the room while she collected her thoughts. Eastleigh's chambers were rich in masculinity, but with a great depth of character—if one could say as much about a room. The rich dark woods, luxurious carpets, and lovely pieces Eastleigh had collected from his travels had been placed just so—all his doing. It was a large room, yet cozy with its fire blazing, two large chairs flanking the fireplace, and a shelf full of books.

A sense of belonging bloomed in her and brought a smile to her lips. "Yes, I do recall, now."

Eastleigh settled his gaze on her. "I wouldn't have wanted you to be anywhere else but here." His voice caught, then grew husky. "With me. In this very bed."

He moved from the chair and sat beside her, the mattress

giving beneath his weight. "It's been a frightfully long couple of days, darling. In more ways than you can imagine."

The very sound of his voice would have been enough to soothe her, but the scent of him, the heat radiating from his body, and oh, his fingers tracing a line down her cheek comforted her even more. A simple act, but a slice of heaven nonetheless. "What of Mum?"

"She'll be fine. A mild attack is all." He moved his fingers to her mouth and outlined the edges of her lips, setting them to tingling.

"She's already nagging Hemphill. Claims we drained her supply of good gin when he poured it through your wound before stitching you up. So now she's decided to settle for cherry cordial." A brief smile touched his lips. "Hemphill's not letting her have any just yet, however."

Lilith lifted a hand to cover his. Stilling her movements, he kissed her fingertips. "Is that what happened? He was able to remove the stick and then poured gin through the hole left in my leg?"

"That's some of what happened. Stubborn little piece of wood, that. Left enough debris inside your leg to mulch a garden, so the whole ordeal took a bit more time then he'd anticipated. Would you care for a bit of laudanum to dull the pain?"

"Not at the moment." They fell silent. He cared deeply for her. She was certain of it now. And with so great an intensity, the very essence of his devotion vibrated in the air between them. The heady notion washed through her like fresh rain on a spring day. She'd never felt such as this from anyone before. Hadn't a clue what she'd been missing. And to think how foolishly close they had come to throwing it all away.

Tears clogged her throat. "You're right. It has been a very long few days." She took in a breath to try and ease her urge to cry. It did no good. "Do you recall I said one day I would feel the need to crawl into your arms and weep?"

"Is now the day?" The husk in his voice trickled through him clear to his skin and into hers. His fingers slipped from beneath her hand and slid over to run along the side of her jaw, soft as an angel's kiss.

"I do believe so." She patted the other side of the bed and forgot about trying to swallow her tears. "Come. Climb in beside me and hold me."

"Give me a moment." He moved to an enameled cabinet across the room and returned carrying a small black velvet box. "I had wanted to take you to a jeweler in France to have a special wedding ring made, but since we have yet to make the trip, I thought you might like this in the interim."

His eyes filled with promise, he took a deep breath and opened the box.

Lilith gasped. A gold ring with a large, multi-faceted stone surrounded by seed pearls sat in the center of the black velvet. "Oh, my," was all she could manage.

"It was Mum's. The stone is a rare alexandrite that came out of an emerald mine in the Russian Urals. She'd like you to have it. If it doesn't suit you, we can have something made once we get to Paris."

Lilith lifted the ring from the case and slipped it on her finger. "How could I ever want something other than this? It's exquisite. I've never seen anything like it."

"The special thing about an alexandrite is, if you observe the color during the day, it is a lovely blue, but in the evening, it turns nearly purple, as you see it now. I don't know how it works, but I always thought it was lovely."

Lilith looked up at her husband and, with tears falling freely, patted the bed once again. "Now, I really do need to crawl into your arms."

· · ·

Morning greeted Lilith with breakfast in bed brought by Tildy and her mother. Eastleigh, up and already dressed, followed behind them, supervising their every move and acting as though she'd never been banished from Easton Park. "You'll not stay long. I don't want my wife tired out."

"Oh, Eastleigh, I'm already frightfully bored, and it's not even nine of the clock. I could use some company seeing as how you've been gone since the crack of dawn."

He grinned. "I'd think twice about extending an invitation if I were you. We've a house full of Malverns, all itching to hear your side of things. Especially the part about meeting up with Rob." He shot her a curious look. "Which I've wondered about, as well."

Oh, dear. She got busy with her eggs and kippers. Had Rob said anything about what occurred at his house? Eastleigh wouldn't be *that* forgiving. "Speaking of your cousin, what happened to him after Doctor Hemphill had me placed in the back of the wagon? I cannot recall seeing him again, and I should like to thank him."

Eastleigh sat in the chair closest to the bed. "Once he saw you were taken care of, he went home straight away. He's accepted an invitation to dinner this evening." He paused to study her for a moment. "About your meeting up with him—there's no need to tell the tale more than once, so if you'd care to inform me, I can relay the facts to the others."

Lilith's mother watched her, waiting quiet as a mouse while Tildy poured a cup of tea, set it on Lilith's tray, and backed away. "If that's all, milady, I'll excuse myself and leave you to your privacy."

A good sip of tea ought to wet Lilith's suddenly dry throat. She took her time depositing the sugar into the cup and stirring slowly while she thought things through. No sense in being specific about *certain* things that had been horribly misunderstood. She took a sip and set her cup down.

And no sense dawdling any further or suspicions would certainly arise, especially where the naughty Sir Crocodile was concerned. "Oh, there's nothing to tell, really. The storm had grown quite fierce by the time I got to Rob, so I notified him of Mum's having taken ill. After that, I hurried back ahead of him, only to have the tree tumble over right when I got there and toss me into the river. Since he was not far behind me, he saw what happened and dove right in."

She looked at her mother and her husband and smiled. There, that was indeed the truth, as it were. "I do need to thank him." *And see to it he does not elaborate any further.*

Eastleigh's eyes narrowed, and he opened his mouth to speak, but a knocking on the door stopped him. "Blast it all, the locusts have descended."

"How do you know it's a Malvern and not the doctor?" Lilith asked.

"Because there's that irritating little one tap, followed by four, and then two more." There it went again, precisely as he'd said. "Come in, for God's sake."

The door opened a ways, and a hand shoved through,

holding a bouquet of flowers—all whites and blues, with a single red rose in the center. It had to be Sebastian, the big flirt. "How lovely! Do come in."

Lady Willamette stepped over the threshold.

Lilith's mouth fell open.

Eastleigh snorted.

Lilith's mother stepped forward. "I had better go."

"No," Will said. "What I have to say is for everyone's ears." She approached the bed and held herself straight and proud. "I should not have left Miss Sarah Marks's gardening book on your bed when Eastleigh asked me not to. It was wrong of me."

She dug into her trouser pocket and pulled out a packet. "These are seeds from Miss Marks's own garden. I do hope you will see fit to planting them in yours."

Eastleigh's brow shot up. "Hell, Will. I didn't think you had it in you."

"Shut it, Augie." She looked around. "Where's Tildy? I need a bloody vase."

Lilith clasped her hand over her mouth to keep from giggling—at Will for trying to act so surly, for the astonishment on Eastleigh's face, and for Mother's cheeks reddening at Will's use of the word "bloody," as if using the term were an everyday occurrence. Come to think of it, for Will, it probably was.

"I'll see to finding Tildy." Lilith's mother made to slide out the door.

"No need," Will said, crossing over to yank on the bell pull.

Lilith's mother sat in a chair and folded her hands in her lap, looking quite uncomfortable.

"The flowers are lovely, Will. And I can't wait to plant the seeds." She had to come up with something better than that to try and ease Will's obvious discomfort. "And as for you placing the book on my bed, don't let's get buried in the past. We only have the moment, so let us live in it."

"I say, isn't that my line?" Merriment danced in Eastleigh's eyes.

The door, having been left partially open by Lilith's mother, swung wide, and three brothers stepped through. Ridley handed Will a vase. "Need one of these, dear girl?"

Rose, Violet, and Iris rushed in behind them and straight to Lilith's bedside. "We've been waiting in Mum's room," Iris said. "She's awfully upset that she's not allowed out of bed to join in. I think she is about to convince Doctor Hemphill that it is far worse to have her upset in her own chambers whilst we hear all about what happened."

Lilith looked about the room and at everyone gathered around, so obviously glad to see her. Life was good. More than good. She thought of her visit to Lord and Lady Ardmore's home and his daughters lying about their father's bed while Rose read to them. Her throat got a little tight, so before she lost her nerve, she patted the bed. "Come, ladies. Join me, and I'll tell you all about it."

• • •

Eastleigh entered his bedchamber four days later, carrying a box Mum had given him. "The locusts have departed, and with Hemphill's permission, Mum has called us to high tea. I'll carry you."

Lilith tossed back the covers. "You mean I can finally

leave this room? No wonder you were so anxious to get up and about after you took that nasty fall. What's in the box?"

He set it on the bed and removed the cover. "Something from Mum's travels that should prove to be a sight more comfortable than a corset and stuffy day dress."

"Why would I need anything but a dressing gown if everyone's gone and we're merely going down the corridor to Mum's chambers? Besides, Mum said she and Lady Hester Stanhope dressed in men's clothing while abroad, so I doubt I'd be at all interested."

"Darling, she managed to pack away a lady's frock or two. You're going to like this. Mum's below, by the way, waiting for us."

He lifted out a silky-looking, pale turquoise garment in two pieces. "And look, you have slippers to match."

"Oh, my. The color alone is worth the wearing." She reached over and took the fabric between her fingers. "So soft. Would you mind calling for Tildy to help me into it?"

"I can manage this." He leaned over and touched the tip of his tongue to her earlobe. God, he loved the taste of her skin.

Her breath escaped with a small hiss. His groin tightened. The days coming up, before those stitches in her leg were removed and he could get his hands all over her, were going to grow mighty long. "Here, let me help you out of your gown."

"I'll need my chemise and drawers. Tildy knows where they are. Or I can manage since Doctor Hemphill has me walking a few steps."

"You won't need them. Can you manage to stand?"

"I see." She scraped her teeth over her bottom lip, and a

flush rose to her cheeks.

Hell, the mere mention of going without her underthings, and she was as ready as he to do more than hold one another through the night. She rose from the bed and lifted her arms over her head.

He removed her nightrail and dropped it to the floor. Then groaned. "You're so incredibly beautiful."

She took his hand and placed it against her breast. "I think I'd like one of those delicious kisses you're so good at giving."

"Take care with your leg, Lilith." But his thumb had already rubbed across her nipple. It grew taut beneath his touch.

She leaned into him and, pressing her body against his, set her mouth to his lips. Their tongues touched, and his cock jumped to attention. Her hand found the front of his trousers and slid up and down. A wild, primal urge cut straight to his core. He was so hard now, he hurt. A husky moan slipped past his lips. He pulled away. "We can't do this."

"We just did." She grinned and stepped back. "Now dress me."

He chuckled and looked at Lilith standing before him, wearing nothing but a bandage around her thigh, her mouth swollen from their kiss, her hair in wild disarray, and the tips of her round breasts still peaked. "God, you're stunning. But you're beginning to sound like me giving orders, so I think I might have unleashed a wildcat."

He picked up one of the pieces of fabric and turned it about. "This seems to be the skirt, but how do you suppose it's going to work getting it on with your leg the way it is? Should I pull it over your head or bring it up from the bottom?"

"I think if you kneel and let me lean on your shoulders, I can lift my bad leg enough to slip it on."

He crouched down, only to find himself staring straight at that glorious triangle of soft, blonde curls. A raw, naked edge of lust shot right through him. "Get this thing on fast, Lilith, before I toss you back on the bed and show you what else I can do with my tongue."

She giggled and stepped into the skirt, slower with her bad leg. "And here I thought you were a man of finesse."

He stood, holding her shoulders, and pressed a quick, hot kiss on her mouth. His gaze slipped back down to those splendid breasts. Who knew when they had first met that she looked so good beneath all her clothing? "Talk to me about finesse in two weeks, and we'll see what you have to say."

"You're staring, dear. You might want to help me into the other part of the...whatever it's called."

He grabbed the top half of the costume and slipped it over her head. As her naked chest disappeared beneath the loose frock that fell to her hips, he let go a blatant sigh. "I'll have you know it was with great reluctance that I did that."

She shoved a hand through her hair. "Now what to do with this?"

He lifted her up and carried her to a chair, and after tucking her feet into the matching slippers, he picked up her brush lying on a toilette tray. "Let's leave your hair down."

The moment stretched between them, with him combing through her silken locks, and her sitting quietly while he tended her. His chest tightened. In the years to come, there would be other moments like this. He would do this for her after their children were born. He'd do so when her hair no longer held its sheen and was white as the shirt he wore.

Lost in a wave of pleasure that nearly took him under, he bent and kissed the top of her head. He had to clear his throat to speak. "Have you written to Mrs. Hazelthorpe and thanked her for playing the matchmaker?"

Chapter Twenty-three

Doctor Hemphill bent over the side of the bed, a pair of spectacles perched on his nose. He held a pair of scissors in one hand and long, shiny tweezers in the other, ready to snip away. Lilith found it hard to believe only ten days had passed since the accident—it seemed so much longer. At least the stitches were finally being removed.

He clipped at the first set and gave a sharp tug to pull it free from her skin.

She winced.

He paused, studying her eyes. "Hurts?"

Eastleigh, his body tense, grunted and stepped from the end of the bed to stand on the side opposite Hemphill. He slipped his hand into hers and scowled at the doctor.

She bit her lip. "Like bee stings, but please, continue."

Eastleigh squeezed her hand. She squeezed back and turned from the doctor to her husband. He gave her an encouraging smile. How comforting. This was home. *He* was home. Here was her world now and he was in it—every step of the way. Even his family, who'd returned—the men boisterous below, Rose, Iris, and Violet scampering around in the upper hallways, and Mum calling for tea—was part of it. Even Lilith's mother had settled in and was softening daily. Here was a bright thread in the tapestry of Lilith's life. Here was something she had never had—or knew existed. The preciousness of what she now possessed would never be lost on her.

"How are you faring?" Eastleigh's rough voice was filled with concern.

She smiled reassuringly. "Not so bad, after all. I think I was more apprehensive of what I didn't know to expect. I'm fine."

Ah, her husband. Could she possibly have fallen more deeply in love in only ten days? Despite a house full of Malverns, she and Eastleigh had managed to live in a world of their own while she healed. He was constantly by her side, insisted on carrying her to the garden each sunny day until she complained she was no cripple. After that, he walked her there, to sit among the weeds, he'd say, but his sultry grin left no doubt he took great joy in pampering her. He made it clear he'd do anything to see she healed properly, yet the broad stroke of his strong will told her he was no weakling to be manipulated or made to bend to her wishes.

On the contrary.

Yes, here was her home. No longer was it an edifice or a space to be occupied by noisy people intent on out-shouting or out-laughing one another. And hopefully, there would be free-spirited children running around in the corridors, playing in the fields. Oh, how she wanted that for her and Eastleigh.

He'd insisted on being the one to change her bandages daily, making certain she was discreetly covered when Doctor Hemphill examined the wound. Lilith had laughed when Eastleigh announced to a proud Mum that for once her home-brewed gin was worthwhile. Even Hemphill said pouring the throat-burning rot through Lilith's open wound rather than down her gullet was just the thing. No infection had set in.

Another snip of the scissors, a brisk tug, and the last stitch broke free from her leg. She hissed.

Eastleigh grunted and gave her hand another squeeze.

"Good as new." Hemphill stepped away from the bed. Slipping his scissors into his worn black leather bag, he nodded to Tildy, who gathered the used bandages. On their exit, Doctor Hemphill said, "You're free to do anything you wish, except ride a horse."

Lilith laughed. "Oh, dear, you have no concern of that occurring. I do thank you for everything."

The door closed silently behind the doctor and Tildy, leaving Lilith and Eastleigh alone. She glanced at the mantel clock. Only noon? Good heavens, would nightfall ever come to pass? Soon there would be a meal, and then Mum's high tea with all the rowdy Malverns gathered.

"I expect you had better get off the bed so we can make our way downstairs," Eastleigh said. "I'm famished."

Silence stretched between them as he regarded her with what she knew pounded in her own veins, as well. Night after night, he'd held her in his arms, not daring to cross a line lest he injure her leg. But he'd touched her—intimately at times—and he'd ignited flames in both of them that nothing but each other would extinguish.

"I am famished, as well." She tapped the bed next to her.

He regarded her, passion in his eyes. "You're certain?"

"I should be asking you that question. Have you any concerns about another terrible episode occurring? Look what you had to contend with after the last time we made love."

"My dear, the shock of nearly losing you should have triggered something, but I haven't had an episode in ten days."

A sultry grin touched his lips. "Besides, if one of those blasted things were to come along, didn't we agree that we'd see each other through whatever happens in our lives?"

Her heart tripped a beat. "Have I failed to mention that I am glad you delivered me to your chamber after the surgery? This isn't merely a bed, Eastleigh. This is our world now, and it will bear witness to many lives who will follow after us. Come. It's time."

His breath left his lungs in a great whoosh.

"I've had a lot to think about lying around in this bed for so long," she said. "I want you to teach me another lesson. Do you have it in you?"

Loosening his cravat, he tossed it aside. Without taking his eyes from hers, he removed his jacket and unbuttoned his waistcoat. "I want more than to simply lie with you, Lilith. I, too, want to make something beautiful of our lives that will remain long after we are gone."

His words were a verbal caress, and the tenderness of their meaning drew a mist into her eyes. "Only an artist would speak in such a poetic way. Another reason for me to be grateful I sent that letter off to our matchmaker."

He offered her a sultry grin and shrugged off his shirt. Then he worked at removing his shoes and trousers. The muscles in his arms and across his broad chest rippled.

Watching his movements, her body sprang to life. This close to him, her mind was unable to focus on anything but his physical presence. Her breasts tightened and her thighs heated—and then that little bud between them ached for more of what he'd done to her all these nights she'd curled next to him.

The pulse in her neck beat in furious arousal, and then the beat ran rampant through her. A little moan escaped her lips

He glanced at her and chuckled, low and throaty. Divested of his clothing, he slipped her robe and drawers from her and slid between the sheets alongside her. His naked heat seeped into her. His subtle musk—all the more enticing bereft of cologne, enveloped her.

His arms wrapped around her, and he kissed her. There was no prelude to this kiss. They'd had plenty of those while waiting for her leg to heal. She knew his taste, knew his scent. All familiar. The rest of it was far too long in coming. His mouth assaulted hers in a full, hot-blooded exchange— kiss for lethal kiss that drew their heated bodies together.

"I love you," she cried out.

He withdrew, just enough to lift his shoulders and peer deep into her eyes. Something close to pain settled in his. "I needed to hear that."

And then he thrust into her, so deep she felt his pelvis connect with hers. He didn't move, but held himself completely still inside her, filling her. His large body, a contrast to her smaller one, hovered against hers, weightless, while his arms caged her in and his scent surrounded her.

He nestled his mouth into the curve of her neck and murmured, "Before we go any further, while my body is fitted inside of yours, I want you to know I fell in love with you the day you could not remember who I was. You were so vulnerable, yet so strong. And so incredibly beautiful."

His words, hoarse and filled with intensity and tenderness, fell quietly upon her ears. "But my commitment to you came long before that, Lilith. I need you, and now I know you need me, as well. You, dear wife, are my forever."

Epilogue

Lilith sat abed, devouring the luscious sight of her husband in the act of dressing for the day. He gave one last tug at his waistcoat, and then ran his hands through his hair with a flourish. Those supple curls she loved to touch fell magically into place. "Have you ever thought of using a hair brush, dear?"

He wiggled his fingers at her. "Just did."

Tossing her a wink, he strolled over to where she'd propped herself against a stack of pillows. Sinful thoughts leapt from her mind and landed in her belly, turning into heated deliberations. She would seduce him before he walked out the door.

She shifted about at the very idea. The bedding pooled around her waist, exposing the silk negligee he'd given her the night before. French, pale blue trimmed in a froth of white lace. His was an act of worship when he'd draped it on her—an act of sheer lust when he'd removed it barely an hour later.

A kiss on her forehead, and he motioned with his head toward a letter lying on her bedside table. "Are you going to keep that blasted thing under our noses until it turns to dust?"

She glanced at the missive. "I've been debating whether or not to inquire of the smithy as to which horse trampled my father."

Eastleigh scowled.

"Oh, dear," she said. "Did I sound terribly shallow just then? I hadn't meant to. It's just that I can't help wondering how the horse fared after being beaten half to death. I imagine my father thought the poor thing a convenient substitute on which to vent his rage since my mother and I were no longer available as his whipping posts."

"He should've known a horse would only take so much abuse before it turned on him."

A shudder ran through her. "Still and all, his death must have been a horrific one."

Eastleigh brushed the back of his hand across her cheek. "I've got better use for this letter than having the blasted thing stare us in the face every day."

He strode across the room and tossed it into the fire. The paper curled brown at the edges and then burst into flame. "The entire sordid affair is nearly four months passed, Lilith. It's time to let it go."

As the paper turned to ash, a quick pain pricked her heart. But then the small black cloud that had hovered over her since the letter arrived dissipated. "You're right. Yes, of course."

She took in a slow breath, and in relief, let it go all at

once. One lacey strap fell off her shoulder. "Speaking of months, dear."

At her quick change of subject, Eastleigh wheeled around. "I don't recall the word *months* being an entire subject." Amusement sketched a near-smile on his lips, and faint lines appeared at the corners of his eyes. "What are you up to?"

She granted him her sauciest smile. "It's been eight months since Rob saved my life and..."

"Since *Rob* saved your life? What the deuces was I doing at the scene, dancing a jig?"

Her laughter, soft and low, filled the air between them. "You know perfectly well what I mean. Skewered on that branch like I was, I would've drowned before your arrival had it not been for him."

Eastleigh crossed one booted foot over the other and leaned onto his elbow parked on the mantel. He set to lazily flicking at his chipped tooth and regarding her through veiled lids. "Something's grinding away in that rather dangerous mind of yours that has me on virtual tenterhooks."

Her gaze roved his indolent stance. "I can tell."

Yes, seducing him before he got out the door was just the thing. Participating in a wanton act while fully clothed could be quite delicious at times. Like sinful French chocolates. She'd grown to adore all things French since he'd introduced her to them. "I feel a reward is in order for your cousin having saved me."

Eastleigh's brow lifted. "Do tell? And by the manner in which you are regarding me, what do you have in mind?"

"Don't be crude. How I look at you has nothing to do with your cousin."

"Ah, do I suspect Mum's tutoring at work here? How

well she's taught you the tricks of witchery."

Even with her gaze trapped in his, she could easily take in his full form. Good. She had him aroused. "Do you realize you haven't had one of those dreadful episodes since you recovered the missing pieces of your memory? Not one megrim since you found peace with Rob?"

His jaw dropped. "No, I hadn't realized."

"You owe him. I'd like you to give part of your land to him. He's not got — "

Eastleigh shot forward. "Bloody hell, give him my land!"

"Oh, lord love a duck, Eastleigh. Why do you need so much dirt? Don't be greedy."

"Madam, I earned every inch of land I possess. I rode that damn donkey until I had blisters on my arse for weeks."

Now it was her turn to lift a brow. "Indeed? And will you have earned all that you will one day inherit merely because of your birth order?"

"That's different."

Pushing the covers aside, Lilith slipped from the bed and waltzed over to where her husband stood. Sliding her arms around his neck, she fitted her body against his. He was so warm, and smelled so clean. "Will we reside here or there when you become the earl?"

His fingers, gentle as a breeze, swept the length of her silk-clad hip, sending more heat streaking through her. "Here."

Her hands wandered from his neck to his chest. His heart thudded heavy in her hand. "Well and good, because I love it here. But what will become of all you inherit if — "

"Whatever you have in mind, cease. Will is to remain in residence there with Mother. God knows my sister will require a place of her own since she'll never marry. Besides, there's no better person to take care of the property."

He'd slowly worked Lilith's negligee above her hips while they spoke. When had he flipped open the buttons on his trousers? "By the way, dear wife," his voice rasped, thick and husky. "I have *already* parceled off a good portion of land to Rob."

"Do tell?"

He grasped her waist, turned her around, and bent her over the foot rail of the bed. His hand drifted along her bare hips, and tiny shivers danced along her skin already flush with yearning.

His breath brushed hot against her nape. "My solicitor awaits downstairs, darling. And I'm to meet Rob this afternoon if you care to join us. In the meantime, I've rather enjoyed your blatant teasing to the point of disrupting my schedule. Care to have a go at a quick and wild ride?"

• • •

Lilith sat in front of the curricle alongside Eastleigh while Mum, pleased as a child with a new toy, rode in the rear, chattering endlessly about the fine scenery and the crisp autumn air painting the leaves in shades of gold and orange. But mostly, she carried on about how the apple crop was exceptionally fine this season—which to Mum, translated into an abundance of apple cider.

"Who might that be?" Lilith squinted at a couple meandering along a path leading to Hemphill's cottage. A shockwave ran through her. "Why, that's Mother and Doctor Hemphill!"

She turned to Eastleigh, her jaw slackening. "Are they

holding hands? With her in mourning?"

"Oh, it's quite all right," Mum called from behind. "She's wearing black."

Eastleigh grinned and leaned toward Lilith's ear. "You aren't the only woman Mum's been tutoring. Better close your mouth, dearest, there are flies about."

When the curricle turned onto the lane leading to Rob's home, Eastleigh groaned at the sight of the two horses' rear ends planted on either side of the drive.

Lilith couldn't resist a tease. "Haven't they weathered nicely? The green patina and all."

Eastleigh scowled.

Mum tapped Lilith on the shoulder. "Robbie made a mistake when he created those two horses' arses."

"Isn't that the profound statement of the ages." Eastleigh's words dripped with sarcasm.

"They'd have been perfect," Mum replied, "if Robbie had engraved your name on one fat rump and his on the other."

Lilith passed a gloved hand over her mouth. Little good that did to stifle the giggle.

Eastleigh shook his head. "Enjoy the ride, Mum."

"Lovely day, isn't it?" she responded.

When they arrived, Rob stood next to the stable, turning a piece of glowing metal into some kind of art form. Like the first time Lilith had wandered onto his land, he wore no shirt, only a leather apron to prevent flying sparks from burning his flesh. He set down his hammer and the branch of hot metal. Removing his gloves and apron, he donned his shirt, but not before Lilith caught sight of the garish scar on his side. A little quiver of revulsion rippled over the skin on her arms.

He regarded no one in particular. "I don't suppose you'll be staying long?"

"Stuff it, Rob," Eastleigh growled. "I've come to deliver the deed. However, I should be more than content to have my solicitors rearrange things, if you are so inclined."

A smirk lifted one corner of Rob's mouth. "Does this mean I have to be cordial and invite you in?"

Mum danced forward, her countenance filled with joyfulness. "I could go for a bit of cordial, if it's cherry."

Rob grinned and jerked his head toward the house. "Got some good French brandy inside, Mum."

"Even better." She turned to Eastleigh, her huge blue hat bouncing about and threatening to disgorge the fresh flowers she'd planted there. "He's got French brandy. Do come along."

Before he and Rob disappeared into the library, Lilith and Mum were escorted into the very room Lilith had entered the day she'd sought Rob out. This time, she took her time looking around.

As sumptuous as the surroundings were, Rob's home lacked something. Or was it someone? "He doesn't seem to have any servants, Mum. Why is that?"

"Oh, he employs them, dear, but they are sent off to their homes by late afternoon. Cook leaves an evening meal for him. Robbie keeps to himself."

"Since the war?"

Mum poured herself another brandy and leaned forward. "I'll have you know, Sir Crocodile and the prince were holy terrors when they caroused together in London. See that half-finished portrait? Word got back to me on more than one…"

The door to Rob's study opened. Mum's mouth shut. When they rose to leave, Lilith turned to Eastleigh. "Might you escort Mum to the carriage? I'd like a moment with Rob."

Eastleigh's brow cocked, but he said nothing and took Mum's arm. Lilith waited until the door closed behind them. "I have never told Eastleigh about a certain incident which took place between you and me when I came here to tell you Mum had taken ill. I thought you should know."

Rob said nothing, but something passed through his eyes that looked as though it might be relief.

She lifted her chin. "Mind you, I would never keep anything of consequence from my husband, but since what occurred was merely a slight misunderstanding, I thought it not worth the mention."

A brief smile passed over Rob's mouth. "Clever girl. What do you want?"

"Would you give consideration to replacing those two distasteful equine back ends with something a little more seemly?"

He paused for a long while, regarding her with those dark eyes that never failed to penetrate. Mischief settled in, and his lids grew heavy. "No."

Stubborn fool. "I'm appealing to your sensibilities as a fine artist."

He gave a little snort. "Just because I'm good at what I do, doesn't mean I'm not a bit wicked."

Blast it, all. "Well, then. I'll be on my way."

"I'll see you out." They were passing the stable in silence when he paused, picked up the huge leather bellows, and giving them a good couple of blasts, set the fire to flaming and sparking as though it sprouted wings from hell.

Lilith turned on her heel and made for the curricle. "Oh, if he isn't the very devil doing that," she grumbled as Eastleigh handed her into the carriage.

"Care to spend the night, Mum?" Rob called out, his arms folded across his broad chest, an impious grin on his face.

Mum nearly bolted from the back seat of the carriage. With a chuckle, Eastleigh eased her to the ground and climbed aboard.

"That man is nigh on impossible," Lilith grumbled. "And he has secrets. Dark ones. Who's that woman in the painting?"

Eastleigh turned the two grays toward home and, without a backward glance, lifted a gloved hand in farewell. "He wouldn't agree to remove the horses' arses, would he?"

"How would you know what I was up to? And do answer my question."

He leaned over and pressed a kiss to her cheek, his breath fanning her skin. "Darling, allow the man his secrets. We should all have a few."

She gave him a sweeping glance. "You have secrets?"

"Do you?"

She tried to swallow a giggle but failed. "Do I?"

The carriage came to a sudden stop. "Lilith?" His voice broke in the middle of her name and his gloved hand tugged at her chin, forcing her to look his way.

Was that hope shining in his eyes? Her heart set to beating wildly. Oh, how she loved this man. "I don't suppose I'll have my greatest secret much longer, will I?"

"Don't tease me, Lilith."

She laughed and threw her arms around him. "Oh, my darling. This child I carry will be so very blessed to have you as a father."

Acknowledgments

I actually dreamed this entire story one night. I woke up amazed that I had watched a movie in my sleep. Even though I wrote a couple of novels before I managed to get to this one, the story remained as a bright spot in my heart. When I sat down to finally put it to words, the characters and the story came alive as though the dream had occurred the night before.

I have a passion for collecting stories of eccentric women throughout history who were daring enough to step outside the dictates of society. Mum is my representative of these unconventional women who lived during the Regency and Victorian eras. All the stories Mum tells about her past are based on actual events belonging to the wilful daughter of an earl, Lady Hester Stanhope (12 March 1776—23 June 1839). Niece to William Pitt the Younger, she acted as his assistant while he was prime minister. Upon his death, the government awarded her a lifetime pension, which she promptly used to pursue a scandalous life in the Middle East, never to return to England. Wild and daring, Lady Hester thought nothing of traipsing around the desert in men's clothing, or of taking a string of lovers, including one twelve years her junior. Given the opportunity to write whatever stories I enjoy telling, I simply had to include Mum in all those wild adventures.

I want to thank my agent Jill Marsal of the Marsal Lyon Literary Agency for placing *The Seduction of Sarah Marks* in the right hands. You are my rock.

Many thanks to my wonderful editor, Erin Molta, who showed me how to make this story even better. I also thank you for your bright and cheery support that shines through, even in the briefest of emails.

Thanks to my wonderful RWA® Hearts Through History critique partners: Wendy, Anne, Tess, Averil, Renee, Barbara, Joan, Sam, Cari, and Deb for helping me put the right words into the story. What an amazingly talented and caring group of women you are!

Thanks to the awesome 2012 Firebirds. As fellow finalists in the prestigious Romance Writers of America Golden Heart Contest®, we've stuck together and supported one another through thick and thin. Thanks for being there when I needed you most.

To my Beta readers, Jennifer Arp and Nancy Linehan. Your precious input and catching those niggling little typos and sentences that didn't make sense saved me on more than one occasion.

To the Lalalas and The Dashing Duchesses, I'm in the best of company!

Thanks to my wonderful Hungarian neighbor, Edit

Meszaros. A fantastic cook who lived for a time in England, she makes her own liqueurs. Without you, Mum's "tipples" wouldn't have been authentic. And thank you, Edit, for those scrumptious meals when I was too busy trying to finish a manuscript to cook. And hey, you even lent me your cat to prance around on my desk. What more could I ask for?

And since you, dear reader, have chosen to read my story, my heartfelt thanks. Without you, there'd be no point, would there? I hope you enjoyed the story.

About the Author

Kathleen Bittner Roth is a PAN member of Romance Writers of America® and belongs to the Hearts Through History Romance Writers chapter. Kathleen was a finalist in RWA's prestigious Golden Heart contest and has won numerous awards for her writing. She is the founder of Inner World Perceptions, an international well-being center. She has worked in the media for many years (television and radio, including The History Channel, and all four major networks). Kathleen has also been a contributing editor of an online romance magazine and a guest on many blogs.

Made in United States
North Haven, CT
01 February 2022

15527364R00162